Lisa could feel his body shaking as much as her own

Tony put his arms around her and pulled her close to him, bending to kiss her forehead and cheeks, her eyelids and throat and lips, with lingering, gentle kisses that took her breath away.

This is the nicest thing that's ever happened to me, she told herself. *This is the sweetest feeling I've ever had.*

But just as that thought occurred to her, she came abruptly back to reality and pulled away in confusion.

"Would you...would you like a cup of coffee or something?" Lisa offered shyly.

"What I'd like," Tony said with quiet deliberation, "is for you to go out with me tonight, Lisa. I'd like to take you to the movies or something. Is that possible, do you think?"

She forced herself to look at him then, stabbed cruelly by the image of what he was offering. He was suggesting that she could have a normal, happy relationship with a decent, attractive young man. How simple it seemed, and how completely impossible it was for her!

"No," she whispered, miserable. "No, I'm afraid I can't do that, Tony. Not ever. Please don't ask me again."

Margot Dalton is acknowledged as the author of this work.

Special thanks and acknowledgment to Sutton Press Inc. for its contribution to the concept for the Crystal Creek series.

ISBN 0-373-82528-5

SOUTHERN NIGHTS

Margot Dalton

SOUTHERN NIGHTS

Harlequin Books

TORONTO • NEW YORK • LONDON
AMSTERDAM • PARIS • SYDNEY • HAMBURG
STOCKHOLM • ATHENS • TOKYO • MILAN
MADRID • WARSAW • BUDAPEST • AUCKLAND

DEEP IN THE HEART Barbara Kaye	March 1993
COWBOYS AND CABERNET Margot Dalton	April 1993
AMARILLO BY MORNING Bethany Campbell	May 1993
WHITE LIGHTNING Sharon Brondos	June 1993
EVEN THE NIGHTS ARE BETTER Margot Dalton	July 1993
AFTER THE LIGHTS GO OUT Barbara Kaye	August 1993
HEARTS AGAINST THE WIND Kathy Clark	September 1993
THE THUNDER ROLLS Bethany Campbell	October 1993
GUITARS, CADILLACS Cara West	November 1993
STAND BY YOUR MAN Kathy Clark	December 1993
NEW WAY TO FLY Margot Dalton	January 1994
EVERYBODY'S TALKIN' Barbara Kaye	February 1994
MUSTANG HEART Margot Dalton	March 1994
PASSIONATE KISSES Penny Richards	April 1994
RHINESTONE COWBOY Bethany Campbell	May 1994
SOUTHERN NIGHTS Margot Dalton	June 1994
SHAMELESS Sandy Steen	July 1994
LET'S TURN BACK THE YEARS Barbara Kaye	August 1994
NEVER GIVIN' UP ON LOVE Margot Dalton	September 1994
GENTLE ON MY MIND Bethany Campbell	October 1994
UNANSWERED PRAYERS Penny Richards	November 1994
SOMEWHERE OTHER THAN THE NIGHT Sandy Steen	December 1994
THE HEART WON'T LIE Margot Dalton	January 1995
LONESTAR STATE OF MIND Bethany Campbell	February 1995

Dear Reader,

Reviewers and readers alike can't seem to get enough of Crystal Creek!

"The McKinney family just gets more and more fascinating. I have read every book in the collection.... Just when I think the next one can't be as good as the previous, I am surprised to find it is just as, if not more, satisfying than the last."

—Melissa Barnes,
South Carolina

Margot Dalton's NEW WAY TO FLY is a "fine and fitting successor to the first ten Crystal Creek books. May they go on forever!"

—*Rendezvous*

The talented Ms. Dalton returns to Crystal Creek via Las Vegas in *Southern Nights,* our sixteenth Crystal Creek installment. The bizarre circumstances that bring Lisa Croft to the Double C will keep you on the edge of your seat, but save some smiles for Cynthia's unique antidote to the ennui that's causing so many sleepless southern nights!

Next month, author Sandy Steen will introduce you to Rio Langley, a loner who comes back to Crystal Creek to settle his late mother's affairs. He gets way more than he bargained for, the least of which is a bundle on his doorstep whose contents are astounding! Watch for *Shameless,* available wherever Harlequin books are sold. And stick around in Crystal Creek—home of sultry Texas drawls, smooth Texas charm and tall, sexy Texans!

Marsha Zinberg
Coordinator, Crystal Creek

A Note from the Author

I have many wonderful memories of the trips I made to Texas while planning and researching these books, but one is especially vivid. Late in March, after a long day of brainstorming in a hotel room, our weary group of writers and editors set off to roam the streets of Austin in search of some really good Texas barbecue. It was quite late in the evening, and the tree-lined streets were dark and silent. All at once, directly above us, one of the trees burst into song. It was the most amazing moment. I forget what kind of birds filled that tree, but I've never heard any birds sing after dark ... except in Texas! The image of the singing tree in the darkness will always remind me of "southern nights" and starry skies filled with mystery and romance.

Margot Dalton

Who's Who in Crystal Creek

Have you missed the story of one of your favorite Crystal Creek characters? Here's a quick guide to help you easily locate the titles and story lines:

DEEP IN THE HEART	J. T. McKinney and Cynthia
COWBOYS AND CABERNET	Tyler McKinney and Ruth
AMARILLO BY MORNING	Cal McKinney and Serena
WHITE LIGHTNING	Lynn McKinney and Sam
EVEN THE NIGHTS ARE BETTER	Carolyn Townsend and Vernon
AFTER THE LIGHTS GO OUT	Scott Harris and Val
HEARTS AGAINST THE WIND	Jeff Harris and Beverly
THE THUNDER ROLLS	Ken Slattery and Nora
GUITARS, CADILLACS	Wayne Jackson and Jessica
STAND BY YOUR MAN	Manny Hernandez and Tracey
NEW WAY TO FLY	Brock Munroe and Amanda
EVERYBODY'S TALKIN'	Cody Hendricks and Lori
MUSTANG HEART	Sara Gibson and Warren
PASSIONATE KISSES	J. T. McKinney and Pauline
RHINESTONE COWBOY	Liz Babcock and Guy

Available at your local bookseller, or see the Crystal Creek back-page ad for reorder information.

SOUTHERN NIGHTS

CHAPTER ONE

CYNTHIA MCKINNEY WOKE from a troubled sleep and gazed at the fluted plaster cornices that bordered the antique ceiling. J.T.'s humped body beneath the bedclothes hid the face of his bedside clock, but Cynthia guessed that it was about five-thirty.

She sighed, nestling under the covers and longing to catch a few more minutes of sleep, though she knew there wasn't much point in trying. In a little while Jennifer would be awake, yelling for her early feeding, and then another long day would begin.

Another long, hot day, Cynthia thought wearily, looking at the sly fingers of sunlight that already poked their way around the edges of the window shade. The August heat was a living thing, a malevolent presence that stalked the ranch, waited up on the hills and slipped down into the house whenever a door was opened.

This was her second summer in Texas, but Cynthia had never gotten used to the heat. Summer had always meant something so different to her. She craved cool, leafy shade beneath avenues of tall trees, sunlight dancing on water, the salty tang of the sea at

the cottage on the island where her family tradition-
ally spent their holidays.

Back home in New England, summer was a wel-
comed season, rich and golden, full of gentle out-
door pleasures. Here in Central Texas, though,
summer was more like an enemy, a thing that you hid
from and fought with air-conditioning, drawn shades
and gallons of cool liquids.

At least she wasn't pregnant this year. Cynthia
shuddered when she thought about the previous August. Her first experience of the Texas summer had
come when she was six months pregnant, swollen and
blotchy with heat rash. She rolled her head on the
pillow and grimaced with distaste at the memory.

Her husband opened his eyes, saw the grimace and
gave her a lazy smile, reaching toward her. "Are you
making faces at me while I'm asleep?" he whispered.

"Obviously not," Cynthia said, drawing away
from his embrace. "You're awake, aren't you?"

He caught the sharpness in her tone and his smile
grew wary. "You know, you could still come with us,
Cynthia," he said at last. "Why don't you change
your mind and toss some things in a suitcase? We
won't be leaving for a few hours."

Cynthia felt a tightening in her stomach, a reluctance to take up this familiar argument. "I've told
you a hundred times," she said coldly, "that I hate
riding in that little plane."

"Oh, come on. You're a bright girl. You know the statistics. Flying in that plane of mine is far safer than driving a car on the highway."

J. T. McKinney was smart enough to understand that his wife could never argue with statistics. Cynthia felt a flare of annoyance, and fought to control it. "I can't leave Jennifer behind, J.T., and you know it. She's still nursing."

"Just once a day. You told me yourself it was time to wean her from that last feeding. She's almost nine months old."

Cynthia hated having her own words turned against her in an argument, and J.T. did it more effectively than anyone she'd ever met. Her annoyance grew and her stomach began to churn.

"Besides," he went on when she hesitated, "if you don't want to leave her behind, it's easy to take her with us. There's lots of room in the plane."

"Oh, sure," Cynthia muttered bitterly. "Lots of room for a stroller and playpen, a daybed, her formula and equipment, ten cartons of disposable diapers..."

"We can buy diapers when we get there, Cynthia," her husband said mildly. "I'm sure they have such things in California."

Cynthia began to feel increasingly cornered and irritated. "Look," she said tightly, "I really can't think of anything I'd enjoy less than going away for two weeks with you and Ruth and Tyler and a cranky baby! That's not exactly my idea of a holiday, J.T."

"I don't know why not," he said, his jaw taking on that stubborn set that she knew so well. "It's the only holiday we're likely to get this year, Cynthia. I don't have time to take another two weeks off anytime soon. We have to make this trip to California, so I don't see why we can't make it enjoyable."

"That's just it." Cynthia turned away from him to look at the clock again. "You don't ever see much of anything, do you?"

J.T.'s long body tensed and he appeared on the verge of a sharp retort. But he restrained himself and reached for her, drawing her into his arms and kissing her throat. "Let's not fight, sweetheart," he whispered. "Not just before I have to leave. I love you so much. I love you. . . ."

His hands moved against her breast, fumbling with the tiny buttons on the front of her nightgown.

Cynthia's body turned rigid. She looked down in growing anger at his silvered temples, his tanned cheek and the muscular line of his shoulder.

The same heat that sapped her energy seemed to arouse J.T., to wake some kind of sleeping, lusty demon within her husband. In the summertime, he'd make love every day if she let him.

She pulled away and turned her back on him. "Jennifer will be waking soon," she muttered.

"Let her yell a while," he pleaded, nuzzling her nape and reaching around her body to cup and fondle her breasts.

Cynthia shook him off and drew herself to the extreme edge of the bed. "I'm not in the mood, J.T.," she said briefly.

He leaned up on one elbow and gazed down at her. "Look, are you really upset about this trip to California? I don't see how I can get out of going, Cynthia. I promised Don I'd be coming, and we need to get a handle on this winery thing. We need to watch his harvesting procedures and get a look at a few of the other producing wineries out there in the Napa Valley. It's vital to our whole operation."

"I know all that," Cynthia said wearily. "I'd just like a holiday that's a real holiday, for once."

"Lots of people go to California for their holidays," J.T. argued. "Why can't we?"

"Because I don't want to."

"Well, I don't know what you want these days," he said coldly, rolling out of bed and reaching for his jeans. "But I sure as hell know that it isn't me."

Cynthia watched him as he dressed. "What's that supposed to mean?"

"You know goddamn well what I mean! Seems like I can't even touch you anymore. Maybe it's just as well I'm going away for a while."

He slammed out of the room, buttoning his shirt as he went, and Cynthia listened to the distant clatter of his boots on the stairs. She lay staring at the window, so flooded with unhappiness that it was a relief when she heard the first sound of Jennifer's plaintive crying.

She stumbled out of bed, belted on her dressing gown and hurried into the next room. Jennifer stood shakily upright in a pink terry cloth sleeper clutching the bars of her crib and howling.

Cynthia breathed deeply of the familiar morning smells—milk and talcum powder and wet diapers. She smiled down at her baby, who stopped crying abruptly when she saw Cynthia. Jennifer's face creased into a happy grin, displaying her two bottom teeth, and she bounced on the crib mattress. Cynthia picked up the child, murmuring softly to her, forgetting the argument with J.T. in a flood of maternal tenderness.

"Sweet little girl," she whispered against the baby's fragrant neck. "Mommy's little sweetheart. Did Jennifer have a good sleep? Did she have a nice long sleep? Come, baby, let's change this wet old diaper...."

Still murmuring, Cynthia laid the little girl on the crib mattress, deftly changed her sodden napkin, then carried her to the rocking chair in the corner, unbuttoning her nightgown as she went.

She sat in the chair and nestled the baby close to her, sighing with pleasure as Jennifer's small mouth fastened on her mother's breast and she began to nurse greedily.

Actually, J.T. was right, Cynthia thought, caressing the baby's soft, downy head. It was probably time to give up this final nursing. Jennifer had never taken to a bottle very well, but she drank readily from a cup by now and was eating a lot of solid foods.

Cynthia knew that she clung to the early-morning nursing mostly for her own sake. It was nice to pick up the baby and feed her so effortlessly, without going down to the kitchen to heat milk. And it had always been precious to Cynthia, this early half hour with her baby in the hushed light of dawn before the rest of the house was stirring.

She rocked and gazed at Jennifer's soft pink cheek flattened against her breast. The past year had been a strange experience for Cynthia Page McKinney, a time when she had ceased to be a logical, intelligent woman and had become a kind of mindless, nurturing animal. She had never been so physical, so preoccupied with the rhythms and changes of her body.

She and Jennifer had spent this time locked together in a mystical, milky world of warmth and tenderness, so closely tuned to each other that when the baby cried, Cynthia felt an actual pain in her own body, an aching at the core of her where Jennifer had come from.

For nine months she'd been absorbed with her pregnancy, with the awesome changes in herself that were creating a new human entity. And then for another nine months she'd been wrapped up in Jennifer, totally engrossed by the wonder of that tiny perfect body, the little hands like dimpled starfish, the soft fan of eyelashes on round pink cheeks, the dainty ears nestling like shells against her baby's head.

But in recent days, Cynthia had gradually begun to rouse from her trance, to wake up and look around, and she was dismayed by what she saw. While she had been wrapped up in pregnancy and mothering, the world had rolled on without her. Everything had become more crowded and complex, fast-moving and busy, and it seemed that there was no room for her anywhere.

Cynthia stroked Jennifer's soft, fluffy head and gently squeezed the baby's little toes, fighting back an irrational flood of tears. These weepy times came over her often now, it seemed, attacks of blues that made her feel almost sick with their dark intensity.

She couldn't believe how lonely and isolated she felt, living here as mistress of the beautiful home she'd helped to restore.

J.T.'s children were much kinder and more accepting of their stepmother than they had been at first, but sometimes Cynthia even missed those grim old days when they'd been cold and suspicious of her. The bitter sparring, the silent battles for control and position—at least they'd been exhilarating. They had made Cynthia feel like a real person, engaged in a vital conflict. Probably that was why she'd been so surprisingly desolated by the growing weakness of J.T.'s grandfather, old Hank Travis. His caustic personality had always been a bracing presence, utterly genuine and passionately infuriating. With his decline, Cynthia could feel another part of herself quietly dying and drifting away on the hot Texas wind.

Soon there would be nothing left. Even Jennifer was growing up and slipping away from her, developing into a noisy, happy member of the household. Sometimes, even now, the baby pushed her mother aside and demanded to be held instead by her father or one of her tall brothers.

"You belong to them, don't you, baby?" Cynthia whispered, looking into her daughter's drowsy brown eyes with a little shock of recognition. "You're a McKinney, and a Texan, just like all the rest of them. My God, soon you'll be shutting me out, too, and I'll be the loneliest woman in all the world."

She wiped a tear of self-pity from her cheek and drew a deep breath, disgusted with herself for all these maudlin emotions that she just didn't seem able to control.

Jennifer was beginning to relax in her mother's arms. Her lips barely moved against the breast, but each time Cynthia tried gently to disengage the baby, she frowned and stiffened, flailing her small fists in sleepy outrage.

"All right," Cynthia whispered. "A little while longer, then. Just till you fall asleep."

She rocked and gazed at the dancing bunnies on the opposite wall, then tensed when she heard J.T.'s familiar tread on the stairs. He appeared in the doorway, dressed in a plaid shirt, faded jeans and the scuffed leather work boots that he wore around the ranch. Cynthia's throat tightened as she gazed up at him, and her heart swelled and throbbed with love.

There had never been a man like J. T. McKinney. Until he came into her life she had never known love, never experienced the heights of sexual desire or the glory of fulfillment. She also hadn't known how much pain two people could cause each other....

"Look, I hate to leave you like this," he said quietly, standing in the doorway and looking down at her. "It's a sick feeling, going away after a fight. I love you, Cynthia. I don't know why it's so hard for us to get along these days."

Cynthia looked away, blinking to keep the tears back so they could talk. If she started crying, J.T. would get tense and awkward, and then he'd vanish. He couldn't bear her tears.

"I just..." She bit her lip and paused, forcing herself to look up at him again. "Sometimes I feel like I'm invisible, J.T. Like I don't even exist anymore. It makes me resent my life so much, the way it's gone and stolen my whole self away from me."

"And me?" he asked quietly. He walked into the nursery and leaned against the baby's changing table, arms folded, long legs extended. "Does it make you resent me, too, Cynthia?"

"Sometimes," she confessed. "When I get this way, I hate everybody. I just feel so lonely."

"I don't understand," he said in that same gentle tone. "The house is full of people, and we all love you. How can you be lonely?"

"Because I don't *exist* anymore!" Cynthia told him in despair.

His mouth tightened, and she could see him struggling to control his impatience.

"Don't you understand, J.T.?" Cynthia pleaded. "As adults in this world, we're mostly defined by what the people around us think about us. For instance, everybody looks on you as a hell of a man, a top-notch executive, a high-powered rancher with a good brain and a ton of responsibilities. You enjoy being defined in those terms, don't you?"

He nodded, watching her face.

Cynthia shifted in the chair, moving the sleeping baby away from her breast and reaching up with one hand to button her nightgown. "Well, when I lived in Boston, it was the same for me. I had an office with my name on the door. I had clients, appointments, really serious responsibilities. The people in my world looked on me as a shrewd investor, a smart, capable banker. And it felt so good."

"Doesn't it feel just as good to be my wife, and Jennifer's mother?"

"It doesn't seem *real*," Cynthia told him, trying passionately to make him understand. "How can you be a real person if you're only defined in terms of what you are to someone else? I don't want to be described as being somebody's wife or mother, J.T. I want to be a person in my own right. I want to have something just for me."

He grinned. "Should I pick a room downstairs, make you an office and put your name on the door in big gold letters?"

"Don't make fun of me!"

"I'm not making fun of you. I'd sure like to have you back, Cynthia. I could use your advice about a lot of the financial decisions we're facing, but you haven't been interested for a long time."

"That would just be playacting. None of it's really mine, is it?" Cynthia said in despair. She knew that she was sounding irrational and that J.T. would soon grow annoyed with her if she persisted, but she couldn't let it drop. "The ranch is yours, and the winery is Tyler's, and the boot shop is Cal's."

"So what do you want? You want a business of your own? Do you want to open your own consulting firm in Austin, or what?"

"I don't *know*," Cynthia said. "I don't think a business of my own would be a practical idea right now," she added. "I just want . . . something for me. Something special and exciting, something that makes me feel alive again."

J.T. cocked an eyebrow at her. "That's what the women always say in movies just before they go off and start an affair with some young stud," he commented, only half-joking.

Cynthia's jaw dropped. "How could you say such a thing?"

J.T. shrugged and picked up a small stuffed bunny, absently smoothing its velvet ears. "You're a real sexy woman, Cynthia. Or you used to be, God knows, but you haven't shown much interest for a long time.

Maybe it's my fault. Maybe I just don't turn you on anymore," he added, looking desolate.

She turned away and shook her head impatiently, wondering how men could always manage to do this. No matter how hard a woman argued, no matter how passionately she tried to express her point of view and make him understand what she was feeling, her man always rearranged the focus so that he was the wronged party and she was supposed to feel guilty over her treatment of him.

She got up and moved across the room to lay the baby in her crib. Jennifer immediately rolled over onto her tummy, elevated her little bottom in the air and lay humped like a pink snail, sleeping deeply in the filtered morning light.

J.T. stood by his wife, leaning against the crib and gazing down at his little daughter.

"Sweet baby," he murmured huskily, drawing the soft blanket up over her rounded bottom. "Sweet little Jennifer Travis. I'm sure gonna miss you for two whole weeks, darling."

Cynthia's throat tightened at the tenderness in his voice. She wondered if he was telling the baby the things he wanted to say to his wife, but was afraid to because of her prickly attitude these days.

Suddenly she felt a wave of longing for him, a hungry thrusting urge to be with her husband, twined around him, warm and sweet and close. He was right. It had been far too long.

"Oh, J.T.," she whispered, reaching for him. "Please, let's..." But he was no longer paying any attention to her. A rush of noise had broken out in the ranch yard below, a sound of crashing boards, of hooves and bellows and shouted cries.

J.T. hurried over to the window, then turned to dash from the room. "Those damn bulls have broken out the corral fence again," he said over his shoulder. "They're into the meadow and we've already got the plane out there on the airstrip. We have to get them headed back into the corrals before they get close enough to damage a wing or something!"

Then he was gone, rushing downstairs and through the lower floor, until finally all that was left of him was the hollow clump of his boots and the distant slamming of a door.

Cynthia stood at the nursery window and watched the flurry of activity below her, men running and shouting instructions and dust clouds swirling around the bulls as their heavy hooves thundered across the parched earth.

"I hate this place," she whispered, resting her face against the glass to cool her flushed cheeks. "Dear God, how I hate this place."

A FEW HOURS LATER Cynthia stood by the edge of the small airstrip, squinting into the brilliant morning sunlight as J.T., Ruth and Tyler got ready to board the plane.

Jennifer was with her, protected from the sun by a wide-brimmed cotton hat as well as the big fringed shade on her stroller. Both of them watched as J.T. slung a couple of suitcases up into the body of the plane, then turned and strode across the airstrip toward his wife and baby.

"My girls are sure looking sweet today," he whispered huskily, smiling down at Cynthia. "You've always looked better in shorts than anybody, girl."

"I'm almost thirty-seven years old," Cynthia said dryly. "I think that's probably a bit of an exaggeration, J.T."

Again she saw that wary look in his eyes. He gazed at her thoughtfully for a moment, then bent to pick up Jennifer, who crowed and kicked her little bare legs in delight.

Cynthia watched them, deeply moved by the sight of J.T.'s brown hands on her child's tender body in the white ruffled sunsuit.

"You be a real good girl, you hear?" J.T. whispered into the baby's neck. "Don't you go making your poor mama all worn-out. If I get home and find out you've been a problem, you'll be in big trouble, little lady."

Ruth approached, smiling, and took the baby from J.T.'s arms. "She won't be bad, will she?" Ruth murmured, kissing Jennifer's round cheek beneath the brim of the bonnet. "She's just a little sweetums. She's such a darling."

Cynthia smiled fondly at the younger woman. Though Ruth was already in her fifth month of pregnancy, she was just beginning to show signs of a gentle bulge at her waistline beneath a baggy T-shirt.

"Ruth," she asked, "are you sure you'll be all right? The flight won't be too choppy for you?"

"I'll be fine." Ruth kissed the baby again, then handed her on to Tyler, who came up beside them and beamed down at his wife. "I can hardly wait to see Dad and the winery," she added. "It's the most exciting place in the world at harvest time."

Cynthia nodded, thinking with a pang of envy about how easily Ruth had made the adjustment to life on a Texas ranch.

But then, she told herself, Ruth had a vital contribution to make. She had all that valuable knowledge about wine making, and the men recognized it. They hardly made a decision without consulting her. Ruth and Tyler were full partners in business, in marriage, in life and in their approaching parenthood.

J.T. and Cynthia, on the other hand, had spent the past two years just sort of muddling along, fighting and arguing and loving each other passionately but never really finding a way to merge their personalities, to blend together and become a working team.

Cynthia watched Tyler, who was swinging the baby high in the air until Jennifer squealed and kicked in excitement. She curbed a familiar impulse to speak sharply to him, and admonish him not to play so roughly with the baby.

There was no sense saying anything, Cynthia realized. Tyler wasn't going to change the way he treated
Jennifer. Neither was Cal, or J.T. for that matter.
Besides, Jennifer loved this rough-and-tumble kind
of play. She was probably going to grow up to be one
of those hard-bitten female rodeo riders, swaggering
around in leather chaps and ragged denim shirts.
Again, Cynthia felt a deep loneliness, a desolate sense
of abandonment.

J.T. glanced at his wife's face, took the baby from
Tyler's arms and nodded briefly to his son and
daughter-in-law. The young couple moved forward to
hug Cynthia and murmur farewells, then vanished
into the plane, laughing together and embracing as
they climbed the steps.

When Cynthia and her husband were alone on the
matted strip of grass, J.T. put Jennifer tenderly back
in the stroller, patted her dimpled bare shoulder and
then took his wife in his arms.

"Cynthia," he pleaded in a hoarse whisper. "I love
you, darling. Can't you give me something to take
away with me?"

Cynthia stood rigid in his embrace, thinking miserably about all the walls between them, all the anger
and hurt and confusion. It would take weeks of talking to sort things out, and he wouldn't even give her
a weekend. He refused to go away to Galveston for a
few days of tenderness and communion, or even to
drive into Austin for a weekend at a hotel, away from
all the demands and pressures of family life.

There wasn't time, he kept telling her. The ranch and the winery needed all his attention, every day. Maybe later, in the winter, when things slowed down, they could get away for a holiday.

But maybe that was going to be too late, Cynthia thought grimly, as they stood together in the blazing noonday sunlight.

"Cynthia?"

Automatically, she raised her face and kissed him. "Goodbye, J.T.," she said quietly. "Have a nice holiday. Say hello to Don for me."

"That's all?" he asked, leaning back to study her face. "That's all you can say to me?"

She nodded wearily. "That's all I can say."

He released her and stood watching as she bent to fasten the strap across Jennifer's plump middle. She spent a long time at it, fighting back tears, waiting until her face was composed before she straightened and looked at him again.

"Goodbye, Cynthia," he said formally. "Keep well. I'll call you tonight when we get to Las Vegas."

She nodded, and J.T. turned and strode toward the plane without looking back. There was no need anymore to hold back the tears. His tall figure in jeans, white shirt and Stetson blurred in front of Cynthia's eyes as he vanished into the aircraft, seated himself at the controls and started the engines.

Cynthia stood watching and waving while the plane rose into the air, circled and drifted off into the sun. Then she wiped her eyes, turned the stroller around and bumped it across the dusty grass toward the house.

Virginia came around the corner of the garage, her arms loaded with flowers, and caught up with Cynthia near the veranda steps. "Are they gone?" she asked, bending to give Jennifer a kiss.

Cynthia nodded. "I thought you and Lettie Mae would be out there to say goodbye, too."

"Lettie Mae's making dill pickles, and I hate telling folks goodbye," Virginia said, her sweet face puckered with concern. "Especially when they're going off in that damned little plane. Poor Ruth, do you think she'll be all right?"

"She says she'll be fine. She's certainly had an easy time with this pregnancy so far."

"I think she's just too busy to be sick," Virginia commented, seating herself in one of the wicker chairs on the veranda and jamming the flowers into a plastic bucket of water. She began to strip leaves from the stalks, smiling down at Jennifer, who watched in wide-eyed interest and reached out a chubby hand to grab one of the daisies.

"Don't let her have that. She'll probably eat it," Cynthia said automatically. She lowered herself into another chair, still thinking about Ruth and Tyler and their vital, loving marriage.

"Are you all right, dear?" Virginia asked, glancing at the mistress of the house.

The gentle concern in the older woman's voice was too much for Cynthia's frayed emotions. Her throat tightened and tears began to trickle down her cheeks again.

Virginia reached out and squeezed her hand. "He'll be home before you know it," she murmured. "Just wait and see."

Cynthia nodded, struggling to get herself back under control.

"You should have gone with him," Virginia went on, frowning at a broken flower stalk. "I could have looked after this little lady for a couple of weeks."

"It's just too much to ask of you, Virginia. You're supposed to be retired, and you're still working almost full-time."

In fact, Virginia's situation was becoming a major concern to Cynthia. She knew the housekeeper wanted to be relieved of her duties at the big ranch house. Virginia was more than ready to retire to the little house J.T. had provided for her in Crystal Creek, take in a couple of young women as boarders and begin enjoying a life of well-earned leisure.

But Cynthia couldn't manage the big house without help, not while Jennifer was still such a handful. Nor could she expect Ruth to take on a lot of household duties when she was busy with the winery and with the house that she and Tyler were building for themselves near their vineyards. Lynn was fully absorbed in her horses and her marriage to Sam Russell and Lettie Mae seldom ventured out of the kitchen anymore.

"I wish we could find somebody else," Cynthia said. "This really isn't fair to you."

"I can manage for a while," Virginia said comfortably. "We've got the word out everywhere that we're looking for some household help, and eventually somebody will come along."

"But who knows how long that might take in a little place like this? And in the meantime, you're still working so hard every day," Cynthia told the housekeeper with a worried frown.

Virginia ignored the comment, squinting down at a bunch of flowers in her hand. "Do you think these daisies are too ratty to go in the front hall? The heat's been awful hard on them this year."

"Virginia, don't change the subject. I've seen how tired you look sometimes, and how you rub your back when you think nobody's watching."

Virginia glanced at the younger woman and her face softened. "Is that so? Well, I've seen how sad you look, sometimes, when you stare off into space like that. Is everything all right, Miss C?"

Cynthia swallowed hard and shook her head. "It's just... it's kind of hard," she confessed, "having to make so many adjustments in such a short time. I had to learn to be married, live in Texas, adjust to J.T.'s heart condition, then motherhood, all within a few months, it seemed. I'm still kind of dizzy, Virginia. I know it's silly, but sometimes I feel like I've been run over by a truck and there's nothing much left of me."

Virginia reached out to squeeze her hand. "Texas can have that effect on folks. It's all larger than life, somehow. It leaves you feeling small."

Cynthia looked at her in surprise. "But, Virginia...you've lived in Crystal Creek all your life."

"That doesn't mean I don't have eyes to see how things are for other folks. I think I know how hard it is for you. Marriage to a man as stubborn as J. T. McKinney...well, it can't be an easy thing."

Cynthia's amazement grew. As far as she could recall, this was the first time she'd ever heard one of the longtime household help say something to her about J.T. that could be construed as even faintly critical.

"I wasn't married long enough to learn much about it," Virginia went on, smiling dreamily at the distant hills, obviously remembering her young cowboy, killed so long ago in a riding accident. "But I've noticed that the brighter and stronger and more interesting two people are, the harder it usually is for them to get along. They're harnessed together but they keep wanting to pull different ways, and it's a powerful struggle."

"These days I always feel like it's my fault," Cynthia murmured, her voice so low it was almost inaudible. "Like he's this big, strong, intelligent man and I'm just a silly, emotional woman who should be getting over her nonsense."

"I know. That's the way they want us to feel, all those men, but it isn't always so."

"It isn't?" Cynthia felt a growing sense of unreality as the conversation progressed. She would never have suspected their pleasant, cheerful housekeeper of harboring such philosophies.

"No. I think lots of your problems are J.T.'s fault, and there's times I'd just like to take him by the ear, sit him down and tell him so."

Cynthia gazed at the other woman in fascination. "What would you tell him?"

"Oh, lots of things," Virginia said with a shrug. "Like that he should take you off for a holiday every now and then, just the two of you. He should pay some real attention to you like he did when you were courting. He should see that you have some responsibilities around here that make you feel alive. I'd tell him that it's not enough just to marry a woman, set her up in the house and give her a baby and then expect her to be fine from then on."

"Is that what he did with Pauline?"

"More or less. But that was different. She went through considerable hell to get the man she wanted, Miss Pauline did. But once she had him, she was a real traditional wife and mother. She expected to be treated that way, and she probably wouldn't have been comfortable with anything else. Actually..."

Virginia fell silent for a moment, then smiled at her employer.

"I never thought I'd hear myself say these words, but I'm ready to retire and I've seen a lot of living. I'm getting old enough to see things clearer now."

Cynthia waited tensely while Virginia organized her thoughts.

"I loved Miss Pauline dearly, and I always will. But in a lot of ways, Miss Cynthia, you're a more interesting, complicated woman than Pauline was. And you need more from a husband. And if J. T. McKinney doesn't realize it pretty soon, I truly fear that he's riding for a real bad fall."

With that, the housekeeper picked up her bucket of flowers, lifted the baby from the stroller and vanished inside the house, leaving Cynthia gazing into the sunlight in troubled silence.

CHAPTER TWO

J.T. GRIPPED the telephone receiver and stared at an ugly oil painting above the bed. It was a matador in a red velvet jacket, standing haughtily in front of a huge black bull quivering with banderillas. J.T. observed that the frame was solidly bolted to the wall. That was one of the things he hated about hotels, the way they nailed down everything that could be moved. It gave him the depressing feeling that the whole world was full of thieves.

"So did she have a pretty good nap this afternoon?" he asked.

"Not really," Cynthia said. Her voice sounded low and faraway. J.T. almost had to strain to hear her words. "It was so hot. Even with the air-conditioning, she's all sweaty when she wakes up from her nap. I worry about her getting a chill."

"It's sure hot out here, too," J.T. said, trying to keep his voice cheerful. "When we touched down at the airport, my landing gear practically sank into the asphalt."

"Is Ruth all right?"

"She was looking a little peaked by the time we landed. Lucky we decided to make a stopover here in

Vegas rather than going all the way to California in one day. I don't think Ruth could have stood a trip that long.''

Cynthia was silent for a moment at the other end of the line. "Is your room nice?" she asked in a small, wistful voice.

"It's a room. The picture's nailed to the wall above the bed. Makes me want to get a crowbar from the plane and pry the damned thing off.''

He waited for his wife to chuckle or make a droll comment, but she didn't.

"Cynthia?"

"I'm all right," she said, sounding distant again. "I'm just so tired. It's almost midnight, J.T.''

"Damn, I guess it is. We're two time zones behind you, aren't we? It's not even ten o'clock here in Vegas. The streets are full of people, and the whole town's running full blast.''

"Will you be going out?"

J.T. shrugged. "I doubt it. Ruth and Tyler said they were going down to the casino for a while, but it's sure not much fun doing Vegas on your own.''

He gazed out the window at the laughing throngs in the street below, assailed by a sudden wistful image of what this evening could have been. He saw himself with Cynthia on his arm, saw her laughing and glowing with golden loveliness as they swept through lounges and casinos and attended a couple of the fabulous shows that were playing.

"God, I wish you were here," he said. "You should have come, Cynthia. You should be with me tonight."

Slowly the image of the casinos and clubs faded. He saw another picture, of Cynthia coming out of the bathroom into the muted light of the room, wearing a transparent lace nightgown that showed the curves and shadows of her body, that whispered as she moved. She crossed the room, letting the gown slip from her shoulders, and stood naked before him, her dark eyes mysterious and warm with promise....

J.T. groaned aloud and shifted awkwardly on the chair.

"J.T.?" Cynthia asked with a note of anxiety in her voice. "Is something the matter?"

"Nothing," he said, still almost breathless with the fiery surge of lust that roared through his body. He was tense and rigid, aching with need, almost in pain.

More like a kid of seventeen than a man in his fifties, he thought in despair. When in hell did a man ever get over this?

Maybe it would help, he reflected bitterly, if his wife would ever make love to him. These days, lovemaking in his marriage was like a snowy day in the Hill Country. J.T. couldn't remember the last one, but he knew it was a rare and marvelous occurrence.

"J.T., the baby's crying. I'll have to go."

"Cynthia... God, I wish you were here. Can't you come?" he pleaded. "Look," he added, energized by his thrusting, overpowering desire, "have Ken or somebody drive you in to Austin tomorrow and get on a commercial flight. We'll wait for you here in Vegas. Call me and I'll meet you at—"

"J.T., that's just ridiculous. If I'd wanted to go with you on that trip, I'd be there now. Please, I have to leave. She's really yelling."

And in fact J.T. could now hear the distant wails that never failed to distract his wife's attention, no matter how much he needed her or wanted her. "Sure," he said wearily, slumping back in the chair. "You go tend to her, honey. I'll call you tomorrow from California, all right?"

"All right."

"Cynthia?"

"Yes?"

"I love you, girl. I love you so much."

"Good night, J.T. Travel safely, all of you."

Across a thousand miles of high plains, mountain ranges and desert, J.T. could hear the remote sadness in her voice. He hung up, still feeling hollow and miserable, and wandered over to stand looking out the window.

The street below looked more like high noon than nighttime. Tourists strolled past in shorts and T-shirts, thronging the wide sidewalks and intersections, brightly illuminated by the vivid glare of a million neon lights. Down the street at the Mirage, the miniature volcano was about to erupt. Hundreds of people crowded the fenced area, laughing and waiting with uplifted faces as the fast-moving lanes of traffic roared by.

J.T. held the curtain aside, watching the flare of the volcano, the cascades of molten lava, the brilliant light show. He heard the distant sound of cheering as the spectacle faded and the lighted gardens and waterfalls around the casino came back into view.

A couple in evening dress strolled past and crossed the street, heading for the huge moving staircase, all enclosed in glass, that spanned the grounds and delivered guests to the casino. J.T. watched them idly, thinking that the woman looked a little bit like Cynthia. She was tall and graceful, with shining golden hair that fell smoothly around her head, and she laughed and hugged her companion as they entered the walkway.

J.T. watched them disappear, battling another stormy flood of sexual desire that left him feeling weak and restless. Abruptly he reached for his Stetson, fitted it on his head and walked out the door.

In the lobby he stepped from the elevator and almost collided with Tyler, who was waiting to go up, a brown paper grocery sack cradled in his hands.

J.T. grinned at his son. "Coming back from the casino with a sack of money, are you?"

Tyler chuckled. "Yeah, that's real likely," he said with cheerful sarcasm. "I can't even make money on the nickel slots. Ruth and I lost our shirts down there after dinner."

"How much?" J.T. asked.

Tyler grinned. "Twenty bucks. Our entire gambling allowance. We're cleaned out, so we're staying in the room to watch TV tonight. Ruth's up there now, having a bath."

J.T. felt a pang of envy as he looked at his son's handsome, smiling face. Tyler was here with his wife and the two of them were playing and having fun, enjoying their holiday like a couple of children released from school. Tonight they'd settle comfortably in their room to watch television, then go to bed and hold each other with loving tenderness, whispering together in the darkness...

"So," he asked abruptly, pointing at the package in Tyler's hands, "what's in there, if it's not cash?"

Tyler looked embarrassed. "Strawberries."

"Strawberries?"

"Ruth has a craving," Tyler said. "She wants fresh strawberries in the worst way. We called room service, but they didn't have any in the kitchen."

J.T. chuckled. "So you've been out wandering around Las Vegas at night, all by yourself, looking for fresh strawberries?"

"It's amazing," Tyler said. "Everything around here is open all night long, Daddy. Grocery stores, novelty shops, clothing stores, everything. These people never go to bed."

J.T.'s smile faded and he felt a touch of sadness, gazing into his son's face. Tyler looked as he used to when he was a small child on some kind of adventure. The boy didn't get away from the ranch very often, J.T. realized. And he'd been working so hard the past few years. Tyler was certainly entitled to a vacation with his pretty wife, and J.T. was happy for them.

But he felt so damned lonesome.

"Well," he said aloud, "you kids have fun. And don't keep her up all night. She needs her rest."

Tyler gave his father a wolfish grin. "I'm hoping the strawberries will wake her up a bit. I think I'll order a bottle of champagne to go along with them."

"Well now, that just might work," J.T. said dryly, watching as Tyler disappeared behind the sliding door of the elevator. He hesitated briefly, glanced into the crowded casino and then headed out onto the street, surprised by the blast of warm air that hit him.

This might be desert country, but it was still a lot hotter outside at ten o'clock than it was in the air-conditioned hotel lobby. J.T. wandered down the busy street, feeling more and more isolated as the crowds pressed around him.

He drifted into a casino and played a few hands of blackjack, depressed to find that he couldn't seem to lose. If he held at fourteen, the dealer broke. If he hit seventeen, he was dealt a three. In less than half an hour, J.T. won three hundred dollars, cashed in his chips and left, feeling worse than ever.

It wasn't much fun, winning all alone. Unless gambling was your thing, you needed someone along with you to enjoy this experience. And for J. T. McKinney, gambling definitely wasn't a thrill. There was enough financial risk in the day-to-day operation of a ranch to take any excitement out of playing cards.

He moved off down the street again, not even sure of where he was going. The wave of lust that had overwhelmed him when he heard Cynthia's voice didn't seem to be diminishing at all. Maybe it was the heat, or the holiday atmosphere, or the brilliant neon lights glancing off the skimpy summer outfits most of the younger women were wearing.

J.T. found himself gazing hungrily at tanned legs, at the curve of buttocks under brief shorts and the swell of young breasts beneath T-shirts and halter tops.

Just like a dirty old man, he thought miserably, turning off the Strip to wander down a side street where the light wasn't as glaring and the sidewalks were less crowded.

"Hi, cowboy," a soft voice said nearby. J.T. paused and squinted into a darkened alcove under a ragged hotel canopy.

"Hi," he said automatically when he realized that the words were being addressed to him.

"Are you lonesome?" the voice asked.

It was a low, husky voice, a little halting and incredibly sexy. "Yeah," J.T. said reluctantly, as if the words were being dragged from him. "Yeah, I'm real lonesome. Does it show?"

A woman emerged from the shadows and came toward him. J.T. peered at her, but the light was too dim to get much more than a blurred impression of her looks. He saw long shapely legs in a suede mini-skirt that barely covered her crotch, a slim waist and an ample curving bosom only partially concealed by a low-cut suede top.

The woman's face was hidden under a cloud of dark hair. She moved nearer to J.T. and took his arm, pressing close against his side. He looked down at the mass of shining black hair, surprised that, despite her high spike heels, this woman came just about to his shoulder. She had to be at least four or five inches shorter than Cynthia.

In fact, she was different from Cynthia in every way....

She stood so close to him that he could smell her perfume, a surprisingly light and delicate scent that reminded J.T. of the flowers that dotted the hillsides around his ranch in the springtime. He looked down at her, watching the play of distant neon lights on her curving, half-naked bosom.

Compelled by an urge that he couldn't have con-trolled to save his life, J.T. reached out a tentative hand and touched one of the woman's breasts, cup-ping the warm flesh in his hands. Hunger stabbed through him, an unbearable surge of sexual longing that made his knees feel weak and shaky.

"Come on," she whispered in the darkness. "Come with me. I'll treat you real good."

Numbly, J.T. turned and followed her through the door of the hotel, across a deserted lobby and up a narrow, grimy staircase.

They were almost at the top of the stairs before he regained a semblance of control, stopped and realized just what he was doing.

J. T. McKinney had never once been unfaithful to either of his wives. Dogged fidelity was a characteristic of the men in his family. It was unimaginable to think of Tyler cheating on Ruth, and even Cal, who'd had hundreds of girlfriends in the past, had now settled in with Serena as if she were the only woman in all the world.

In fact, if one of his sons had been caught in adultery, J.T. would have been deeply disappointed and probably very angry.

Yet here he was, like a panting dog, following some Las Vegas hooker up to her room.

"I can't do this," he muttered, pausing on the stairway. "Sorry. I just can't."

The woman turned to him, a dim shadow in the pool of darkness at the top of the stairs. "Please," she whispered urgently. "Please don't go away."

"Look, I'm sorry. I don't know what came over me. I can't go with you."

"Please," she whispered again, moving back down the steps and pressing close to him. But there was no passion in her manner or her voice. There was nothing but fear, a terror so real that J.T. could almost smell it. "Please," she urged him in that same hoarse whisper. "Please don't go away."

J.T. tried to disengage himself from her clutching hands, feeling increasingly trapped and panicky.

"I'll give you some money," he muttered, reaching for his wallet. "If that's what you want, I can give you some. I just can't..."

"If you give me money," she whispered, "you don't have to...to do anything. Just come to my room for a little while. Please."

Again he was conscious of her fear, and the desperate tremble in her voice. He yielded, feeling helpless and a little frightened himself, and followed her down the hall and into a shabby room.

As the woman locked the door behind them, J.T. looked around warily in the dim light, wondering if this whole thing was some kind of trap. What dark menace lurked beyond the curtained alcove by the bed, or through the door of the little bathroom?

Part of his brain was poised and cautious, rapidly assessing the situation and his own danger. The other part, strangely, was thinking in a detached fashion that it would be a horrible thing for Cynthia to have her murdered husband's body found in some prostitute's room on a gritty street in Las Vegas.

"Switch that light on," he said sharply.

The woman obeyed, then crossed the room awkwardly in her high heels and stood looking up at him in tense silence. J.T. stared at her face in astonishment. He'd expected garish makeup, a hard glittering smile and a shopworn look. But this woman was lovely.

Not a woman, J.T. corrected himself. She was just a girl, a delicate creature with creamy skin, a sweet, childlike mouth and wide brown eyes that gazed at him with fear and pleading. In the bright light, her sexy garb looked forced and artificial against the fresh innocence of her face, as if she were a little girl playing dress-up.

"Lord," he whispered. "How old are you?"

"I'm . . . I'm twenty-five."

"Like hell. My daughter's about that age, and you're a lot younger than she is. How old are you?"

"Nineteen," she murmured, clearly on the verge of tears.

J.T. felt a hot surge of disgust with himself, and with all men whose uncontrolled sex drives created this terrible situation. His storm of lust had completely vanished, replaced by self-loathing and compassion for the girl who stood trembling by the shabby bed.

"Why are you doing this?" he asked gently.

She shook her head. "Do you want . . . do you want to get undressed?" she whispered, reaching for the fastening on her skirt. "I can . . ."

"No, dammit! I don't want to get undressed. You're just a little girl. You should be at the high school prom, not here in this room."

She gave him a brief, bitter smile, then jerked her head around nervously when a car horn blared in the street below.

"What are you so afraid of?" J.T. asked.

"Please," she whispered, looking down at the stained carpet. "You said that if we didn't do anything, you'd still . . . you'd give me some money."

"How much?" J.T. asked, taking his wallet from his hip pocket.

"It's a . . . a hundred dollars," she murmured. "If we just . . . do it. But it's more if you want anything special."

J.T. felt another jolt of revulsion, thinking about this lovely young creature being forced to do "special things" for lecherous old men.

"Why are you doing this?" he asked again, peeling off some of the bills he'd just collected from the casino. "You're a beautiful girl. Why don't you get a job and make a life for yourself?"

Again she refused to answer, just bit her lip and shook her head. She accepted the money from him and stood watching as he moved toward the door.

"Could you . . . could you stay for a little while?" she murmured as he reached for the doorknob. "Please? Just . . . fifteen minutes or so? I could make you some coffee," she added shyly, waving her hand in the direction of the small alcove behind its sagging curtain.

J.T. paused and looked at her. "Why do you want me to stay?"

"He's watching me," the girl whispered. "If you leave right away, he'll know we didn't do anything, and he'll be so mad at me."

"Who will?"

"Ramon," she said. "His name is Ramon."

"That's your..." J.T. hesitated. He'd been about to say "your pimp," but the words sounded harsh and out of place when he looked at the girl's delicate face. "Your boyfriend?" he concluded lamely.

Her mouth twisted. "Hardly," she muttered.

Again J.T. saw that look of naked terror in her eyes, coupled with a kind of wretched, trapped misery that was more than he could bear. He moved slowly back into the room.

"You know, I think I could use a cup of coffee," he announced, dropping into the only chair in the room, a big faded armchair near the window. He shifted abruptly when a loose spring stabbed his hip.

The girl's face brightened with a look of childlike gratitude that tore at his heart. He watched as she hurried into the little alcove, her slender legs coltlike and awkward in the high heels, and turned the heat on under a kettle on a tiny stove.

"What's your name?" he asked.

"Lisa," she said over her shoulder, taking a mug down from the sagging cupboard and spooning instant coffee into it.

Silence fell, broken only by the sound of the kettle as it hissed and began to boil. "So Lisa, tell me about Ramon," J.T. said with forced casualness. "How did you happen to meet up with him?"

She came back into the room, carrying the brimming mug carefully in two hands like a child. "Do you take cream or sugar?"

"This is fine." J.T. accepted the mug gravely. "Why are you so scared, Lisa?"

The kindness in his tone was clearly difficult for her to bear. Tears began to gather on her eyelashes, and she brushed at them with the back of her hand. "I came here to get a job," she said finally, seating herself on the edge of the bed and looking earnestly at J.T. "Just a month ago."

"Where did you come from?"

"New Mexico. I grew up in a little town west of Albuquerque."

"Does your family still live there?"

"My mother lives there with my stepfather. They have four little boys. My half brothers, they are." Her expressive face shadowed again at the mention of her stepfather, and J.T. had a pretty strong suspicion about why she'd left the little town in New Mexico. "It was real hard," she added simply. "There never was much money at home."

"So you came here to get a job."

The girl nodded. "I came on the bus. When I got here, Ramon was at the bus depot with a woman called Sally. They told me they could help me find a job."

"But they didn't tell you what kind of job?" J.T. prompted her gently when she fell silent.

"They said they'd get me a good job at one of the casinos, helping with tour groups. They said I just needed some training. I didn't have anywhere else to go, so I went with them."

"Then what happened?"

"I never saw Sally again," the girl told him simply. She looked at him with childlike misery, her eyes wide and tragic. "Ramon brought me to this room and beat me up every day. He took my clothes and everything else I owned. He hardly ever brought me any food. I was starving, and it hurt so bad all over that I could barely move."

"My God," J.T. whispered, staring at her. "Why didn't you run away? Why didn't you go to the police?"

"Ramon watched me all the time. Every minute," the girl told him. "After a long time he brought me some clothes and told me I had to...to go out on the street."

J.T.'s coffee was suddenly sour in his mouth. He set the mug on the floor, unable to drink any more. "But once you were out on the street, why didn't you run away? Why don't you get away now?"

"He still watches me all the time," Lisa said. "He sits in that coffee shop across the street and watches who I talk to, when I take men up to the room and how long they stay. Then he comes and gets the money from me, and I have to go out and do it again. If I tried to run away, he'd kill me."

"Even if you went to the police?"

"If I went to the police," the girl said bitterly, "I'd file a complaint and be back out on the street in half an hour, and then how could I hide from him?"

"But . . . why don't you leave the city? Just get on the bus and go somewhere else?"

Lisa gazed at him. "I never get to keep any of the money," she said simply. "And he'd find me no matter where I went."

J.T. felt his anger rising. "What does he look like, this Ramon?" he asked abruptly. "Maybe I'll just go over to the coffee shop and have a little talk with this bastard."

The girl's face turned pale with terror. "Oh, no," she whispered. "Oh, please, don't do that. If he ever knew I told anybody about him . . ."

J.T. watched her in silence, entertaining wild thoughts of packing her up and taking her to California with them. But how could he explain her presence to Ruth and Tyler without endangering his marriage? And how did he really know that her fantastic story was even the truth? After all, he was in pretty deep waters here. Maybe this setup was just some kind of elaborate Las Vegas scam, and he was swallowing it whole, like any gullible tourist.

"Look," he said at last, "if I give you all this money . . ." He took out his wallet again and peeled off a few more fifty-dollar bills. "If I give you this, will you promise me you'll get on a bus and leave town? He can't track you across the country. Once you're out of here, he'll forget about you."

The girl's eyes widened as she looked at the money. There was a brief silence, and then she surprised J.T. by getting to her feet in a businesslike manner, tucking the bills inside her bra and moving toward the door.

He followed her, wondering with wry humor if he'd just been royally fleeced.

Easy come, easy go, he thought philosophically, following the girl's slender form down the stairs and out onto the street.

In front of the hotel, Lisa startled him again by reaching for his arm, tossing her head in a flirtatious manner and beginning to walk with him up the street in the direction he'd come, cuddling close against his side.

"Look," J.T. said uncomfortably, "Lisa, I have to get back to my hotel now."

"Where is it?" she asked.

"It's on the Strip," J.T. said.

"Point to it," she whispered. "Pretend you're taking me somewhere." She smiled brightly and gazed up into his face, but her eyes were dark with fear. J.T. could feel the tension in her slim body.

He glanced across the street at the lighted windows of the coffee shop. Lisa jerked harshly at his arm.

"Don't look!" she whispered. "Pretend you're talking to me. Laugh and have a good time. Please," she added, her voice breaking. "Just for a little while, till we're out of sight."

"What should I talk about?"

The girl hesitated, laughing and tossing her head again as they came abreast of the coffee shop. "Tell me . . . tell me where you grew up," she said at last, in a low tense voice. "You sound like Texas. Did you grow up in Texas?"

"I sure did."

Her dread was infectious. J.T. began to feel nervous and frightened, too, especially when they were past the coffee shop and he couldn't look around to see if they were being followed.

"Where? Where did you grow up? Please talk to me," Lisa whispered.

J.T. swallowed hard and forced himself to smile down at her in a casual way. "Well, I grew up in a little place called Crystal Creek, not far from Austin," he said. "My folks had a ranch outside town."

"Was it nice? Were you happy when you were a little boy?"

"Yeah," J.T. said. "It was real nice. I had a lot of friends, boys from town and from other ranches. We used to spend the summer at the swimming hole, and gallop our ponies up and down Main Street, playing cowboys and Indians. We had a real good time."

Lisa nodded and smiled. They rounded the corner and headed out onto the Strip, merging into the colorful throngs of people who still crowded the sidewalk, even at midnight.

A taxi was cruising slowly in their direction amid the traffic a block up the street. The girl disengaged herself from J.T.'s arm and glanced wildly over her shoulder in the direction they'd come. Then she bent down, whipped off her high heels and sprinted up the

sidewalk to wait at the curb, waving her hand frantically.

J.T. stood alone in the crowd, watching as the cab
stopped and Lisa's slim body vanished inside the vehicle. The last he saw of her was a terrified white face
and a cloud of dark hair as the cab drifted past him
on Las Vegas Boulevard, heading into the glittering
ocean of neon lights.

INSIDE THE CAB, Lisa settled against the hard vinyl
seat and drew a couple of deep breaths, worried that
she was going to faint. She felt dizzy and light-
headed, and she couldn't seem to catch her breath.
Her heart still thundered so hard within her chest that
it sickened her with its noisy pounding.

"Where to, lady?" the driver asked.

"The...the Greyhound bus depot," Lisa whispered. "Please hurry." She gazed blindly out the
window as the cab rounded a corner and headed
downtown. The streets looked normal, just a typical
Saturday night in Las Vegas. Nobody knew that
something momentous and terrifying had just happened, and the whole world was turned upside down.

Lisa felt anxiously inside her bra for the money,
wondering if she'd actually succeeded in fooling Ramon. Did he really believe that the tall cowboy had
been taking her with him to a party somewhere?

Ramon always told her to ask the men if they had
any friends who might be interested. "Turn one trick

into two," he said. "It saves your time and my money."

He'd certainly been watching from the coffee shop, and he'd seen her walking away with the cowboy. Hopefully he believed that they were going on to another hotel to meet a group of the Texan's friends.

In situations like this, Lisa was supposed to check in with Ramon when she arrived at the new destination so he knew where she was. He would be waiting for her call, and it wouldn't be long before he realized that he'd been deceived.

She just had a little while. Unless there was a bus leaving right away, he would find her before long.

Lisa shuddered at the thought of Ramon's fury, and the terrible punishment he would inflict on her when he caught her. He would kill her without hesitation, but first he'd make sure that she suffered enough to serve as a hideous example to other girls who might try to run from him.

Lisa folded her hands in her lap in a childlike manner and lowered her head in a brief, desperate prayer. "Please, God," she whispered. "I know I've done bad things, but I never wanted to. Please, please, help me get away. Please don't let him find me." Then she bent and fitted her high heels back on her feet, still fighting to get her breathing under control.

"Here we are," the driver said, glancing back at her.

"Do you..." Lisa's voice broke. She paused, shaken by a deep, uncontrollable spasm of terror, and forced herself to try again. "Do you have change for a fifty?"

"Is four tens all right?"

"Whatever," Lisa said in growing desperation, handing the bill over the seat and receiving her change. She bolted from the back seat of the cab and ducked inside the lighted bus terminal, feeling as vulnerable and exposed as if she were stark naked in the glare of searchlights.

A long line of people waited at the ticket counter. Lisa couldn't bear to join them and stand out in the open under those bright lights.

She hurried into the washroom and leaned over a sink to splash cold water on her face and wrists, then gazed in wonder at the white face in the mirror.

Was it really her, this half-naked woman in the seductive clothes? A month ago, she'd been a completely different person. But that was before she'd slipped off the edge of the world and found herself living in a hellish nightmare of brutality and exploitation....

She felt a wave of nausea and lowered her head, bracing her hands against the sink, trying to fight down the rising sickness. After a few minutes she moved nervously back out into the terminal and saw that the line had dispersed. "Are there any buses leaving right away?" she asked at the ticket counter.

A bored young man consulted a chart at his elbow without looking up. "There's a coach leaving for the southeast in fifteen minutes," he said. "It's boarding now at gate six."

"I'd like . . . I'd like a ticket."

The young man looked up and suspended his gum chewing in startled appreciation when he saw Lisa. An unpleasant smile spread across his face as he glanced over the counter at her swelling bosom, her long legs and shining dark hair.

"Would you, now? Where you going, sweetheart?"

Lisa hesitated. "Can't I just get on the bus?"

"You need to tell me where you're going, doll. I need a destination on the ticket, see?"

A destination.

Lisa's numbed mind moved slowly, grappling with this new problem. The adrenaline rush that had accompanied her escape was beginning to wear off, and she felt sluggish and sick with dread.

"C'mon, baby. Maybe you don't want to go away after all," the ticket clerk suggested with a leer. "Maybe you just want to go home with me instead. I get off shift in half an hour."

"Southeast?" she whispered.

"What?"

"You said the bus is going southeast. That's Texas, isn't it?"

"Yeah, I guess. Among other places."

Lisa had a brief yearning image of lazy summer days, of small boys laughing and splashing in a swimming hole and racing their ponies up and down the sleepy main street of a little town. The scene was remote and sun-washed inside her mind, warm and shining with innocence and purity. It seemed as far removed as a person could get from the squalor and depravity of Lisa's brief sojourn in this glittering nighttime city, of the things she'd done in the past weeks and the things that had been done to her.

"Crystal Creek," she said at last, drawing a deep ragged breath and watching as the young man leafed through his destination book. "I want to go to Crystal Creek, Texas."

CHAPTER THREE

CYNTHIA WRESTLED the baby's stroller along a dusty path behind the ranch buildings, heading for the leafy coolness of the riverbank. Inside the stroller, Jennifer kicked her small bare legs and chortled with pleasure as she grasped at the trailing grasses that lined the path.

The rugged banks of the river gave way after a while to a gentle slope, shaded with rustling cedar trees so the grass underfoot was still soft and green in spite of the baking heat of summer. Cynthia moved the stroller off the path, set the parking brake and took a blanket that was folded over the handle, spreading it out on the grass.

Jennifer watched from beneath the lacy frill of her bonnet, wide-eyed with interest.

"Da?" she asked hopefully. "Dada?"

Cynthia gave her daughter a brief sad smile. It wasn't particularly surprising that the baby's first word had been Daddy, considering how much she adored her father. But it seemed miserably ironic that Jennifer would start saying this word just the day after J.T.'s departure for California.

When he'd called yesterday to report their safe arrival at the Napa Valley winery, Cynthia hadn't told him that Jennifer was talking. That would be such a delightful surprise for him when he came home, to have his baby daughter greet him by name.

"Daddy's far, far away," Cynthia told the baby, lifting her out of the stroller and setting her on the blanket. "He won't be home for almost two weeks. It seems like an eternity already, doesn't it?"

Jennifer chuckled and looked around, drumming her heels on the blanket. Then she turned over, dropped onto all fours and crawled briskly off toward the trees.

"Oh, no you don't," Cynthia said, grasping the baby's plump middle and hauling her back into a sitting position. "Not off the blanket. There's snakes and bugs and all kinds of awful things out there."

Jennifer's smile faded. She opened her mouth to wail, but subsided when Cynthia rummaged in her bag and produced a cookie and a few bright plastic toys. While Cynthia settled herself, the little girl sat chewing thoughtfully on the cookie. She grasped one of the rattles in a fat dimpled fist, murmuring to herself in her unintelligible baby language.

Cynthia leaned back and moved slightly so her legs were in the sun, thinking about J.T.

This was the first time in their marriage that he'd gone away for more than a night or two at a stock sale, and she missed him terribly. The bed seemed vast and empty. She ached for his touch, his hands and mouth and body, with an urgent physical need that was almost painful.

And yet, she thought wryly, when he was home, she usually didn't want him to touch her.

Maybe this whole irrational conflict really *was* just some kind of postpartum depression. That was what Nate Purdy had suggested when Cynthia had tentatively broached the subject on her last visit to the family doctor.

"I've seen all manner of strange things, Cynthia," he'd told her comfortably. "Women who can't abide their husbands, women who don't even want to be in the same room with their babies, women who suddenly start believing that the old family housekeeper is out to steal their man...it goes away after a while."

"How long?" Cynthia had asked. "Jennifer's going to be walking soon. It's a little late for postnatal blues, isn't it?"

"There's no telling," he'd said, shaking his handsome, silvery head. "Just no telling."

But Cynthia hadn't really believed him. The doctor's explanation seemed so careless and facile, typically male in its approach to the complexities of a woman's personality. Cynthia knew that her strange disturbed feelings had nothing to do with hormone imbalance or the demands of late motherhood. In fact, she was certain of this, because her feelings about other aspects of her life hadn't changed at all. She was the same person, with the same tastes, outlooks and abilities that she'd always had.

The only real difference lay in her relationship with J.T. And no matter how she looked at it, how hard she tried to be fair about her own emotions, Cynthia truly believed that the growing tensions in their marriage were his fault, not hers.

She understood her husband a little better now that Carolyn had taken the time to let her know the truth about his first marriage. Cynthia had been so amazed to discover that Pauline hadn't been the paragon of womanly virtue she'd always supposed, and J.T. hadn't been an unfailing tower of strength and devotion.

After that talk with Carolyn, things had been better between Cynthia and J.T. for quite a while. They grew closer, and had some really sweet times together. But a lot of their amiability in those months was probably because Cynthia was still wrapped up in her baby, willing to be a wife and mother and nothing more.

Willing, Cynthia thought, smiling grimly at the irony, to be more like Pauline.

J.T. couldn't help it. He was designed to live more comfortably with a woman like Pauline who followed the unspoken rules and used feminine wiles and subterfuge to get her way. Pauline had ruled by appearing to yield, and J.T. had accepted her behavior. He just couldn't understand what Cynthia wanted from marriage, because their views of life were so vastly different.

J.T. saw himself as a warrior and provider, out doing battle with the world to protect his helpless wife and babies. The role of his woman was to nurture and comfort, giving him strength to face his adversaries and slay all those dragons. When he came home to his castle, she was supposed to heap praise on him for his success, and reward him with her sexual love.

Cynthia, on the other hand, saw marriage as a partnership. She saw a man and woman walking side by side, shoulder to shoulder, facing the dangers of the world together. When one faltered the other was strong, so the two of them united could overcome anything. There was no role differentiation in Cynthia's mind. Women could make tough business decisions without help, and men could care for sick babies. Each partner turned a hand to what needed to be done at the moment, and together they moved from strength to strength.

J.T. could never seem to accept that image, and Cynthia couldn't give it up. How were two stubborn people supposed to arrive at a compromise and find a way of getting along together?

Cynthia didn't want to be an ornament in J.T.'s house and a tempting morsel in his bed. She wanted to be a vital, exciting, necessary part of his life, a person who delighted and intrigued him because of who she was and what she was capable of, not because she was the woman currently occupying the slot in his existence marked Wife. That was what Cynthia had meant when she told J.T. she didn't feel that

she existed anymore. His powerful stereotype of how
a wife should think and act was beginning, with insidious power, to blur the lines of her own personality, to swallow up the woman she really was in some
shadowy image wearing an apron in the daytime and
sexy nightgowns after dark.

"I'll leave him before I let that happen," Cynthia
told the baby. "If he can't give me some of himself,
bend a little and make me a full partner, he's not getting any of me."

The words were defiant, but misery flooded her as
she spoke. She was lonely and terrified of what the
future might hold whenever she considered a life
apart from J.T.

The baby chuckled and pounded the cookie against
the blanket. Cynthia rescued it automatically, handed
it back to Jennifer, then glanced along the path when
she realized somebody was approaching. It was
Jimmy Slattery, the young nephew of Ken Slattery,
ranch foreman at the Double C.

Jimmy was ten years old. His parents, Ken Slattery's brother and his wife, had taken high-paying
summer jobs on an oil field in Alaska, and Jimmy
couldn't possibly go with them, so he'd been sent
down from Oklahoma to spend the holidays with Ken
and Nora. He was plump and dark-haired, pale and
heavily freckled, and wore thick glasses that caught
and reflected the sunlight, giving him a remote,
watchful look.

Cynthia felt some sympathy for the child because in many ways they were both exiles here, struggling to fit into a way of life that had been established for a century and had scant room for either of them. But Jimmy Slattery, she'd discovered, was a hard child to develop a relationship with. He didn't get along with the other children at the ranch, so he was always alone, and he apparently spent his time spying on people, slipping among the trees and the ranch buildings, making mysterious markings in a little notebook.

"Hello, Jimmy," Cynthia called as he approached. "What are you up to?"

Jimmy paused by the blanket and stared down at Jennifer, who smiled broadly and waved her cookie. "Nothing," he said, gazing off into the trees with a secretive squint.

Cynthia looked at the child helplessly, wondering what to say.

There were two other boys on the ranch close to his age, but they were already miniature rodeo hands, riding steers and following the weekend circuit with their fathers. They had no time for Jimmy, with his thick glasses and his mysterious, solitary pursuits. And Jimmy himself was openly contemptuous of the younger boys, like Rory Jones and little David Milne from over at the Gibson place.

Jimmy moved closer to the two on the blanket, seated himself on the grass and took the notebook from his pocket. He leafed through it and consulted one of the entries, frowning importantly.

"I saw a UFO last night," he told Cynthia in a lofty tone.

"You did? When?"

"It was..." Jimmy paused to look at the notebook again. "It was eleven fifty-six. It circled the sky to the north of the ranch buildings, hovered above the hay meadow for six minutes and departed in an easterly direction."

"Eleven fifty-six? That's almost midnight, Jimmy. Isn't that a little late for you to be up?"

Jimmy cast her a cold, pitying glance. "Yeah, like I'm supposed to see UFO's in the *daytime*," he suggested with heavy sarcasm.

Cynthia controlled the urge to speak sharply to the child. After all, he was a guest at the ranch, and his parents had abandoned him for the entire summer. No wonder he seemed troubled and defensive.

"What did it look like?" she asked.

"The UFO?" Jimmy looked at her suspiciously. "Are you making fun of me?"

"Of course not. I'd love to see a UFO," Cynthia said, hugging her knees and gazing dreamily at the sparkling river below them.

"Do you believe in them? Most grown-ups think they're just silly."

"Certainly I believe in them. How could there possibly not be intelligent life out there in the universe? When I look at all the stars at night, and think that every star is like our sun, and has its own system of planets—"

"And the stars we see are just a fraction of how many there really are," Jimmy interrupted eagerly. "There's billions and billions of them."

"I know." Cynthia smiled at the boy, who suddenly seemed much more human and likable. "I think it's only logical that there are thousands of advanced civilizations out there, and one of them will eventually find us. I think it would just be wonderful."

She watched the sun-dappled water, lost in a wistful dream of silver airships, of shimmering rainbow towers and distant worlds too strange and exotic for human imagination.

Jimmy hesitated, then glanced at his watch and got abruptly to his feet. "I have to go," he said, pausing to make another notation in his book. "If I see the UFO again, I'll tell you about it, okay? Maybe you can come and watch it, too."

"I'd like that, Jimmy."

Cynthia smiled as the boy pocketed his notebook and hurried off toward the ranch buildings with a little swagger of importance.

"Do you believe in UFO's, Jen-Jen?" she asked the baby, bending to kiss the top of the little girl's lacy bonnet. "Will your generation be the one to learn about the mysteries of other worlds out there?"

Jennifer wriggled and held up the remains of the cookie in her fist, solemnly offering it to her mother. Cynthia pretended to nibble at the sodden mess, making noisy sounds of appreciation, and the baby laughed out loud in delight.

Insects hummed in the grass nearby, but the air was locked in golden midday stillness, hushed and silent under the shimmering waves of heat. Cynthia hugged her baby, still lost in dreams of faraway worlds without pain and conflict, infinite light-years away from the miserable little day-to-day problems that kept people apart and destroyed their love.

LISA HUDDLED in her seat at the back of the bus, gazing into the sunrise as it spilled over endless miles of sagebrush and saguaro cactus. She felt strangely light, as if she were disembodied and floating in some unreal world of sand and air.

A woman brushed past her, carrying a small baby, and headed toward the tiny, cramped washroom at the rear of the bus. Lisa looked up at the woman's tired face and realized with quick sympathy that this fellow passenger was very young, probably not much older than Lisa herself.

"I'll hold him if you like," she offered shyly. "There's not much room in there to set him down anywhere."

The other girl's eyes flickered uncertainly over Lisa's exposed bosom and long, silk-clad legs. Lisa felt a rush of hot embarrassment, but the young mother was obviously too weary to make moral judgments.

"Sure," she said, lowering the sleeping baby into Lisa's arms with a sigh of relief. "Thanks."

She disappeared behind the swaying metal door and Lisa looked down at the baby, smiling gently. He was about five or six months old, his drowsy face as pink and sweet as a flower. She thought about her little brothers, how tender and pure they'd been at this age, and felt a wave of sadness.

It would be so nice to have a home to go to, some place where you knew you'd be loved and protected. But Lisa had no safe haven. Her life at home with her stepfather had been almost as terrible toward the end as those captive weeks with Ramon. Sometimes Lisa wondered if there was a safe place anywhere in all the world, or if men everywhere were cruel and greedy, bent on satisfying their own desires no matter how great the cost to others.

The young woman came out and collected her baby with a grateful smile. "Thanks," she whispered.

"That's all right. He's such a sweet little thing."

"Where are you going?"

"Crystal Creek. It's a small town west of Austin."

"We're going to Houston. His daddy..." The girl kissed the baby's cheek and gave Lisa a wan smile. "His daddy finally got a job and sent for us. I haven't seen him for three months."

Lisa smiled back, feeling another aching flood of loneliness. "If he wakes up and you get tired of looking after him," she murmured, "just bring him back to me for a while. I'd love to hold him."

"Thanks. That's real nice." Lisa watched as the other girl moved back up the aisle to her seat near the front, then turned to stare out the window again.

A few hours later the bus stopped for breakfast. Lisa sat alone at a table near the back of the little restaurant, miserably self-conscious in her sexy garb. She escaped into the washroom as soon as she finished eating and took the money from her bra, counting what was left.

So far, her cab fare, bus ticket and breakfast had used less than half the money the Texas cowboy had given her. Lisa looked at the bills in her hand, surprised by the power that came with money.

No wonder Ramon was so greedy, she thought. These crumpled bills were tremendously valuable, the key to freedom and a life of dignity and happiness. They made all the difference in the world.

Lisa got back on the bus, avoiding the curious stares of other passengers as the world lightened and the sun climbed higher in the desert sky. At the next stop she bypassed the cafeteria and went into a little tourist shop that was open for business even on this sleepy Sunday morning.

She bought two pairs of jeans, some running shoes, a couple of printed T-shirts and a plaid shirt, and a nylon knapsack to carry her things. After a brief hesitation she peeled off another bill from her dwindling supply and purchased a comb, some lipstick, a toothbrush and toothpaste and a few other toiletries.

Then she returned to the bus depot, hurried into the washroom and locked herself in the largest cubicle. Lisa peeled off her skimpy suede outfit with a grimace of distaste and dressed herself in jeans and one of the T-shirts, packing the rest of her purchases away in the knapsack. She looked at the costly suede skirt and top for a moment, then folded them neatly and set them on the floor in the corner along with her high-heeled shoes.

Maybe somebody else would have a use for them, but not Lisa.

Never again, she thought, moving out of the cubicle to look at herself in the mirror.

Lisa gaped in wonder at her reflection, astonished by the transformation that clothes could make. She looked like herself again, a slim, pretty teenager in jeans and running shoes, wholesome and shy. There was no trace of the painted siren who'd picked up men on street corners and sold her body for money.

Nothing in her life had ever felt as good as ridding herself of that dreadful image.

Lisa took a deep breath, shouldered her knapsack and moved back out into the coffee shop, sensing a tentative wave of a feeling so unfamiliar to her during these past few years that she hardly recognized it.

The feeling, she realized after a brief startled examination, was happiness.

DONNIE KIENZLE STOOD at his wicket, bored almost to tears, as he always was on slow nights. Sundays were usually busy, with people heading out on the bus to start the week somewhere else, or going back home after weekend trips. But tonight, caught in the oppressive heaviness of the August heat in Las Vegas, nobody seemed to be going anywhere.

"Hey, kid," a voice said softly. "You Donnie Kienzle?"

"Yeah," Donnie said, looking up. "Who wants to know?"

He saw the man standing on the opposite side of the counter and stiffened instinctively.

There was nothing openly dangerous or unpleasant about the man, Donnie realized. In fact, he was quite handsome in a dark, Latin kind of way, with shining black hair that was carefully combed, and a full, sensual mouth. He wore a soft leather jacket that probably cost two months of Donnie's salary, and an open-necked silk shirt in a stylish print that made him look like a well-dressed young executive.

But there was something in that smiling mouth and in the cold stillness of his eyes that was unspeakably menacing. Donnie shivered, thinking that this man would cut your heart out without batting an eyelash, and enjoy your pain while he was doing it.

"Can I help you?" he asked nervously.

"My name's Ramon," the young man said, fixing Donnie with a dark, hypnotic gaze. "I'm looking for a friend of mine who might have gone on a little bus trip late last night. They tell me you were selling tickets on the night shift."

Donnie swallowed hard and tried to keep his voice from shaking. "I sold lots of tickets," he said. "It was real busy last night."

"My friend looks like this." The man in the leather jacket opened a folder and took out a glossy eight-by-ten photo of a beautiful young woman with brown eyes and a cloud of dark hair.

Donnie remembered the terrified girl in her sexy suede outfit, and realized instantly what kind of situation this was. He'd suspected it all along, of course, but confronted with the reality of this cold-faced man, he felt a little awed just the same. It was like being in the middle of a movie.

"So, do you remember her, Donnie?"

Donnie licked his lips and clenched his fists nervously behind the counter. He thought about the look of fear in the girl's eyes, her shy delicate face and lovely body. What was this man going to do to her when he caught up with her?

Donnie felt a brief impulse to protect her. He could easily lie to Ramon, tell him he was certain the woman had gone to Los Angeles or some other place out west. There'd be no way to prove afterward that Donnie had lied deliberately. And it would give her a little more time to get away....

While he hesitated, the man rummaged in the pocket of his leather jacket, then reached casually through Donnie's ticket window. Donnie's eyes widened when he saw the hundred-dollar bill dangling from Ramon's well-manicured fingers.

"She..." Donnie choked, still eyeing the bill longingly. "She went to...to Texas," he whispered finally. "To a little town called Crystal Creek. It's west of Austin."

Ramon gave him a cold, measuring glance while Donnie trembled with dread. At last, the dark-haired man dropped the bill onto the counter, turned and strode out of the bus depot into the darkness, leaving the door swinging behind him.

VIRGINIA PARKS SAT patiently on one of the hard vinyl benches in the bus depot at Crystal Creek. Her niece, Angela, crossed the room and flopped heavily down beside Virginia, her plump face creased with annoyance. "It's almost half an hour late," Angela complained loudly. "When the hell is it coming?"

"Don't swear, dear," Virginia said automatically. "They said it's just a brief delay. You'll still get there in lots of time."

Angela flounced and glared out the window again.

Virginia sighed, wishing devoutly that the bus would arrive so she could rid herself of this unpleasant teenager and get on with her day. There was still so much to do....

She shifted her body wearily on the bench and smiled at the young woman opposite them, who was busy tending a small baby lying next to her on the bench.

This girl, Virginia thought, probably wasn't much older than Angela, but she had an air of maturity and composure that set her apart. In fact, she seemed like a member of a different generation, even though she wore the usual jeans, running shoes and T-shirt. Her face was beautiful, and her wide, dark eyes were gentle with affection as she deftly powdered and changed the baby.

"How old is your baby?" Virginia asked.

"Oh, he's not mine," the girl said, glancing up with a shy smile. "He's Sally Jo's. She's in there having a cup of coffee before the bus comes to take them on to Houston."

"I'm going to Houston," Angela announced. "If the freaking bus ever *gets* here."

Virginia and the young dark-haired woman exchanged a quick glance that was eloquent with sympathy and understanding.

"Are you going to Houston, too?" Virginia asked.

"No," the girl said in her soft voice. "I'm staying here."

The eastbound bus pulled up at that moment and Angela rushed to board it. She pushed her way past other travelers standing patiently with their luggage, anxious to make sure that she grabbed the very best seat. The baby's mother appeared, relieved the girl of her charge and also boarded the bus.

Finally, Virginia stood alone in the sunshine, waving with relief at the big vehicle as it lumbered down the street and around the corner. She became aware of the pretty, dark-haired girl, who also stood waving at the bus with tears running down her cheeks.

"He was such a sweet baby," the girl said apologetically to Virginia, brushing at her eyes with a trembling hand. "I've been helping Sally Jo look after him ever since I met them yesterday in Arizona. His name is Joshua."

Virginia smiled back and fell into step beside the girl as they returned to the empty depot.

"Do you have family here?" Virginia asked, watching with interest as the young woman shouldered a nylon knapsack and stood looking uncertainly out the window.

"No, not really."

"A job, then?"

The girl flushed and looked awkward. "No, I don't. I was hoping to find a job when I got here. I came because..." She paused, glanced briefly up at Virginia and continued. "I met somebody who used to live here and he... he made it sound so nice. I just decided I wanted to live in Crystal Creek, that's all."

Virginia gave the girl a thoughtful glance. She seemed awfully young to be crossing the country on the whim of a friend. Still, nobody knew better than Virginia Parks that young people these days were wildly unpredictable creatures. She thought about the girl's gentle manner and her deft handling of another woman's baby, her tears of genuine sorrow when the baby moved on out of her life again.

On another wave of fatigue, Virginia thought as well about all the inescapable duties and heavy chores at the ranch these days. There was the relentless care of the big house, and poor Cynthia was growing more and more burdened and worn-out with her constant responsibility to little Jennifer....

"What kind of work do you do?" she asked the girl. "I guess first I should introduce myself," she added. "I'm Virginia Parks."

"I'm Lisa Croft." The girl smiled shyly. "I'll do any kind of work," she added. "Waiting on tables, cleaning, baby-sitting, anything like that."

"Do you have references, Lisa?"

Virginia watched, her curiosity growing, as the emotions played across Lisa's expressive face. This poor child was certainly terrified of something, Virginia realized. She felt a warm surge of the deep, motherly compassion that was an essential part of her nature.

"I...no, I don't," Lisa murmured. "I had letters from my high school English teacher, and from the lady I baby-sat for these last three years, but I...I lost them."

"Where was that, Lisa? Where did you go to school?"

"In...over in New Mexico," the girl whispered. "That's where I grew up."

"Well, could we call them, do you think? Your teacher and the lady you worked for?"

The girl's delicate face brightened. "Yes, of course!" she said. "I could get the numbers right away. Are you...do you know of a job somewhere in town?"

Virginia paused, wondering if this wasn't a terribly rash and impulsive thing she was doing. But then she remembered Lisa's gentle, confident handling of the baby, and her resolve strengthened.

"Well," she said, "not exactly in town. I work at a ranch just a few miles out in the country, but I'm supposed to have retired long ago. We just can't seem to find anybody else to help with the housework and the baby."

Lisa's face blazed with excitement. "Oh," she said, "I'd love a job like that! It's out in the country, you said? And there's a baby?"

"There sure is. Just about the sweetest baby in the whole world. She's nine months old, the little darling, and her name is Jennifer."

"Oh, Mrs. Parks . . ."

"Now, it's not up to me," Virginia warned. "The lady of the house will have to talk with you, and we'll certainly have to call these references of yours. But if you'd like to come out to the ranch with me now, maybe we could . . ."

To Virginia's surprise, tears gathered in the girl's beautiful eyes once more and began to roll slowly down her cheeks. "Mrs. Parks, do you believe in God?" she whispered.

"I certainly do. Why?"

"Because it's been the most wonderful thing. The past couple of days, I feel like somebody's been watching over me and leading me just the way I should go. I've never felt like that before."

All doubts about what she was doing vanished from Virginia's mind. It didn't matter what this lovely child had suffered, or what she was running from. Virginia was suddenly determined that the fear deep in Lisa's eyes was going to be banished in time, and she was going to smile as happily as any other girl.

"Come along with me, Lisa," she said gently. "I'll take you out to the ranch."

They chatted about everyday things as they drove along the winding road to the Double C. Virginia glanced at her passenger from time to time, increasingly touched by the girl's gentleness and air of shy reserve.

Lisa was visibly shaken when they swept through the wide stone gates and up the circular drive to the ranch house.

"Oh, my," she whispered in awe, taking in the pillared facade of the big house. "It's like a castle. Like those places on television."

"It's just home to us," Virginia said comfortably. "Now, J. T. McKinney, that's the boss, he lives here with his wife and baby. He has three grown children as well, but you won't meet all of them right away. Seems like they're scattered all over the country just now."

Lisa followed the older woman into the house, gripping her knapsack nervously in her hands. They passed through the quiet foyer and into the sun room, where Virginia indicated one of the flowered sofas.

"If you'll just wait here, Lisa, I'll go find out if Miss Cynthia has time to talk with you right now."

But Lisa wasn't listening.

Virginia glanced at the girl in puzzled surprise. Lisa stood transfixed in front of a long oak console that was covered with family pictures. Prominently displayed in the middle was a big studio portrait of J.T., Cynthia and Jennifer, taken earlier in the year when the baby was just a few months old.

"Lisa?" Virginia said.

"Excuse me?" Lisa glanced at the older woman, her brown eyes wide with shock.

"Do you want to wait here while I find Miss Cynthia?"

"All right," Lisa whispered, sinking tensely onto the edge of a nearby couch and gripping her bag tightly in her hands. "Yes, I'll wait here."

What a strange reaction, Virginia mused, as she trudged up the stairs to look for Cynthia. When the poor girl looked at that picture of J.T. and Cynthia, she'd turned as pale as if she'd seen a ghost.

CHAPTER FOUR

MANNY HERNANDEZ CROUCHED in a corner of the Double C horse barn, applying steady pressure to a rope stretched from the heels of a sorrel two-year-old. The colt lay on his side on the floor, dark eyes rolling with terror until Ken Slattery moved closer and placed a clean burlap sack over the young horse's face. As soon as his eyes were covered, the colt's nervous trembling stilled and his sides stopped heaving.

"Ready, Tony?" Manny asked his young assistant.

Tony nodded, testing the rope that secured the colt's forelegs, and probed with gentle fingers at the animal's lacerated chest. Then he reached over to rummage in his bag for a suture kit.

Manny leaned back on his rope and watched the younger man's actions with quiet satisfaction.

This was the best move he'd ever made, Manny thought, taking on an assistant for his growing veterinary practice.

Second best, he corrected himself with a sudden flash of white teeth in his dark face, as he recalled Tracy waiting for him back in the house in Crystal Creek. There wasn't much doubt that Tracy Cotter was the best thing that had ever happened to Manny Hernandez.

But Tony Rodriguez was turning out to have been a pretty good choice, too.

Manny knew he'd taken a considerable chance on this young man, hiring him just out of veterinary school and burdening him with a lot of heavy responsibilities so early in his career. But from their first interview he'd been impressed with Tony's clear-eyed manly gaze, his air of politeness and quiet confidence, and the fact that, like Manny, Tony had worked hard and struggled for years, fought his way out of an impoverished background to make something of his life.

And as the weeks passed, Manny was growing more and more convinced that he'd made the right decision. Tony was always pleasant and reliable, good with customers and neat in his habits, both around the clinic and in the field. Best of all, he had gentle, healing hands. Sometimes it seemed that Tony just had to touch a suffering creature, stroke it and examine its injuries, and the animal would brighten and begin to respond.

Manny watched now as Tony started to install a series of careful sutures in the colt's torn forequarters. Tony's brown hands were strong and precise as he gripped the forceps and knotted the ligature with quick expertise, his dark face intent with concentration.

The boy reminded Manny of himself at that age, with his shock of glossy dark hair, his quiet black eyes and lean face with its blunt, prominent cheekbones. But Tony was taller and bulkier than Manny. His biceps flexed and knotted beneath the white cotton T-shirt as he tugged at the forceps, and his tanned forearms were corded with muscle.

"You know, J.T. should get rid of that barbed wire and go to rail fences if he's going to run expensive animals like this on his land," Manny commented to Ken, still gripping the rope as Tony continued to stitch the gaping cuts.

"We're working on it," Ken said, watching the young veterinarian's hands in fascination. "But it takes a lot of time and money to install rails on ten thousand acres, Manny."

"Everything takes money," Manny said with a rueful grin. "Wouldn't it be nice if just once, there was enough to go around?"

Ken nodded, then turned as a plump boy approached them. He wore khaki shorts and a bulging green pack over his shoulders, and gripped a notebook tightly in his hands as he stared down at the trussed, blindfolded horse.

The child's eyes widened behind his thick glasses when he saw the blood darkening the wooden floor and Tony's brown hands plying needle and forceps.

"What happened?" he asked.

"A couple of colts up in the north pasture got to running, and this one got tangled up in some barbed wire," Ken told the boy briefly. "Cut himself up pretty bad, trying to get loose."

"Will he have scars?" The boy leaned closer, his mouth open, gazing at the neat stitches.

"Not many. Not when he's lucky enough to have Tony stitching him up," Manny said cheerfully, and was rewarded by a brief shining smile from the young man with the forceps.

"Manny, this is my nephew, Jimmy," Ken said, dropping a hand onto the child's shoulder. "My brother's boy. Jimmy's folks are way up in Alaska this summer, so he's staying with Nora and me."

"Hi, Jimmy. I'm Manny, and this is Tony, who works with me. Do you like animals?"

Jimmy shrugged. "I had a dog once, but it died," he said briefly.

Manny looked at the boy's withdrawn face, wondering what to say. There was something funny about the kid, he mused. Not at all like his calm, easygoing uncle, who stood next to Jimmy, squinting out into the sunlighted ranch yard. The boy seemed tense, almost defiant as he clutched his notebook and stared down at the horse on the barn floor.

"I have to go," Jimmy said abruptly, looking up at Ken. The light glanced off his thick glasses so his eyes were impossible to see. "I prob'ly won't be home for lunch."

Ken turned his full attention to the boy, and Manny could read the concern in the man's quiet craggy face.

"Nora doesn't like it when you're not home for lunch, Jimmy," he said mildly.

"There's something I have to do," the child said, his mouth taking on a stubborn look. "I have to climb up and explore some clues on the hill over there," he added with an air of considerable mystery and self-importance. "It's something I'm doing for Mrs. McKinney."

Ken still frowned uncertainly, but the mention of Cynthia's name had apparently been enough to sway him. "Okay," he said. "Stop by the house and pick up a lunch so you don't get hungry. You can have yourself a little picnic," he added, trying to smile.

The child regarded his uncle coldly for a moment, the sunlight flashing from his glasses again. Then he turned and marched off into the yard, still clutching his notebook with exaggerated importance. Tony Rodriguez squatted back on his heels and flexed his hands, watching the little boy disappear.

Strange kid, Tony mused, just as his employer had a few moments earlier. Jimmy looked to be about ten years old, but he didn't seem very much like a regular ten-year-old. And with six younger brothers and sisters back home, Tony had considerable experience to back up his observations.

He washed disinfectant over the neatly stitched wounds and touched the animal's glossy neck, stroking it gently while he studied his handiwork. After a moment, he nodded to Manny and Ken.

"All done," he said, getting to his feet with lithe grace. "You can let him up now."

The two vets watched as Ken removed the blindfold and ropes. The colt struggled to his feet, standing for a long moment with forelegs awkwardly braced and head hanging.

The animal took a few unsteady paces across the floor, then gathered confidence and trotted out into the sunlight with a soft whinny of relief.

Tony smiled and crossed the barn to the little stone sink installed in a corner near the tack rooms. He ran water over his bloodstained hands and gazed absently out into the ranch yard, still watching the boy, who had stopped to talk to somebody near the house.

Suddenly Tony's dark eyes widened and his heart began to pound heavily beneath the white cotton T-shirt. He paused, gripping a coarse towel in his hands and staring at the scene in the yard.

Jimmy was by now deep in conversation with a young woman pushing a baby stroller. There was a baby in the stroller, too, a cute little thing in ruffled pink sunbonnet and rompers, who laughed and clutched at a pair of yellow butterflies dancing nearby on the wayward breeze.

But Tony wasn't looking at the baby or the boy. He was staring at the woman pushing the stroller. Time stood still, and the summer morning was rich and throbbing with music as Tony Rodriguez stared at the girl across the ranch yard.

He had never seen anything so beautiful.

She was wearing baggy denim shorts, a plaid shirt and sandals, but the casual clothes couldn't hide the dainty curves of her body, or her slender loveliness. She had soft dark hair pulled back and tied loosely at her neck with a blue scarf, and even from this distance Tony could see the gentleness of her smile, the sweetness in her face as she bent to speak with the boy, then stroked the baby's plump cheek with a gesture of tenderness that brought a lump to Tony's throat as he watched.

"She's working at the big house," Ken said quietly, coming up beside Tony and looking at the woman with the two children. "Just came last week, and everybody loves her already. She's sure good with kids."

Tony felt like a swimmer struggling up from the depths, trying frantically to find the light and grab a mouthful of air before he drowned.

"What...what's her name?" he asked when he was finally able to speak.

"Lisa Croft. Hey, Tony, come on," Ken added with a brief grin over at Manny, who nodded and smiled. "I'll introduce you."

Like a man in a dream, Tony followed the ranch foreman out into the sunlight and across the crushed rock to the edge of the house fence. Lisa knelt by the stroller, frowning at one of the chrome wheels. She laughed and dodged the baby's plump fists as the little girl tried to grasp a handful of her hair.

Jimmy watched their approach with an impassive expression. He turned as they drew near and headed away from the ranch buildings at a brisk pace, apparently reluctant to get into any further discussion with his uncle.

Lisa glanced up at them and smiled shyly. "I think this wheel is stuck, Ken," she said, in the sweetest voice that Tony had ever heard. "It doesn't want to turn properly."

Tony's eyes were fixed on her. He felt awestruck and tongue-tied in her presence, more like a kid of Jimmy Slattery's age than a competent man of almost twenty-five.

Tony Rodriguez had met lots of girls during his college years, though he'd been too busy studying and too broke to date very much. Still, he'd generally had a vague impression that girls found him attractive enough, and that if he were to ask, he wouldn't often have been turned down.

But this girl was unlike any he'd ever encountered. There was an air of sweetness about her, of delicacy and purity and a kind of shining childlike innocence that made Tony almost afraid to speak to her, nervous that even a careless word might damage the bloom on her face or bring a look of fear to her shy, dark eyes.

He shifted awkwardly on his booted feet, feeling big and clumsy, watching as Ken knelt beside the girl to examine the wheel on the stroller.

"By the way," Ken said absently over his shoulder, probing at the inner side of the plump rubber tire, "this is Lisa Croft, who helps out up at the big house. Lisa, this is Tony Rodriguez. He's our new veterinarian, and he's one pretty good hand, let me tell you. Just stitched up one of Lynn's colts as neat as a church lady doing needlework."

Lisa glanced up at him with a shy smile. "Hi, Tony," she murmured, a soft pink blush touching her cheeks when she caught the intensity of his gaze.

"Hi, Lisa," Tony said. He searched his mind for something else to say, something bright and witty that would impress her with his sophistication. But she had already turned away, and was gravely accepting a small plastic rattle offered to her by the happy baby in the stroller.

"Well, isn't this the damnedest thing?" Ken muttered, still peering at the tire. "Look, Tony. A piece of string off a feed bag or something has got all tangled up here between the axle and the bushing. It's wound so tight I can't get it off."

Grateful for the diversion, Tony squatted by the other man and studied the tight mass of dirty string. "It'll have to be cut out," he said. "You want me to get a scalpel from my bag, Ken?"

Ken grinned and got to his feet. "We sure can't afford vet fees to operate on the machinery," he said cheerfully. "Bad enough paying for the work you do on the stock."

Tony grinned back at him. "Free surgery," he offered. "No charge for baby strollers."

Ken chuckled and shook his head. "Say, Lisa, if you'll just take Her Highness out of there for a minute, I'll haul this machine down to the barn and get it fixed up, okay?"

Lisa nodded, unfastening the straps and lifting the baby into her arms while Ken took the stroller in hand.

"Tony, you want to keep Lisa company while I tend to this?" he asked, giving the younger man a quick, meaningful glance.

Tony glanced at the quiet ranch foreman, startled, then smiled with boyish gratitude. "Sure thing, Ken," he said huskily. "Would you like me to hold her?" he added, turning to Lisa as Ken ambled off with the damaged baby stroller.

Lisa looked up at him uncertainly, then down at the wriggling infant in her arms.

"I have six little brothers and sisters," Tony said, when she hesitated. "I know all about babies."

The dark-haired girl smiled at him, a smile so warm and enchanting that Tony actually swayed on his feet and felt a little dizzy. "In that case," she said ruefully, "please take her. She weighs a ton, especially when she squirms like this."

She handed the baby over and Tony gathered her into his arms, moved by the tender, precious feeling of the little warm body in his hands. He settled the infant into the curve of his arm, where she nestled and studied him, wide-eyed and solemn. At last she grinned, showing dimpled cheeks and three or four shiny new teeth.

Tony grinned back at her, then looked at Lisa. "What's her name?"

"Jennifer. She's only nine months old," Lisa said proudly, "and she can already stand up all by herself."

"Then she'll be walking soon," Tony said, with the confident air of a man who knew what he was talking about.

Lisa nodded and fell into step beside him, moving slowly off toward the barn, where Manny and Ken could be seen working over the stroller. "She can't quite let go and do it alone, but she walks all around the coffee table, and in her crib, and she'll walk across the floor if I'm holding her hands."

"My littlest brother walked when he was eight months old," Tony said, grinning down at the baby, who was thoughtfully tugging at his ear, her ruffled sunbonnet bobbing against his shoulder.

"My goodness," Lisa said, impressed. "That's really early."

Tony nodded, amazed that he was actually having a conversation with this beautiful creature. In spite of his nervousness, he felt soothed by her presence. There was something so gentle about her that simply being close to her was a pleasure, like walking outside on a spring morning or enjoying a lovely sunset.

"Do you have any kid brothers or sisters?" he asked, suddenly hungry to know all about her, everything that had ever happened to her in all her life.

Lisa looked away, following Jimmy's small body in the distance as he toiled up one of the hills behind the ranch. "Four little brothers," she said. "Not as many as you, but still a handful, sometimes."

Something in her voice troubled him, a distant hint of sadness. Tony was preparing to ask her more about her family when she paused and looked up at him with childlike curiosity.

"Are you really a veterinarian?" Lisa asked shyly. "Not just a helper or something?"

"I graduated this spring," Tony said, unable to keep a note of pride from his voice. "I have my license and everything."

"My goodness," she said, clearly impressed. "That's just like being a doctor, isn't it? I mean," she added awkwardly, "you have to go to school for so many years, and study so hard."

"It sure wasn't easy," Tony said, his face darkening for a moment as he recalled those grueling years of study, and the dreadful poverty and self-denial that he'd endured. "But it was worth it," he added firmly. "Every bit of it."

Lisa nodded and looked down at her feet. "I wish I'd had the chance to go on to college," she murmured. "I always dreamed about it, but I just... couldn't."

"Well, there's still lots of time," Tony said, pausing near the entrance to the barn and holding Jennifer tightly in his arms as he looked down earnestly at the slim, dark-haired girl. "You're just a kid. You could go to college any time, Lisa. Your whole life is still ahead of you."

Her lovely face shadowed abruptly with a pain that was difficult for Tony to bear. She met his eyes for a brief moment, and he was stunned by the sorrow and hopelessness he saw reflected in them. "Sometimes I feel like my whole life is already behind me," she said quietly.

Then, as if regretting her words, she reached up, took the baby from him and moved into the shadowed interior of the barn, walking quickly over to stand next to the two men by the stroller.

Tony watched her slim, straight back and wondered what had gone wrong. They'd been getting along so well, talking together almost like old friends. And now she was gone, and the moment was over so completely that he wondered if she'd ever talk with him again.

JIMMY TOILED UP the face of the hill, heading for the limestone outcroppings far away at the summit. The day was so hot that the rimrock shimmered in the distance, dancing and swirling before his eyes until he felt dizzy just looking up at the hilltop.

He paused, sweating and puffing, then moved over to sit on a rock under the shade of a grove of rustling oak trees. The leafy coolness was a welcome relief after the hot sun on the path, and the boy leaned back and rested, his breath coming in ragged gasps.

Far below, he could see Lisa moving out of the barn, pushing the baby stroller in front of her. She was heading for the house, and Jimmy noted with considerable relief and satisfaction that she was all alone. The big, black-haired man who'd stitched up the horse wasn't anywhere near her, though Jimmy could see him standing in the barn door, watching her leave as Uncle Ken talked with the other man.

He flipped open his notebook, popped the button in his special ballpoint pen and made a careful entry.

11:20 a.m.: L. going back to big house with J. Suspect still observing her.

Jimmy examined his handwritten note, wondering if it was really accurate to call Tony Rodriguez a suspect. After all, he'd never even seen the young veterinarian before today, and he wasn't quite sure what he suspected him of.

Jimmy had been a little jealous when he noticed the way the man had gazed at Lisa with such burning intensity. But it was obvious, Jimmy comforted himself, that Lisa wasn't the least bit interested in Tony. She wasn't even looking back at him as she took Jennifer to the house.

He settled on the rock and looked all around, wondering what other observations he could record in his notebook.

On another hill across the valley he could see men and machines toiling over the site chosen for the Double C winery, and for Ruth and Tyler Mc-Kinney's new home. It appeared that on this hot August morning, concrete was being poured and other areas were being leveled with small earth-moving equipment.

Jimmy felt a tug of nervous anxiety as he took a pair of binoculars from his pack and observed the busy scene. Normally on days like this, he preferred to be concealed somewhere near the construction site, watching and making notes on everything that happened.

One of Jimmy's fondest dreams was that someday there would be a lawsuit, some big important conflict involving millions of dollars, that could only be settled in court with a judge and jury.

"If only there was a witness," they'd all say, all the lawyers and judges. "*Any* kind of a witness to what actually happened."

And he, Jimmy, would have the evidence in his notebook to incriminate the guilty party. He'd stand up right in front of the crowded room—there'd probably even be some girls there in the courtroom—and he'd read:

1:07 p.m.: Concrete being poured into west re-
taining wall. Worker says there's not enough
metal rods to do a proper job. Foreman says,
"Oh, that's okay, we'll go ahead with it anyway.
Whose to know." Witnessed and recorded by
James Everett Slattery, August 8, Double C
Ranch.

Jimmy felt a little nervous, not being in position to
monitor the construction site. But his present mission was just as important, actually a lot more important. Besides, he liked to think about the kindness
in Mrs. McKinney's dark eyes when they'd sat on the
blanket by the river and talked together about UFO's.
Jimmy could never recall being treated with such re-
spect and warmth by a grown-up.

The thought that he and the beautiful golden-
haired lady from the big house shared this secret was
a precious thing to Jimmy. It made up for all the
loneliness, the anguish and fear he sometimes suffered late at night, his homesickness and the cruel
taunts of the other children, who called him Fatty
Four-Eyes and Weird Jimmy behind his back, and
sometimes even to his face.

If it were possible, Jimmy would have liked to carry
the stars to Cynthia McKinney on a platter of purest
gold, decorated with flowers and gems unseen by human eyes. Failing that, the very least he could do was
find her a UFO, and he was fairly certain that he'd
already done so.

Jimmy heaved himself off the rock and started upward again, sweating heavily as soon as he left the shady grove and began toiling up the rocky path in the blazing sunshine.

"I should have brought more water," Jimmy muttered to a bright-eyed gray squirrel that cocked its head to one side and watched him pass.

Jimmy paused and looked at the squirrel, which tensed on its tree branch a few feet away but didn't flinch. "I thought a canteen would make my pack too heavy," he told the squirrel. "Dumb, right?"

The squirrel nodded sadly and Jimmy moved away, panting. To keep himself from thinking about the harshness of the climb, he tried to concentrate on the miracle he'd seen the previous evening.

It had been very late, later than midnight even, long past the time when the last soul on the ranch had gone to bed and drifted quietly off to sleep. The only sounds out by the haystack were the soft nighttime whinnies of colts separated from their mothers, the rustling noises of small rodents in the coarse straw, and the muffled call of night birds making their mournful hunting cries. The stars had seemed more brilliant than usual, throbbing with light, and so close to where Jimmy crouched at the top of the haystack that he felt the silver dust would smear on his fingers if he reached up to touch them.

And then, suddenly, the miracle had begun to happen. One of the stars from a wide nebula at the edge of the Milky Way detached itself and started to drift across the shining black sky.

Jimmy crouched on the prickly hay and watched, awed and breathless, as the speck of light drew nearer. He soon realized that it wasn't a star at all, not even a comet or meteorite or anything like that. It was going much too slowly, with a steady, deliberate path of descent that was bringing it nearer and nearer to earth.

The little boy on the feed stack gaped upward, his throat tight with longing, the moon washing over his plump cheeks, as the light grew ever closer and more brilliant. It hovered and drifted, it lifted and lowered, it slipped from side to side with a smooth, lateral movement that no man-made craft had ever exhibited.

And then, in utter silence, it dropped to earth beyond the craggy rimrock crowning the highest hill on Double C property.

Jimmy shivered in the hot sunlight, remembering the awesome wonder of the moment when he realized, with absolute assurance, that a UFO had actually landed right here at the ranch. He took out his notebook again, studying the entry for the previous evening. It was hard to read, partly because he'd written it in the dark with the aid of a small flashlight, but mainly because the entire note, on account of its overwhelming importance, was written in Jimmy's elaborate private code.

The boy sat on another rock to concentrate on the messy, encoded message while he struggled to catch his breath. He'd had no idea from down at the ranch buildings that this hill was so high and steep. Down below, it just looked like a gentle climb, a pleasant half-hour journey to the summit.

Jimmy squinted up at the silent rimrock, the craggy monuments of limestone that concealed whatever wonder had landed there the previous night. The path seemed even steeper from this vantage point, and his throat was dry and swollen with thirst. His heart thundered in his chest as if it might be about to burst apart.

Jimmy sighed and opened his notebook to a fresh page.

11:51: Mission abandoned because of inadiquit supplies. Will try again tomorrow morning, at approx. 700 hours. Meanwhile, round-the-clock survaylance will be mounted on the landing area.

Feeling somewhat comforted by this businesslike approach, Jimmy climbed off the rock and gazed wistfully for another moment at the mysterious summit. Then he turned and started to make his way back down the trail toward the ranch buildings, wondering where he could find Mrs. McKinney. His evidence was not yet complete, but Jimmy couldn't wait any longer to tell her all about the wonderful, otherworldly light that had settled gently down on the limestone hilltop in that starry midnight silence.

"WELL, J.T., you've had almost two weeks to study the wine-making business. What do you think so far? And will you drink a whiskey with me?"

J. T. Mckinney leaned back in a soft armchair of maroon leather and accepted the glass of whiskey and soda from his host, Don Holden.

It was evening, and both men were pleasantly weary after a long day of overseeing harvest procedures in Holden's Napa Valley winery.

J.T. grinned amiably. "What do I think? Well, Don," he said, "you may have grape stains on your fingers, but I still think that beard makes you look like a college professor, or maybe an artist with real strange political views."

Don Holden smiled and seated himself behind his old oak desk, raising his moccasined feet and resting them lightly on the shining wooden surface.

"That big woman would chop your feet off at the ankles if she ever caught you doing that," J.T. warned him.

"Mrs. Ward?" Don chuckled, though he felt an automatic twinge of nervousness when he glanced around at the door. "She's quite a dragon, all right, that housekeeper of mine. Ruth's always been terrified of her."

"Not anymore," J.T. said with a complacent grin, sipping his drink. "Ruth lives in Texas now, where everybody's sweet to each other and there's nary a thing to be scared of. What a relief for the poor girl, to get away from this nasty, violent place."

Don choked on his drink and took a moment to recover. "Ah, J.T.," he said at last, smiling at his guest. "Thank God that you never change."

Both men were silent for a moment, sipping their drinks in the relaxed ease of long, comfortable friendship.

"Do you know what I'm thinking, J.T.?" Don said finally.

"What's that?"

"Just how strange it is," Don began, prompted by a sudden need to make his friend understand his thoughts. "This baby we're all waiting for. You know, you and I have been friends since they let us off the ark. And now your blood and my blood will flow together through the veins of Ruth and Tyler's baby. What do you think about that?"

J.T. glanced up, his dark eyes bright, his voice suddenly husky when he responded. "You know, Don, sometimes it just about brings me to tears, if I was to tell you the truth."

Don nodded, observing the sunset colors beyond the mullioned windows. "Me, too," he murmured softly. "Me, too, J.T."

The two fathers watched in silence as Ruth and Tyler came into view, walking slowly, hand-in-hand among the rows of grapevines, the soft pastels of twilight swirling all around them.

"Those two seem so happy together, don't they?" Don commented with a fond smile. "It makes *me* really happy, J.T., just watching them."

"Seems Ruth and Tyler aren't the only thing making you happy these days," J.T. responded, grinning at his friend.

"What? Oh, you mean Irene. Yes," Don agreed, leaning back in the chair, his smile broadening. "Yes, Irene and I get along pretty well together."

"Wedding bells in the future?"

"Maybe. Do you recommend it?"

"Beg pardon?" J.T. asked, startled.

"Marriage. Is it a good idea for old fellows like us?"

J.T. focused absently on the young couple out among the grapevines. He was silent so long that Don shot him a curious glance.

"J.T.?"

The Texan shook his head and took a hasty sip of his drink. "Sure," he said. "Marrying the woman you love is always a good idea, Don. And it looks to me like you love that pretty college teacher quite a bit."

Don regarded his friend steadily. "J.T., is something the matter?"

His friend looked down into the amber depths of the whiskey glass again, and Don felt a brief stirring of uneasiness.

"J.T.?" he prompted.

When the rancher looked up, Don was startled by the pain in his dark eyes. "I don't know," he muttered finally.

Don stared at him, wondering what to say.

"When Cynthia and I first got together, we were crazy for each other," J.T. went on in a low, troubled voice. "Couldn't seem to get enough of each other," he added with a rueful grin.

He glanced briefly at his friend, who nodded, waiting. "I sure wasn't acting my age back then, God knows," J.T. said, still brooding over the swirling liquid in his glass. "But then, right away I got sick, and then she was pregnant and we had the baby, and we started this winery, and it seems like it's just been one damn thing after another."

"So what's the matter?" Don asked quietly. "Aren't you happy anymore?"

"Not the way we used to be," J.T. said, looking bleak. "Everything's so different now, Don. I just can't understand it."

"Do you still love her?"

"God, yes!" J.T. burst out with another quick glance at his friend. "I love her more than I ever did. More than I ever thought I could love any woman," he added in a low voice.

"More than Pauline?"

J.T. was silent a moment. Then he nodded awkwardly, staring down at his hands. "Pauline was a good wife to me. We had some rough times at first, but after the kids came along, she stood by me all the way, and we built a fine life together. I always appreciated her help. But the way I feel for Cynthia... it's...different, somehow."

"In what way?"

"I don't know, exactly. But there's still times now, after two years together, that I'll see her or even think about her, and I'll get as shaky and excited as a kid, just knowing I'm going to be with her soon. You know what I mean?"

Don nodded. "I think I do, J.T. But," he added dryly, "that doesn't exactly sound like a couple with a problem. I don't really understand what it is you're so worried about."

"I'm not the one with the problem," J.T. said flatly.

"You aren't?"

"Hell, no. I feel the same as I always have, only more so, if that's possible. I love my wife, I'm nuts about our baby, and I'm real excited about this winery idea, now that they've all got me talked into it. My life would be perfect if only..."

He fell abruptly silent, and turned to the square of pearly gray sky beyond the window.

"Isn't Cynthia happy anymore, J.T.?" Don asked gently.

The other man's handsome face tightened and a small nerve began to twitch along his jaw. "She doesn't seem to be," he said without expression.

"Why not?"

"How should I know?" J.T. asked with a sudden flare of impatience. "Seems to me she's got everything she ever wanted, but she's just getting more miserable all the time."

"You must have asked her about it, haven't you? Talked with her about what's bothering her?"

"I've tried," J.T. said bitterly. "About a hundred times."

"And what does she say?"

The Texan gave a despairing shrug. "Who knows? She either starts to cry, or else she tells me all this woman stuff about not being fulfilled, not feeling *real* anymore.... Don, what the hell does that mean? Not feeling *real?*"

"What do you think it means?" Don asked, giving his friend a sudden, alert glance.

"I think it means she's tired of me. I think she's wishing she hadn't left Boston and her high-powered job to take on a man who's twenty years older than her, and has a shaky ticker besides. I think she maybe wants something different. Or somebody else."

"J.T. ...." Don began, but paused, considering his words carefully.

"Yeah?"

"J.T., maybe that's not what she's saying at all. Maybe the problem is that you're just not listening carefully enough."

"I'm listening," J.T. argued stubbornly. "And what I'm hearing my wife say is that she's not happy

with her marriage anymore. I think that's pretty
straightforward, Don."

Don tried another tack. "Is she tired, J.T.? It must
have been hard for her, after all, first looking after
you, and then looking after the baby and the house
and all."

J.T. nodded. "It's been real hard. And I know she's
tired. But they just hired a new girl last week, a few
days after I left, so things should be getting better
now."

"A new girl? I don't believe you mentioned that
before."

J.T. waved his hand carelessly. "I forgot. When I
called home the other night, Cynthia told me that
Virginia finally found a girl to help with the baby and
the housework. Somebody from New Mexico, I think
it was, who came to town looking for work."

"They hired a *stranger* to look after little Jennifer?"

J.T. grinned briefly, though his eyes were still dark
and miserable. "Yeah. It surprised me, too, the way
the women at my house guard that baby like a bunch
of lionesses. But this girl is terrific, apparently. They
checked her hometown references and nobody had
anything but good to say about her. I guess she's just
fitted right in and taken a whole lot of the burden off
everybody. Cynthia sounds more rested already."

"But not any warmer?"

"No," J.T. said, his smile fading. "Not a hell of a
lot warmer, Don. The worst thing is," he added in

despair, "I honestly don't know why she's still mad at me. I don't even know what I'm doing to upset her all the time."

She's trying to tell you and you won't listen, Don thought, looking at his friend's lean, weathered face, the powerful jaw and wide stubborn mouth. *Dammit, man, why won't you listen?*

Don Holden felt a helpless flood of sympathy for the gracious blond woman he'd met briefly at the ranch when he'd flown down for his buddy's wedding. Poor Cynthia, she certainly had her hands full, he thought, trying to make J. T. McKinney understand the needs and yearnings of a modern woman.

But there was nothing Don could say to help her. Unless J.T. would somehow bring himself to see the light, nobody was going to penetrate the man's thick-skulled obstinacy, not even his best and oldest friend. And trying to force the issue would just make J.T. retreat in anger. Reluctantly, Don moved the conversation back to a safe, casual discussion of winery procedures and economics, and the two men sat talking in quiet tones as the mellow California twilight deepened beyond the windows.

CHAPTER FIVE

COLD MOONLIGHT SPILLED through the window, flowing in long silvery rectangles across the floor and the bed. Cynthia stirred wearily and looked out at the starry Texas sky, realizing that she'd forgotten to draw the drapes when she went to bed.

Out here in the country, folks tended to overlook things like windows and drapes. After all, there was nothing all around but miles and miles of empty stillness.

She rolled over and hugged her pillow, shuddering at the thought of all that loneliness. The solitude that surrounded the ranch buildings seemed to be pressing right into the room, creeping through the closets and slithering among her folded underclothes in the dresser drawers. Loneliness filled and crowded her world so there was hardly any place for Cynthia any longer, and she hungered for J.T.'s hearty masculine presence with a longing that was almost unbearable.

"Tomorrow," she whispered aloud, sitting up and hugging her knees under the silken nightgown. "He'll be home tomorrow night. He'll be right here in the bed with me."

She smiled, her face softening in the cool silver moonlight, and stroked his pillow with a gentle hand. She could almost see his face on the pillow, the powerful mouth and laughing dark eyes, the hard line where his neck dipped into a lean muscled shoulder. Physical longing for her husband swept through Cynthia's body in such a hot flooding wave that she felt weak, almost ashamed of her lack of control.

I shouldn't feel this way after nearly two years of marriage, she thought miserably. Not after a baby and a serious illness and all the other things they'd been through. This kind of raw sexual desire really should be dimming now, settling into something easier and more comfortable.

But when Cynthia visualized her husband's face and body, or when she recalled the way it felt to be in his arms, open and abandoned to his love, it was all she could do to keep from moaning aloud and burrowing against his pillow in an agony of yearning.

Cynthia lifted her head after a moment, listening to the silence, wondering absently what was different about the night. She had a twinge of anxiety, thinking about Jennifer, then smiled when she remembered that Lisa was in the house.

The shy young woman had already made a vast difference in Cynthia's life. Ever since Lisa came, Cynthia was able to close her door tightly at night, confident that Jennifer would be cared for if she woke and began to fuss. All those blessed hours of uninterrupted sleep had refreshed her, strengthened and renewed her energy so that she was even ready to examine her life and her marriage with new eyes, and approach the whole situation with fresh commitment.

She got up from the bed and moved restlessly to the window, standing in the pale moonlight and looking out at the shadowed ranch buildings. Tiffany entered from the hallway and padded across the floor, distracted from some mysterious nighttime errand by the movements in the bedroom. She purred softly and rubbed against her mistress's bare ankles. Cynthia stooped to pick up the plump cat.

"Things are going to be different this time, Tiffany," she whispered into the cat's warm fur. "I'm not going to be so awful to him. After all, it can't be easy for him, either, all this unhappiness. I won't be so stubborn anymore. I'm going to make a real effort to be cheerful and loving, and not fight with him all the time. I really am."

Tiffany yawned and struggled to get down. Cynthia finally released her, watching as the cat's long striped tail whisked around the door frame and vanished in the blackness of the hallway. Then she turned toward the window and the moonlit ranch yard again.

Her eyes were adjusting to the darkness and she could make out individual objects... buildings and haystacks, white rail fences and the humped bodies of sleeping cattle and horses.

The sky was black and brilliant with stars, like trails of silver glitter spilled carelessly on an expanse of rich

black velvet. The moon drifted low over the buildings, a pure shining disk just a day or two away from
fullness.

As Cynthia watched, the moon seemed to fade
away, to vanish before her eyes and leave a shadow on
the land. She realized that it was moving gradually
around behind the craggy limestone outcroppings on
one of the high hills to the east.

All at once she drew her breath in sharply and
stared in fear and amazement. Where the moon had
disappeared, another light suddenly materialized. For
a long time it hovered in silence like a second moon,
spilling radiance onto the hilltop, but no heavenly
body had ever looked or behaved in such a fashion.
While Cynthia stared upward in awe, the light began
to flash rhythmically and float with eerie grace from
side to side. It rose and lowered with dizzying speed,
slipped behind the hills where the moon had vanished and then reappeared almost instantly on the
other side of the limestone outcropping. Cynthia
gripped the window frame and looked around wildly,
wondering what to do. Should she wake the household, run to look for a telescope or binoculars, call
the police or the Air Force?

A camera...maybe she could find one of the video
cameras....

She hurried across the room, searching for her
robe, with some frantic notion of calling Ken Slattery's house and telling them to wake Jimmy, to show
him the mysterious moving light and ask what he

thought of it. But at the doorway she stopped, feeling foolish, and moved hesitantly back to the window again.

Ken and Nora would think she'd taken leave of her senses, calling them at this hour and asking them to wake a ten-year-old child to look at a strange light.

Besides, when she got back to the window, the light had vanished completely. The moon drifted back into view, silent and still, spilling its gentle radiance on the sleeping ranch yard again.

"Maybe it was the moon all the time," Cynthia whispered. "Maybe I just saw some trick of light and shadow."

But she knew that wasn't true. She'd seen an actual light, an artificial illumination from some silent, airborne craft that behaved as she'd never seen any aircraft behave in her life.

Cynthia's heart pounded and her breath came in short ragged gasps, as if she'd been running. She felt sweaty and chilled, sick with excitement as she studied the craggy hilltop, its outline silent and unrevealing against the silvery wash of stars.

"I'll talk to Jimmy about it," she promised herself. "First thing tomorrow." Maybe that strange, solitary boy was also watching right at this moment, she thought with sudden hope. Maybe he'd actually seen the same light, and they could share their impressions.

Feeling suddenly more lighthearted and hopeful than she had for a long time, Cynthia drew the drapes and returned to her bed.

The light might turn out to be nothing more than a nighttime fantasy, she thought with a drowsy smile, but it was certainly a welcome relief from all the turbulent emotions she'd been experiencing for so long. For once, she wasn't obsessed with thoughts of J.T. and their troubled relationship, of her own restless dissatisfaction and her erratic feelings about her marriage.

In fact, Cynthia was almost as excited about talking to Jimmy Slattery tomorrow as she was about seeing her husband again, and it felt good to be absorbed, even briefly, in something other than J. T. McKinney.

JIMMY, HOWEVER, was not going to be able to share Cynthia's observations. While she was watching the mysterious light, her UFO consultant was sound asleep on the top of the haystack, wrapped in a couple of blankets he'd stolen from Nora Slattery's tidy linen cupboard.

Taking the blankets was just part of Jimmy's elaborate effort to conceal his nighttime activities. For the past several nights he'd used the pillows on his bed to make a form shaped like a body, just as he'd seen people do in movies, then covered the rounded shape carefully with blankets and stolen some of Nora's other covers to make a bed for himself on the hay-stack.

For a couple of hours he'd lain on the prickly straw, fighting to keep himself awake by reciting songs, scraps of poetry, the plots of movies he'd seen, anything he could think of to keep from drifting off to sleep.

He was waiting for the marvelous light that he'd now seen on two successive nights. Jimmy had made another unsuccessful attempt to climb the hill in the daytime and look for clues, but even early in the morning, the blazing heat had been too much for him. Any trip to the hilltop would have to be made at night, a thought that Jimmy found both terrifying and exhilarating.

But first, he had to be absolutely sure about the light, that it wasn't just some kind of trick of nature, or a passing helicopter or something. If it came again tonight, Jimmy was going to tell Mrs. McKinney about it, and was nerving himself to suggest that to-morrow she could come out with him after midnight so they could watch the UFO together.

Just the idea of this was the most exciting thing that had ever happened in Jimmy Slattery's life. All his waking hours were absorbed in the thought of how wonderful it would be to impress the mistress of the ranch with this fabulous discovery, to be the one who showed her a miracle and to be praised and admired by her. They would be sharing a wonderful secret,

Jimmy and Mrs. McKinney. Nobody else in all the world would know about it.

Unless, of course, they decided to sell their story to the newspapers and the television networks. Then they'd go on all the talk shows, and Mrs. McKinney would tell people in her soft cultured voice that actually, this clever lad beside her had been the first one to see the actual UFO....

But then, just before the light appeared, Jimmy had lost the battle to stay awake. His youth and fatigue won out over his determination, and his eyelids drifted shut. His hands relaxed on the binoculars, and the notebook fell unheeded onto a hay bale at his side.

When the light finally began to shine from the hilltop, it glimmered unheeded across the boy's sleeping, freckled face, reflecting from his thick eyeglasses in flashing disks of brilliance that were not observed by any human eyes.

JIMMY AND CYNTHIA were not the only people on the Double C Ranch who were stirring past midnight on that starry summer night.

Lisa Croft lay in the room that had been given to her when she arrived, on the main floor next to Lettie Mae and Virginia, with one ear cocked automatically in case Jennifer woke and began to cry.

It was a matter of pride to Lisa that not once since she'd come to the ranch had Cynthia been required to get up with Jennifer in the night. The baby was feverish sometimes on these warm summer evenings, troubled with a couple of new teeth and a persistent heat rash. But whenever she woke and began to fuss, Lisa was out of bed in an instant, running up the stairs to soothe the little girl and keep her from waking her mother.

Poor Miss Cynthia, Lisa thought, recalling the woman's beautiful, tired face. She'd been practically worn-out when Lisa arrived, after all those nights of broken sleep and long days of looking after the baby in the summer heat.

Besides, just yesterday Virginia had hinted to Lisa that things weren't exactly perfect these days between Miss Cynthia and her husband, either, and that she suspected the mistress could be fretting over her marriage.

Lisa had listened in silence, her face hidden, concentrating on the stack of snowy cotton diapers that she was folding.

But, of course, Lisa already knew that there was some kind of problem in J. T. McKinney's marriage. Otherwise, why would a man with such a beautiful wife have been up there in Lisa's hotel room in Las Vegas, looking to buy sex with a stranger?

Lisa shuddered and curled up in a tight little ball of agony beneath the covers, trying to push the horrible memory of that encounter from her mind. But she was beginning to understand with miserable certainty that it was impossible to run away from her past.

J. T. McKinney was coming home tomorrow. And as soon as he looked at Lisa, he'd remember that night in Las Vegas. There was no place for Lisa to hide. She rolled over on her back and stared at the ceiling in silent anguish, wondering for the thousandth time what J. T. McKinney was going to do when he saw her.

Would he just stare at her in cold contempt, or would he be furious and yell at her for being in his house, looking after his baby? Would he fire her on the spot and make her leave the ranch in shame, without even having anywhere to go?

He had every right to, of course. He would know the truth, that she was living a lie, and that all these nice people like Cynthia and Virginia and Lettie Mae would be horrified to have her anywhere near little Jennifer if they realized what she really was.

But she was so happy here, and she loved the baby so much....

"How was I supposed to know?" Lisa whispered aloud, gripping the bedclothes tightly in her hands until her fingers ached. "Who could have possibly imagined that he still lived in Crystal Creek? *Nobody* lives in the same place they grew up, not anymore!"

But J. T. McKinney obviously did. And her encounter with him, the hasty decision she'd made based on his casual boyhood memories of a small town in Texas, had drawn Lisa into this dreadful trap. Her situation was all the more cruel because, for the past ten days or so, she'd known a sweet kind of peace and happiness that had been denied her most of her life.

Bleakly, her dark eyes wide and frightened in the moonlight, Lisa tried to think about leaving the Double C and looking for somewhere else to go.

Ramon's face slid into her mind, his cruel, smiling mouth and cold eyes, his carefully barbered hair and expensive clothes and the casual brutality of his actions.

Lisa knew, with the instinct of any hunted animal, that Ramon was already looking for her. Sometimes in the darkness of the Texas night she could actually feel him stalking her, sniffing out her trail and drawing closer all the time. One of these days she'd look up and he'd be there, watching her with his cold eyes, waiting to pounce. And if she didn't even have the safety of this ranch between her and Ramon's grasp, what would protect her?

She sobbed aloud briefly, hugging her arms with a sudden chill.

Another image came drifting unbidden into her mind, banishing the dreaded memory of Ramon. It was the handsome face and tall muscular body of Tony, the young veterinarian.

In spite of herself, Lisa's tears stopped and her mouth curved into a sad little smile when she thought about Tony's lean body in jeans and T-shirt, his strength and gentleness and the way his dark hair fell onto his forehead when he strode lightly across the ranch yard.

He'd come back again to check on the injured colt, by himself this time, and had made a point of strolling up to the house, pausing on the veranda where Lisa had the baby playing in the shade on a blanket.

Lisa remembered the way her heart beat faster and her throat got all tight when he leaned on the veranda railing and smiled down at her.

Just the way he smiled was enough to send a girl into tongue-tied confusion, Lisa thought desperately. She must have seemed like a complete idiot, trying to think of something intelligent to say while he played with the baby and chatted about the ranch, the weather, the animals he'd seen that day.

And all the time he was looking at her with that boyish smile, all she could think of was how strong he looked, how his dark eyes shone and how much she liked the way they crinkled up at the corners when he smiled. He had a dimple, too, that flashed into one of his brown cheeks whenever he laughed....

Lisa moaned and rolled over in bed again, burying her face in the pillow, her body rigid with misery.

Despite his years of education and his manly appearance, in many ways Tony Rodriguez was still just a boy with a heart full of dreams and idealism. Lisa knew what kind of woman a man like Tony was looking for. He wanted innocence and purity, a mother for his children, someone he could be proud of because everybody else respected her.

He certainly didn't want a Las Vegas hooker with a sordid, shameful past. Tears began to gather in Lisa's eyes again, painful tears that burned as they spilled into the pillow.

Struggling to get herself under control, she turned over again and stared absently at the window. Suddenly she sat up in bed, rubbing her eyes and blinking at a strange radiance that filled the sky. But before she could think about the flashing light, she heard a plaintive cry, a muffled wail that came drifting down the dark staircase and through the open door of her room.

Everything else vanished from Lisa's mind, all the troubled thoughts of Tony, of Ramon's frightening cruelty and J. T. McKinney's imminent arrival at the ranch. The mysterious light shimmered and hovered in silence, spilling across her empty room and over the tumbled bedclothes as she grabbed her robe and flew up the stairs to the baby's room.

IN THE NEXT ROOM, Virginia Parks was awake, too, but she wasn't aware of the eerie light because she had her drapes securely drawn, muffling out the moonlight and the night sounds on the ranch. She heard Jennifer's first dismal cries, and Lisa's running feet, and smiled in the darkness.

What a marvelous girl Lisa had proved to be, dropped like a miracle from heaven just when they needed her the most. Virginia nodded with satisfaction, recalling Lisa's own words the day they met at the Crystal Creek bus depot, her shy confession that she felt she'd somehow been led to this place.

Virginia Parks certainly believed in divine guidance. In fact, there'd been quite a lot of it in her own life lately.

First, there'd been the wonderful solution to all her worries about the future, appearing as if by magic when J.T. had offered her the chance to live in his small revenue house in Crystal Creek. *That* had been an answer to a prayer, no doubt about it. And then, just when Virginia had really begun to despair of ever being able to escape her responsibilities here at the Double C ranch house, along had come Lisa, another blessing from a benign Providence.

The girl was truly astonishing, Virginia mused in the darkness, listening to the hushed sounds of Lisa's voice singing to the fretful baby, and the gentle creak of the rocker in the upstairs nursery.

Lisa had a way with little Jennifer that was almost miraculous. Even Cynthia wasn't able to soothe the baby as Lisa could, just by picking her up and cuddling her, murmuring and singing little scraps of lullabies. And when she wasn't busy with Jennifer, the girl turned her hand cheerfully to any other work that needed to be done, from helping Lettie Mae in the garden to running a vacuum cleaner energetically through the big house, saving Virginia's poor aching back and her sore feet.

Again, Virginia nodded contentedly in the darkness. Now she'd be able to leave the house to Lisa and

Lettie Mae, and move to town with a clear conscience. She could take over the pretty little cottage, get it all fixed up to suit her taste, find a couple of nice young girls to board with her and start a well-earned life of ease and pleasure.

Virginia sighed, and her heart flooded with gratitude when she thought about J. T. McKinney and Lisa Croft, the two people who had, strangely enough, made this all possible. Tomorrow they were going to see each other for the first time, and Virginia could hardly wait.

J.T was going to be so surprised and happy to meet this girl, who'd already made herself indispensable in his home by taking such a load off of his wife and the household staff.

"He's going to love her," Virginia whispered aloud, her eyes drifting placidly closed. "He's just going to love her."

JENNIFER Travis McKinney snuggled in Lisa's warm arms and peered fearfully over the young woman's shoulder at the starry black sky where the light shone and hovered. Jennifer didn't know much about lights, except that she preferred to have her small clown-shaped night-light switched on when she slept, and howled with furious energy if it was ever forgotten.

But the radiance in the sky beyond her nursery drew her eyes in some irresistible way, tugging at her like the sight of her mother's smiling face or her father's big brown hands.

While Lisa sang and rocked with her back to the window, Jennifer rested her cheek drowsily on Lisa's fragrant neck and put her thumb into her mouth with a comforting little pop. With her free hand the baby fingered a strand of Lisa's dark hair, pulled and tugged at it gently, trailed it across her own face to enjoy its comforting, silky warmth.

"Li," Jennifer whispered huskily, wanting Lisa to turn and look at the marvel that filled the sky. "Li. Dada," she added earnestly, yearning suddenly for that glorious laughing presence that seemed to have vanished so completely from her life.

"Your daddy's coming home tomorrow, sweetheart," Lisa whispered, stroking the baby's downy head with a hand so gentle that it was like the brush of a bird's wing. "Tomorrow, he'll see his sweet little Jennifer again. He'll be so..."

Lisa's voice broke and she fell abruptly silent, burying her wet face against Jennifer's tummy. Jennifer patted the soft dark cloud of hair and looked up at the light again. Her eyes widened as she saw it flash rainbow colors, drift across the hilltop in a swinging motion, rise and lower and dance like the butterflies she loved.

Something drew the baby girl toward the light, an urge that was almost overwhelming, far within the depths of her infant consciousness. She wanted to creep out of the big house, tumble down the steps and crawl as fast as she could across the dusty yard to the place where the light was shining, calling to her....

"Li," she murmured again, entranced.

"You want to lie down, honey bunch? All right, let's put you down...."

Jennifer protested briefly when she was carried across the room and placed in her crib. She rolled over onto her tummy, the thumb still firmly in her mouth, and gazed at the window. But the light was gone, and the sky was black, flat and faraway, not the least bit welcoming anymore.

Besides, Lisa was rubbing her back with slow, easy fingers that felt mesmerizing to the drowsy baby.

"Fall asleep, sweet Jenny," the girl whispered in a soft, lilting voice. "Fall asleep, fall asleep, fall asleep...."

Jennifer drew in a deep breath, sighed and clutched a corner of the blanket against her face. Her long eyelashes wavered and drifted onto her cheeks, and her little body began to rise and fall in the deep rhythms of sleep.

APART FROM CYNTHIA, only the very youngest and the very oldest residents of the Double C Ranch seemed destined to see the mysterious lights in the sky on that hot August night.

In his little stone bungalow behind the main ranch house, old Hank Travis was having trouble sleeping again.

Small damned wonder, he thought bitterly, struggling to sit upright in his rumpled bed, when a man spent most of the day laid flat out in bed like some poor fool in a hospital. How was he expected to sleep at night, for God's sake?

But the weakness that had come over him these past few months left him little choice. Some days were all right, and he could dress himself, even limp over to the ranch house for breakfast. But other mornings he'd wake feeling as weak as a kitten, and the girls would have to bring him his meals, sometimes even sit and help him to eat.

Hank didn't like to think about it much, but a lot of the spirit had gone out of him since the shocking death of young Jeff Harris. That boy had made Hank feel young again, full of spit and vinegar with all his plans. Nowadays, Hank often wondered if it was worth the effort to heave himself out of bed.

"It's just a hell of a thing, this whole business of dying, ain't it?" Hank complained to his cat, who leapt down from the couch across the room and padded over to jump onto the old man's bed. "Who'd've thought it could be such a damn hard thing to do?"

Hank reached out gratefully, his hands shaking, reassured by the familiar warmth of Hagar's soft rusty fur.

Actually, Hagar had always been Ruth's cat, but Hank had more or less commandeered him, especially recently, when the old man had grown so weak. He and Hagar were happy together, and Ruth hesitated to take away the one bit of comfort that seemed to be left to Tyler's great-grandfather.

"Especially," Hank had pointed out mercilessly, "since *you* already got everything in the world a woman could want. You got your man, your fancy new house coming up, a bun in the oven . . . what do you need with this measly cat besides?"

So Hagar lived almost permanently with Hank these days, and the arrangement suited both of them.

Hagar nestled against Hank's skinny ribs, licking thoughtfully at his wrist while Hank reflectively stroked the cat's fur with a deliberate hand.

Suddenly he felt Hagar tense beneath his fingers and look at the window. Hank, too, looked up, and his rheumy old eyes widened in surprise.

"Well, I'll be," he whispered. "What the jumpin' hell is goin' on?"

Grimacing with pain and effort, he swung his ancient legs over the side of the bed, forced himself erect and reached for his walker. Hank abhorred the contraption, but had given in to necessity when J.T. pointed out, not without some impatience, that it was a hell of a lot better to use a walker than to be laid up with a broken hip.

Hank frowned horribly, got his skinny old body into position, then hesitated, leaning on the bars of the walker and shaking with effort. At last, he took a faltering step toward the window, then another and another.

Finally, he reached his destination, rested the walker against the lower sill and leaned forward, staring out into the Texas night, his mouth slack-jawed with amazement.

He saw the light move just as Cynthia had, watched it lift and lower and dance, watched the flashes of color and the mysterious radiance that flooded over the silent countryside.

But Hank wasn't thrilled by the spectacle. The old man was troubled and frightened, almost terrified. He stood trembling between the walker rails, glinting brilliantly in the moonlight, and watched in dread as the light crept partway down the hillside, then retreated.

Hank knew that it was coming to threaten the people on the ranch, and he was powerless to stop it. There was going to be trouble, pain, maybe even death, and he couldn't warn them because they wouldn't listen anymore. "They never listen," he whispered to Hagar, his leathery old face bleak with pain. "These damned young people, they just never listen."

Hank hovered on his metal supports, almost sick with the sense of menace that hovered over the ranch. Who was going to suffer? Who was that light coming to take?

Slowly, with a yearning tenderness that would have surprised his family, Hank ran through all of them, trying to decide who was in danger.

Not J.T., who would always be first and best-loved in Hank's mind. Not Lynn or the boys, or the pretty new wives, or any of the ranch and household staff...

No, wait… That sweet-faced new girl, the one who carried the baby around—she was at risk. Hank saw her in great danger, threatened by something so brutal and horrible that it didn't even have any shape, just a cold, evil smell. He shivered in the night, then glanced, appalled, at the ranch house.

Cynthia stood framed high in a bedroom window, hers and J.T.'s, also gazing pensively at the light spilling over the craggy hilltop. And as Hank watched, the danger rose up to engulf her, too, enclosing her in choking mists of evil and misery.

Hank shuddered, wiped his forehead with a shaking hand and limped back to the bed, sliding under the covers and clutching the cat gratefully to his chest for comfort.

"Poor girl with her fancy big-city name," Hank muttered to the cat. "Something real bad's coming up for her, but ain't no way to stop it. No way in the world."

He thought about Cynthia's fine, aristocratic face, her golden beauty and her earnest desire to fit in and be accepted at the ranch. In many ways, Cynthia had touched old Hank's heart more in these past two years than he would ever have confessed to anybody.

He wished now that there was some way to protect her from the suffering ahead. But Hank had learned, after a hundred years of living, that everybody had to wade through a certain amount of pain, and survival was a personal matter.

The light faded at last, leaving him feeling a little
more calm and at ease. Hagar nestled close, licking
his fingers with a rough tongue. At last, lulled by the
rhythmic purring of the cat and the drowsy nighttime sounds beyond the window, Hank fell asleep,
too.

Overhead, the stars shone with a cold, impartial
brilliance, waiting for dawn.

CHAPTER SIX

NEXT MORNING, Cynthia sat in one of the wicker chairs on the veranda, frowning through her metal-framed granny glasses at a cross-stitch sampler she was making for the nursery.

Jennifer played at her mother's feet on a soft quilt. Barefoot and happy, the little girl banged a wooden spoon energetically against a couple of aluminum cake tins and beamed with delight at the wonderful sounds she was making.

"Can't nobody stop that damned kid from makin' such a god-awful racket?" Hank asked irritably, glaring at the baby in her diaper and pink cotton shirt.

Jennifer grinned up at him, the broad enchanting smile displaying her new teeth and the dimples in her rounded cheeks. Hank scowled back at her and rocked harder in his chair. Unruffled, Jennifer chuckled and returned to her percussion solo.

Cynthia dropped the needlework in her lap for a moment and smiled fondly at the old man. "You must be feeling a lot better this morning, Grandpa," she observed cheerfully. "You certainly sound more like your old self."

Hank snorted and turned his attention to Lisa, who sat on the step next to Jennifer to make sure the little girl didn't start crawling away and tumble down onto the flagstone path.

Lisa wore a pale denim sunsuit, one of Cynthia's castoffs, and she looked beautiful in the morning light. Her skin, Cynthia thought, was so fresh and delicate that it looked like silk, and her dark hair was rich and glowing with natural highlights. Her eyes were lowered over the little pair of yellow corduroy overalls she was mending, and a fan of dense eyelashes swept onto her cheek in a way that made her look almost as young and vulnerable as Jennifer.

"So, Lisa," Hank said with a grin, "lookin' forward to meetin' the boss tonight, are you? What if he don't like you?"

The girl glanced up at him quickly, and Cynthia was surprised by the sudden look of alarm in Lisa's dark eyes. Trust Hank Travis, she thought with a mixture of annoyance and amusement. The old man had an uncanny knack for putting his finger on the very thing that was making someone nervous.

Virginia must have had the same thought, because she looked up indignantly from the pile of garden beans she was trimming and cutting into pieces for freezing. "Don't be silly, Grandpa Hank," Virginia said briskly. "J.T.'s going to love Lisa. Who wouldn't?"

The housekeeper beamed at Lisa, who gave her an uncertain smile, then reached hastily for Jennifer. The

baby had found a large, dead wasp on the floorboards and was clutching the furry object in her fist,
about to stuff it into her mouth.

"Nasty," Lisa murmured urgently, prying the insect from the baby's fat hand over her strenuous ob-
jections. "Not nice for Jennifer. Mustn't eat. No,
no."

"No?" Jennifer echoed, looking with regret at the
tempting yellow and black creature that Lisa threw
down onto the grass. "No? Dada," she added happily, picking up her wooden spoon again and banging it on old Hank's cowboy boot. "Dada."

"What a mean kid," Hank commented sadly,
moving his foot out of harm's way. "Just a pure little hellion, this one is."

Lettie Mae, who was also trimming beans and who
had been listening in silence, looked up now and
smiled. "She's so much like Cal was at this age," the
cook announced. "Minds me of him all the time."

"Oh, dear," Cynthia said, voicing one of her own
secret fears. "I hope that doesn't mean she's going to
grow up to be a rodeo rider."

"Some kind of criminal, more likely," Hank said
darkly, watching as the baby tried to thrust her bon-
neted head between the veranda rails.

Lisa retrieved the baby and set her back on the
quilt. Virginia returned to an earlier conversation
about the little house in Crystal Creek, which she was
moving into later in the week.

"We're all going to miss you so much, Virginia," Cynthia said. "I just can't imagine this place without you, I really can't."

Virginia gave her employer a grateful smile, then shook her head ruefully. "To tell the truth," she confessed, "I can hardly imagine it, either. But I'm so excited about this house. And as soon as I get a couple of boarders..."

"Where you gonna get a couple of boarders?" Hank interrupted rudely. "What new people are gonna move to this town and wanna live in your house? Nobody ever moves to this town."

"Lisa did," Virginia said in a firm tone. "Lots of people are moving into Crystal Creek," she added. "It's becoming quite a tourist attraction because of Warren Trent's carousel, and the dude ranch and the rock hunting and all."

"Dude ranches!" Hank muttered with withering scorn. *"Rock hunters!"*

"You should have seen the man I met in the post office just yesterday," Virginia went on cheerfully, as if the old man hadn't spoken. "Now, *there* was a big-city fellow if I ever saw one, right in Crystal Creek asking all about the town as if he planned to move here. There's lots of people coming here."

"What was this big-city feller like?" Lettie Mae asked, bending with a gusty sigh to load more beans into her apron. "How can you tell somebody's a big-city feller, Ginny?"

"Oh, just the way he looked," Virginia said vaguely.

"How did he look?"

"Well, he had a purple silk shirt, real silk, and his hair looked nicer that mine ever has, even when Billie Ann's just finished styling it, and he was dark and handsome like a movie star, kind of Latin-looking..."

"Sound like some kinda sissy," Hank commented. "What man goes around in front of people wearin' a purple silk shirt, fer God's sake?"

Cynthia returned idly to her needlework, enjoying the conversation and the ebb and flow of vigorous personalities all around her on this bright summer morning.

Just a few hours, she was thinking, her heart singing as she pictured J.T.'s handsome face and springing step. *Just a few more hours and he'll be home, right here beside me, where I can see him and touch him, and I'll be able to...*

"And he was asking all about opportunities in the town," Virginia was saying, "what kind of jobs there were and who was filling them, things like that."

Cynthia glanced up and was startled to catch the expression on Lisa's delicate face. The girl's eyes had darkened with terror, and her hands tightened convulsively on the spool of thread she was holding.

"Lisa?" Cynthia asked in concern. "Is something the matter, dear?"

But the group on the veranda was distracted at that moment by the sudden appearance of Tony Rodriguez, who came striding up from the direction of the stable, the sunlight gleaming on his curly dark head.

"Morning, folks," Tony said, pausing by the pillared veranda and looking at the group assembled in the shade. "Nice to see you up and around this morning, Hank," he added, smiling at the old man with a flash of white teeth.

Hank grinned back at the young veterinarian, his leathery face creasing with sly humor. "Sure givin' that colt a lot of attention, ain't you, boy?" he asked, with heavy significance and a sidelong glance at Lisa, who blushed and frowned while she tried, with shaking hands, to thread her needle.

Tony shifted on his feet and gave the old man another serene smile. "I just want to make real sure there's no infection under those stitches," he said. "Hi, Lisa," he added casually, looking down at the slender girl on the steps. "Doing some sewing, are you?"

"She . . . she goes through the knees on her overalls so fast," Lisa murmured in a soft, halting voice. "They seem to need patching every few days."

"Care for a glass of iced tea, Tony?" Lettie Mae asked, getting to her feet and shaking out her apron.

"Don't trouble yourself, ma'am," the young man said. "I can't stay. I have to get on over to Carolyn's and check on one of her Santa Gertrudis heifers that's having trouble calving."

"Turrible animals, them Santa Gertrudis," Hank said with satisfaction, reviving an ancient argument.

"I always did say it's no good tinkering with nature. Y'all end up perducing some bastard animal that can't even calve proper. I told Frank Townsend he'd be sorry, gettin' into them ugly animals. Likely what drove him to his death, poor boy, workin' with them irritatin' half-bred cattle."

"Hank Travis!" Virginia said in horror. "What an awful thing to say!"

"Now, Hank," Tony said mildly, smiling down at Lisa as he lifted one booted foot and placed it gently on the step next to her. "The Santa Gertrudis is a marvelous beef animal. One of the best there's ever been, and real hardy besides."

"Bull!" Hank said furiously. "Why, I reckon I've seen more..."

But Cynthia was no longer listening to the argument. Nor was she thinking about Lisa's strange moment of distress, or the imminent arrival of her husband. She'd spotted Jimmy Slattery lurking in the mesquite down behind one of the feed houses, and everything else was swept away by her urgent need to talk to the boy about that mysterious light.

She folded her needlework and her eyeglasses, got to her feet and smiled at the others. "I think I'll just go for a little walk before it gets too hot," she said with cheerful casualness. "Lisa, will you please take Jennifer in and put her down for her nap at ten?"

Lisa nodded, her head bent over the careful stitches she was making. But her face was still pale as ivory, and her hands trembled badly. "Yes, I will," she whispered, her voice almost inaudible. "You don't have to worry about Jennifer, Miss Cynthia."

"And *another* thing about them cattle..." Hank continued hotly.

Cynthia started off toward the cluster of outbuildings. When she was a short distance from the big house, she quickened her steps and began to smile as the lively argument lifted and swirled behind her on the warm summer breeze.

Jimmy sat on an upturned wooden keg next to the windmill, his heart pounding with emotion. He struggled to keep his face calm and expressionless, like a policeman or a private investigator with nerves of steel, when Cynthia began to tell him what she'd seen the previous night.

He smoothed his notebook on his dirty bare knee, flipped it open and took the special ballpoint pen from his pocket. Then he looked over the rims of his glasses at Cynthia, who sat opposite him on the edge of the horse trough.

"Now, this light," he asked with detached professionalism, making a note on the page. "You say it moved from side to side?"

She nodded, her face glowing with excitement. "It flashed all different colors, and flipped from side to side and up and down so fast it almost made me dizzy to watch."

"And it was really bright?" Jimmy made another careful note.

"Oh, it was dazzling," Cynthia said with a distant smile, her dark eyes shining. "I wish you could have seen it, Jimmy!" she added, smiling. "You'd have been so excited."

Jimmy frowned. He didn't like it when she addressed him like any other dumb ten-year-old kid. It totally ruined the image of the cold-faced investigator that he wanted to project.

"And there was no sound?" he asked in a neutral tone, studying his notebook. "Nothing at all?"

Cynthia screwed up her face in an effort to remember. "I don't think so. Of course, the windows were closed and the air conditioning was on, but still, I had an impression of absolute silence."

"I mean for instance, it wasn't like when a helicopter goes by? Would you recognize a helicopter if you heard one?"

Cynthia nodded decisively. "Helicopters go over the ranch all the time, heading up to the military base at Killeen. I know what they sound like, and this didn't make a noise like that at all."

Jimmy felt a sharp pang of regret. If only he hadn't fallen asleep on that haystack, like a stupid baby!

"How long did it last?" he asked.

"I don't know. I was just so caught up in the experience, I hardly kept track."

"Five minutes? Half an hour?"

Cynthia smiled at him. "Probably somewhere in between. What do you think it is, Jimmy?"

"I think it's a spacecraft, doing surveillance," Jimmy said, trying to sound as if he made these momentous announcements all the time. He hesitated, taking a calming breath, then glanced up at her in a carefully offhand way. "Don't forget, I've seen it, too, you know," he said. "The night before last. I would have set up an observation post last night, but I had something else to do. It was something really important, the business I had to do."

"Of course," she answered, her dark eyes widening with excitement. "And when you saw it, did it look just the way I described it?"

"Pretty much," Jimmy conceded. "Of course," he added, consulting his notes again, "a trained observer like me knows more about what to look for, but you did pretty good."

"And you think it's really a UFO? It's not just some kind of... illusion, or something to do with the moonlight, or something?"

Jimmy shook his head. "I think it's real. I wouldn't be surprised," he added pompously, enjoying the way she regarded him with rapt attention, "if the aliens have already landed and established a base up there."

"Right here on the ranch?"

The boy nodded, his chest swelling with importance. "I've actually planned a couple of reconnaissance trips up there, but things keep coming up. I have a lot to do."

Cynthia glanced up at the craggy hilltop, already shimmering and dancing with heat waves in the distance. She shuddered and turned back to the boy. "It's too hot to climb that hill, Jimmy."

"Oh, heat doesn't bother me," Jimmy said, with a look of lofty contempt for physical hardship. "But," he added, "I think I'm going to have to make the trip at night, so they don't see me if they've got surveillance equipment set up."

Cynthia's eyes widened in horror. "Jimmy, you can't go up there alone at night!"

"Sure I can. I do lots of stuff at night."

"But your uncle and aunt would be so upset if you ever did something like that! Promise me you won't try to climb that hill at night unless . . . unless I come with you."

Jimmy considered her words in startled silence. He hated being treated like a kid and told what he could and couldn't do. On the other hand, the prospect of organizing a nighttime expedition, being in charge and having Cynthia trailing behind him, dazzled by his skill and courage, was almost irresistible.

"All right," he said at last, pretending reluctance. "You can come with me. But we better go pretty soon, before the aliens leave. How about tonight?"

Her face lit up with anticipation, then clouded over. "Not tonight," she said slowly. "My husband's coming home tonight, and I'm not sure what time they're getting in. And it won't be so easy for me to get away when he's home, either," she added, looking troubled. "What time would we go, Jimmy?"

Jimmy considered, his throat tightening with mounting excitement that he was careful not to show. "I think we should prob'ly leave sometime after midnight," he said, "because that's when the light usually comes, so that must be when they're active. Let's meet here at the windmill tomorrow night at midnight, and start climbing the hill then."

She nodded, looking suddenly determined. "I'll be here," she said.

Jimmy gave her a warning glance. "I don't want anybody else to find out about this yet," he said. "You won't tell Mr. McKinney?"

She shook her head so firmly that her golden hair swung in a bright arc from side to side. "Tomorrow night he'll probably still be tired from his trip. Anyway, he's always asleep by midnight, and he sleeps like a log, especially if we ..."

She stopped in midsentence. Jimmy wondered why her cheeks turned suddenly pink with embarrassment, but he was too absorbed in the prospect of their nocturnal adventure to spend much time speculating about Mrs. McKinney's emotional state.

He sat on the keg and watched her as she returned to the house. His face was impassive but his head whirled with plans and secrets.

Although Jimmy worshiped Mrs. McKinney, he had no intention of letting her be the first to see whatever was up on that hilltop. Tonight Jimmy Slattery was going to climb the limestone cliff, all by himself. Tomorrow night, after he'd actually seen the aliens, he'd take her along as a witness.

And once the world learned what was up there on that rugged hilltop, nothing on earth would ever be the same again.

J. T. MCKINNEY STRODE through the murmuring summer evening toward his house, on fire with love and longing for his wife.

God, but it was good to be home!

He glanced over at Ruth and Tyler, hurrying along beside him. They were still excited from their trip and had decided a nightcap was in order.

J.T. loved these young people, but he really hoped they wouldn't chat for long. He hungered to be alone with Cynthia, to hold her in his arms and kiss her throat and mouth and eyelids, fondle her rich full breasts....

J.T. shivered with desire and quickened his steps as the big house loomed out of the darkness. Tyler laughed and grasped his father's shoulder.

"Lord, Daddy, slow down! You're loping along here like an old stallion headed for home."

J.T. gave his son a rueful grin. "Reckon I'm glad to be back, son," he confessed. "Going to be real nice to see my girls again."

"Will Jennifer still be up?" Ruth asked hopefully.

J.T. nodded. "Cynthia promised they'd keep her up if they could, and let her sleep late tomorrow."

They climbed the steps and entered the front hall of the big house, heading for the sitting room, where the sound of a television set drifted on cool household air that was pleasantly scented with Cynthia's homemade potpourri.

J.T. breathed deep of the familiar fragrance and paused in the doorway of the sitting room, smiling with pleasure. Lettie Mae and Virginia were side by side on the couch, watching "Wheel of Fortune." Cynthia was across from them, also absorbed in the game show, while a dark-haired girl nestled in another armchair with her back to the door, holding little Jennifer on her knee.

Nobody in the room was aware of the new arrivals, who clustered silently in the doorway, enjoying this placid domestic scene.

"Buy a vowel, you fool!" Lettie Mae shouted at the television screen. "Look at that, Ginny, he's going to spin the wheel again. Can you *believe* it?"

Virginia shook her head sadly. "They're always so greedy. They keep spinning the wheel till they lose everything they've won."

Jennifer's bright eyes peered over the shoulder of the dark-haired girl, then widened in astonishment and delight.

"Dada!" she shouted, bouncing frantically and waving her fat arms. "Da! Dada!"

J.T.'s jaw dropped open and he looked at Cynthia, who had come running across the room to hug him. "Jennifer called me Daddy," he said in amazement.

Cynthia laughed and brushed at her eyes, holding him and touching him as if to convince herself that he was real. "I know," she murmured, beaming proudly at her daughter. "She's been saying it ever since you left. It was her very first word, but she says a few other things now, too. She's started talking months before the average."

"She has? Well, I'll be damned. And how are *you*, sweetheart?" J.T. whispered huskily, pulling his wife into his arms. He thrilled at the feel of her warm curving body in the light cotton dress, her breasts and hips and the long slender line of her waist beneath his hands.

"I'm fine now that you're home," Cynthia murmured, smiling up at him with a private promise of love that made him feel dizzy, almost lightheaded with anticipation. "But I've been so lonely, darling. I couldn't believe how much I missed you."

Relief flooded through him, so sweet and strong that he realized for the first time how tense he'd actually been about this homecoming.

It was going to be all right, he told himself with a powerful surge of happiness. Cynthia was finally over her strange mood and ready to love him again. It was going to be just fine.

He kissed her once more, a long, lingering kiss that made the onlookers smile, then set her reluctantly aside and moved into the room to pick up his daughter, who was shouting for attention.

J.T. bent to lift the little girl from the arms of the new housemaid, then paused and gaped in horror. His heart began to pound with an erratic beat and he put a hand against his chest automatically, as if to protect himself from the shock.

This dark-haired girl who held his child was the hooker he'd last seen outside a seedy hotel room in Las Vegas.

Time stood still while the room swam in front of J.T.'s horrified eyes. He stared down at the girl, thinking rapidly, trying to calculate just what kind of situation he was dealing with.

Was this some insidious blackmail scheme? Would he be haunted his whole life by that one moment of foolish indiscretion?

J.T. thought about the girl's story, the vicious pimp she'd spoken of, and wondered in despair how he could have brought that kind of squalor into the peaceful confines of his home and family. How had she found out where he lived? He was certain that he'd never mentioned his name....

He lifted Jennifer automatically into his arms and snuggled her against his shoulder while his mind continued to whirl and grope for some kind of foothold in this bizarre situation.

Gradually he became aware of the girl's face, of the expression in her eyes. She was looking up at him with the same desperate fear and pleading that he remembered from back there in the Las Vegas hotel.

Don't tell, her dark eyes seemed to urge. *Please, please, don't tell!*

J.T. met those eyes with a steady, measuring look as his equilibrium began to return. He glanced down at Cynthia, who now stood next to him, smiling mistily and holding on to one of Jennifer's plump legs as she leaned against her husband's side.

"J.T.," she said, still flushed and starry-eyed with excitement at his unexpected appearance, "this is Lisa Croft, who's just about the nicest thing that's happened to us in a long time. Lisa, this is my husband, J. T. McKinney."

"Howdy, Lisa," J.T. said formally, extending his hand and noticing how the girl's slim fingers trembled as she returned his handshake. "I hear you're real good with little kids."

"She's also good with vacuum cleaners, sewing machines and just about anything else you can mention," Lettie Mae said with brisk approval. "Come on, Lisa," she added, getting to her feet. "Let's go see if we can rustle up some food for these weary travelers."

The girl stood gratefully and headed for the kitchen, but J.T. caught her arm and turned her briefly away from the others to give her a look of meaningful significance.

"I'll have to have a little talk with you later, Lisa, and get to know you a bit," he said. His voice was deliberately casual but his eyes burned into hers as he spoke. "I like to know a whole lot about the people who look after my family."

She nodded, her face pale with alarm, and then broke away to follow Lettie Mae into the kitchen while J.T. watched in silence.

Finally losing patience with her father's inattention, Jennifer grasped his ear and yanked on it firmly, shouting at him.

"Ow!" he yelled back, holding the plump baby away from him in mock horror. "What kind of bully are you, treating your poor daddy like that when he's just flown clear across the country to see you?"

Delighted by his reaction, Jennifer chuckled and kicked her bare feet against his chest. The room erupted in laughter and his tension began to ease, leaving J.T almost wondering if he'd somehow imagined the whole weird incident with the new housemaid.

A COUPLE OF HOURS LATER, J.T. lay with his hands behind his head, luxuriating in the comfort of his big roomy bed, the crisp sheets and scented pillows, the lazy, contented feeling of being showered and at ease after a long day handling the controls of his plane.

"Lord, this is nice," he called to Cynthia, who was out of sight in the bathroom. "It feels so good to be home, sweetheart. I just can't tell you how good it feels."

"Maybe you can try," she suggested, appearing suddenly in the doorway and switching off the overhead light so the glow from the bathroom shone mistily through her white silk nightgown, outlining her body in all its loveliness.

"Try what?" he asked with a grin, watching as she approached the bed and slipped in beside him. "What should I try?"

She leaned up on one elbow and traced the line of his lip and cheek with her finger. "Try to tell me how good it feels," she murmured, moving her hand down to play with the crisp graying hair on his chest.

He reached up to stroke her shining hair and toy with the strap of her nightgown, easing it down over her shoulder. "What if I showed you instead?" he whispered huskily. "Would that be all right?"

She laughed and nestled against him, then sighed with pleasure as he slipped off the other strap of her nightgown and began to fondle her breasts. J.T. rolled over and knelt above her, pulling the nightgown down over her hips and kissing her breasts, her waist and stomach and thighs. She shivered under his caress, moaning and arching against him, holding his head in both hands and whispering broken words of love as his lips moved across the fragrant softness of her skin.

J.T. was drowning in passion, dazzled by his wife's beauty and thrilled by her warm responsiveness, so hungry for her that everything else slipped from his mind.

Her troubling withdrawal and coldness during recent months, the tension between them and his fears that she didn't love him any longer...even the appalling shock of finding that girl lodged within his home...all of it vanished in a cloud of longing and need that swept him away with the intensity of a hurricane.

Their lovemaking was both stormy and tender, passionate and carefree, as full of laughter and lust and gentleness as it had ever been. J.T. made certain of Cynthia's release, then allowed his own, luxuriating in her silken warmth and smoothness like a man who has come home after years in the wilderness.

"I love you," he whispered into the curve of her neck, collapsing against her with a weary smile. "God, how I love you. There's never been a woman like you, darling. Never in all the world."

He reached up to kiss her lips and felt her mouth smiling under his. "Happy, sweetheart?" he asked, burying his face against her throat again.

"Oh, yes," she sighed. "Yes, I'm happy. You've always been able to make me happy, J.T."

"Sometimes lately I thought maybe I'd lost the knack," he confessed, trying to keep his voice light and teasing. "Thought I'd just forgotten how to please you, girl."

"Oh, J.T...."

"Now, look here," he warned sternly as her hands began to move over his body. "If you start that, we'll wind up doing it all over again, and that's not good for a man my age."

"Oh, pooh," she scoffed. "A man your age. You're lustier than most twenty-year-olds, J. T. McKinney."

"Yeah?" he asked with cheerful belligerence, rolling away from her and grinning. "And what do you know about twenty-year-olds?"

"Not much," Cynthia confessed, turning her head on the pillow to smile back at him. "Just that I'd much rather have you than any number of callow youths."

J.T.'s heart expanded and warmed at this reassurance. But then, suddenly, the talk of youth brought Lisa's image back into focus and he frowned.

"Hmm?" Cynthia murmured contentedly, catching his change of expression. She snuggled against him kissing his shoulder and running her tongue gently along his collarbone to the hollow of his throat.

J.T. cradled her in his arms, staring past her golden head at the play of light and shadow on the ceiling of their bedroom.

"Cynthia..." he began.

"Hmm?" she murmured again, pressing closer, fitting her body into his with loving ease and familiarity.

"Cynthia, this new girl who's looking after Jennifer..."

"Lisa?"

"Yeah, Lisa. How did you happen to find her?"

"Virginia found her at the bus depot. It was like a miracle, J.T. Virginia keeps saying she just dropped into our laps like a gift from the gods."

"No kidding," J.T. drawled.

She propped herself up on one elbow and smiled down at him. "I feel so much better since Lisa came, dear. I think I hadn't even realized how exhausted I was getting. Having her around to help is just wonderful. Especially at night," Cynthia added with a grateful sigh.

J.T. returned doggedly to his careful questioning. "At the bus depot, you say? How did she come to be at the bus depot?"

"Well, she was kind of vague about that. You know how kids are these days," Cynthia told him casually. "I guess she'd met somebody who told her how nice it was here at Crystal Creek, and she was finished school and at loose ends so she decided to come out here and see if she could find work."

J.T. nodded in the darkness, considering this. Maybe the girl was on the level, he thought, remembering his own words that night in Las Vegas, his description of the little town where he'd grown up and the girl's terrified attention.

It could be that she'd done just what she said she was going to. Maybe she'd taken his money, jumped on the bus and escaped, coming on impulse to the place she'd heard about so recently and in such glowing terms.

In that case, J.T. thought, there was no problem. The sinister Ramon was safely back in Las Vegas, J.T.'s marriage was secure and Lisa had a chance at a new life, as long as both of them kept their secret. Still, he was a little worried by the situation, especially when he pictured his baby in the young woman's arms.

"Did she have references?" he asked casually. "Anybody you could use to check up on her?"

"Oh, J.T., come on," Cynthia said with a teasing smile. "You really think I'd hire a stranger without references? I *told* you all this on the phone."

"I know. I guess I wasn't paying real close attention," J.T. confessed.

In fact, back in California when he'd first heard about the new housemaid, she hadn't exactly been a topic of any great interest to him. But now, he thought ruefully, things were different.

"She grew up in a town outside Albuquerque. She'd lost her letters of reference somewhere along the way, but we called her high school English teacher and a lady she baby-sat for the past few years. They had nothing but praise for her."

J.T. relaxed and smiled at his wife, feeling a quick flood of relief and a new sympathy for the girl. If her whole story was true, as it seemed to be, then she really had lived through a nightmare and come out the other side. And though he still intended to have a serious private talk with her, he certainly wasn't going to be the one to wreck her new chance at happiness, not after all she'd endured. The poor kid, he thought with a brief grin, recalling her wide, frightened eyes when she'd first seen him down in the sitting room. She probably hadn't known who he was, either, and had just happened onto Virginia by some kind of weird chance. It must have been a hell of a shock for her when she realized whose household she'd come to work in.

Still grinning, he put aside thoughts of the household staff and turned to his wife, reaching for her with rising hunger.

But she pulled away and smiled down at him, her eyes bright with excitement.

"J.T...."

"Yeah, darlin'?" he murmured. "Come closer. I need to kiss you."

She shook her head and patted his face with a loving hand. "I want to talk about something first. Something I've been working on since you left, that I could hardly wait to discuss with you."

"Okay." J.T. settled back against the pillow and gave her his full attention. "Shoot. I'm listening."

"Well, it's just..." Cynthia sat up in bed and hugged her knees under the blankets. She drew a deep breath, then plunged ahead, speaking rapidly. "Sweetheart, I've been thinking about the huge startup costs for this new business. I think we should consider going public with the winery."

She leaned back and held her breath, waiting for his response.

J.T. looked at her with puzzled surprise. "Go public?" he echoed blankly. "You mean, open up our business to..."

She nodded her head eagerly, bending to kiss him. "Yes! I mean that we should consider forming a public corporation and offering shares on the market to finance the start-up costs."

J.T.'s mind struggled to absorb what she was telling him, but he was numb with shock.

"Cynthia...honey, what are you saying? You mean, let other people in on the action? Sell off our interests in the thing before we even get started?"

She looked at him warily, a bit of the sparkle fading from her eyes. "J.T.," she pleaded, "don't set your mind against the idea right from the beginning. Please, at least consider what I'm suggesting."

He watched her face while she frowned in concentration, staring straight ahead of her as she enumerated her concerns.

"For one thing, J.T., I'm afraid the ranch can hardly bear the debt load we'll have to carry until we move into a profit position with the winery. It's such a long-term project, with huge capital costs. I think the debt could even torpedo the rest of the operation, especially when business is so marginal these days. But with a limited share offering and a good solid prospectus..."

J.T. shook his head stubbornly. "I don't like it," he said.

She glanced over at him. "Why not?"

J.T. sat up and leaned against the headboard, feeling restless and troubled. "I don't know. It's just . . . Cynthia, the winery's going to be here on Double C property. I sure don't want a bunch of Yankees on Wall Street owning shares in the Double C."

Her face clouded. "J.T.," she asked, after a careful silence, "how much do you really know about establishing and operating a public corporation?"

"Enough to know I don't like the idea," he repeated with calm obstinacy. She was silent again for a moment, examining him with a level, thoughtful expression that made him uncomfortable.

J.T. looked away, unable to tell her his real concern. The truth was, he *didn't* know all that much about public corporations, and he didn't want to learn. What he really hated was the feeling that all the old conflicts were going to start up between them again. This was just like those miserable early days when she'd tried so hard to get herself involved in the business of the ranch.

As if she'd read his thoughts, she put a hand to his jaw and turned his face so she could look at him directly. "J.T., the morning you left for California, you said you wanted me to take an interest in the ranch again. You said you missed my help and input since the baby was born. Remember?"

He nodded, meeting her eyes steadily, recalling the conversation.

But not this way, he wanted to plead. *I didn't mean this kind of involvement!*

What he wanted, really, was for her to pay attention to him again, to recognize when he made a clever business decision and praise him for it. That was what he wanted from his wife. Not a lot of disturbing banker's talk about going public with his ranch, selling off little bits of the Double C to out-of-state investors...

Cynthia continued to regard him with that calm, measuring look that made him shift nervously against the headboard. He felt as if she was looking into the depths of his soul, reading all his secret fears of losing control and his panicky aversion to change.

At last she smiled wearily and turned aside to switch off the small bedside lamp, then settled down in the bed. "It's all right," she said quietly. "Never mind, J.T. If the idea bothers you that much, we don't have to talk about it anymore."

He nestled beside her and studied her face in the dim glow from the open bathroom door. "Cynthia darling, you know how much I love you," he whispered. "When I was away these past two weeks, I could hardly stand it, I missed you so much."

"I know, J.T.," she murmured. "I felt just the same way."

She kissed him gently and snuggled against him. He drew her warm body gratefully into his arms, satisfied that the troubling moment was safely behind them.

They kissed and whispered endearments, and J.T. gradually drifted off to sleep, still holding her tightly in his arms.

But an hour or so later he woke and found her gone. The bed was empty, and he felt a wave of sleepy panic. He blinked and looked around, flooded suddenly with relief when he saw his wife standing by the window, staring out at the darkness.

Her body was tense and still, her profile etched with silver by the rising moon. Something in the darkness, a brightness that seemed more than starlight, played and glimmered on her face and body, turning her white nightgown into a shimmering radiance and her skin to pearly fire.

She was so lovely that J.T. shivered under the warm blankets. He wanted to call to her, to tease her and order her gruffly back to bed, but something prevented him from speaking.

He realized with a chill of alarm and terror that while he was sleeping, his wife had somehow traveled far, far away from him. He had the irrational feeling that she wasn't even there in the room with him. To his frightened eyes she seemed impossibly distant, so far removed that nothing he could say or do would be enough to bring her back.

She looked like somebody entranced by another world, he thought.

Or like a woman waiting for a secret lover....

J.T. shuddered and turned away, dry-mouthed with fear, pretending to be asleep so he wouldn't have to ask his wife what she was watching in the stillness of the summer night.

CHAPTER SEVEN

JIMMY TOILED UPWARD in the starry darkness, panting and heaving, his chest on fire with the effort of the climb. Though it was almost midnight, the night was still warm and the boy sweated under the weight of his heavy pack.

He stumbled over a rock in the path, causing a stab of pain to shoot through his toe and all the way up his leg. He paused, whimpering in agony, and reached down to rub his foot in its ragged sneaker, shining the beam of his little flashlight onto the ground.

The path was growing narrower and more sparse up here. He'd have to be careful about where he set his feet. Until now, he'd been reluctant to use the flashlight, fearing that its tiny beam might be visible from the ranch buildings, but he was far enough away now to be safe. He stood silently on the path, stooped beneath the weight of his pack, gasping as he tried to catch his breath.

But when he stopped climbing, Jimmy also grew uncomfortably aware of the murmuring summer night all around him.

He had thought the night would be dead silent, but it wasn't. The soft darkness hummed and throbbed with sounds, alive and dangerous. He heard the rustle of tiny feet in the grass nearby, the whir of wings swooping and diving, the sharp, eerie cry of some night hunter in a grove of trees.

Jimmy looked down at the sprawl of sleeping ranch buildings far below, feeling suddenly wistful. He thought about his bed down there in the little house where the yard light shone like a beacon in the darkness. His pillow was neatly humped beneath the blankets again to create the impression of a sleeping child, and for a moment Jimmy devoutly wished that he was really there, that the sleeping form beneath the blankets was his own body.

He peered anxiously up at the craggy limestone cliffs, faintly etched against the starlight, and shivered. Once more he gazed with longing at the distant safety of the ranch buildings. Finally, he shook his head and took a tentative step downward, then another, almost dizzy with relief.

It was so much easier to go down. Jimmy felt as light as air, like a bit of thistledown carried on the summer wind. He felt that he could fly all the way down the hill and right into the safety of his bed, swooping and soaring gracefully through the window like a comic-book hero.

But suddenly, Jimmy paused in his descent and jerked his head upright. In utter silence, a light had begun to flash from the hilltop, glimmering and reflecting off the lenses of his thick glasses.

Jimmy held his breath and stared, craning his neck upward. The light changed color, flashing blue and green and red, filling the sky with radiance. An eerie glow spilled down the hill like a searchlight, then retreated gradually, still unearthly in its silence.

As abruptly as it had appeared, the light vanished and the night seemed incredibly dark, so thick and black that Jimmy frowned in confusion. He was hardly able to see the parts of his body, his hands and feet and the dull black fabric of his trousers.

He drew a ragged breath, his heart pounding. At last, he turned and began to climb again, placing his feet with cautious deliberation, trying to be as silent as one of those trained outdoorsmen who could pass through the woods without making a twig snap or a blade of grass rustle.

Jimmy was terrified, but also strangely elated. He had never been more frightened of anything in his life than he was of whatever was shining that light from the craggy hilltop, but nothing in the world could have kept him from climbing toward the summit. Whatever was up there, it drew him like a magnet, pulling him upward with relentless force.

His labored breathing sounded loud in the stillness and Jimmy tried hard to be quieter. He wondered a little desperately what had happened to all the night sounds.

Maybe the animals were afraid of the light, too. Jimmy pictured them all hiding in nests and burrows, covering their eyes with shaking wings and paws while they waited for the danger to pass.

Animals had instincts about things like this. Maybe they could smell the aliens. The animals knew that whatever they were, the creatures on the hilltop were not of this earth....

Jimmy shivered again and bit his lip, almost moaning aloud in a sort of delicious terror. But after a brief pause he set his mouth and began to climb again, moving with cautious slowness, taking care to test each foothold in the path before he set his weight on it.

By now he'd reached the level of the rimrock and was weaving among huge scattered boulders, where only a few stunted bushes grew in the thin soil. His feet echoed hollowly on the path and he had to slow almost to a crawl, concentrating all his effort on working his way upward in silence.

He had a sudden confused urge to stop and make an entry in his notebook. This should be recorded for history, Jimmy thought. He should write down the exact time of initial contact, the conditions and location. But he couldn't risk opening his pack and shining the little flashlight, not while he was this close.

Regretfully he abandoned the idea and moved on. At last he hauled himself over the lip of the cliff and moved out among the limestone formations on the summit, squinting into the blackness, flattening himself against a weathered column of rock while he surveyed the hilltop.

Then, suddenly Jimmy gasped and stared, his eyes wide and horrified behind the glasses. His mind moved haltingly, trying to absorb the image in front of him, but he was numb with shock, trembling like a leaf in the wind.

He drew back instinctively and cowered behind the wall of rock, still gaping at the shadowy caverns among the limestone formations.

A light glimmered there, faint and ghostly. Figures moved back and forth in the light, strangely formed creatures unlike anything ever witnessed by human eyes. They shone silver in the eerie light, and drifted about with odd, jerky motions from one patch of shadow to another, carrying trailing shrouds of some substance that shimmered like liquid metal.

One of the figures moved in Jimmy's direction. The boy whimpered soundlessly, sinking down behind the column of rock and cowering with his face buried against his knees. He hadn't been able to look at the creature for more than a second or two, but he'd had a vague impression of an enormous, grossly shaped head and a pair of staring eyes, large and opaque like the terrible dead eyes of a shark.

After that, Jimmy knew nothing more. He sat huddled in the darkness for what seemed like an eternity. It could have been minutes or hours, but he'd lost all track of time. At last, when he was stiff and sore and his head throbbed with agony, he struggled to his feet and crept away down the hill in the darkness, heading for the safety of the ranch buildings, still sobbing from time to time with shock and horror.

LISA CARRIED the baby into the kitchen and set her down in the yellow mesh playpen near the door, where a shaft of morning sunlight fell across the tiled floor and the toy-strewn interior of Jennifer's small enclosure.

"Dada," Jennifer said with satisfaction, settling among the toys and picking up a red plastic hammer, which she pounded thoughtfully against her rag doll's soft body.

"Good girl," Lisa said, bending to kiss the top of the little girl's downy head. "You play nice, honey, while I help Lettie Mae."

"Are you going to help me?" Lettie Mae asked with pleasure. "What a sweetie. With two of us working, these pies will be made in no time."

The cook was busy making apple pies, a dozen at a time, the way she usually did. Her arms were floury to the elbow as she mixed and kneaded the pie dough, and a big yellow plastic bowl heaped with apples stood on the counter nearby.

"I'll peel apples," Lisa offered, taking a small paring knife in her hand and seating herself on a stool at the counter, "while you roll the piecrust. You make such wonderful pies, Lettie Mae."

The cook's dark face creased into a smile as she glanced over at her young helper. "You're a real good girl, Lisa," she said with warm sincerity. "A real good girl."

Lisa flushed and dropped her eyes to the long scarlet trail of apple peel falling away from her knife.

"Dada!" Jennifer shouted, pulling herself upright in the playpen. "Da! Dada."

"That child is sure happy to have her daddy back home," Lettie Mae observed complacently, pausing to beam at the baby. "She loves her daddy."

Lisa shivered in the sunlight and continued with her careful peeling of the apple.

She hadn't recovered from the shock last evening of actually seeing J. T. McKinney, of standing in front of him right in his own house. Ever since she'd arrived at the ranch and realized whose home it was, Lisa had been bracing herself for that moment, but it had still been far worse than she'd expected.

She bit her lip and frowned, concentrating fiercely on her work.

Her distress had a lot to do with her feelings about the ranch and the McKinney family, she realized. They were so good to her, and this place was the nicest home she'd ever been in, the safest and happiest life she'd ever known. For the past couple of weeks, she'd almost been able to pretend that it could be real, that she could stay here and make a place for herself with all these wholesome, warmhearted people.

But when she looked into J.T.'s shrewd, dark eyes, she'd seen herself reflected there in the sexy suede outfit, and quickly recalled all the squalor of her life. She was sickened by the memory. There was no way to change the past, Lisa thought sadly. It was real, and it wouldn't ever go away.

And Ramon was probably edging closer to her right this minute, circling and waiting somewhere beyond the safety of the ranch house....

She felt a brief wave of despair, and was relieved when the outside door opened to admit Jimmy Slattery. The boy stood hesitantly in the doorway, staring at the two women.

"Close that door, boy," Lettie Mae said gruffly. "Don't let all those flies and bugs get in here."

The ranch cook had scant patience for Jimmy, with his pompousness and his sly, secretive ways. He gave her the creeps, she often said, watching people from behind those thick glasses and writing things in his notebook all the time.

Lisa, though, felt a lot of sympathy for the solitary child, and made an effort to be nice to him whenever she could. She smiled at him now as he entered the kitchen.

Jimmy nodded in return and glanced coldly at Jennifer, who stood clutching the edge of her playpen, gazing up at him with wide, solemn eyes.

"I came to see Mrs. McKinney," he announced, turning away from the baby. "Is she here?"

"No, she isn't," Lettie Mae said briskly. "She and J.T. have gone for a walk around the ranch. They won't be back for a while, I reckon."

The boy's shoulders sagged in disappointment, and Lisa looked at him more closely. His face was so pale that the freckles stood out in sharp relief, and the skin beneath his eyes was smudged with fatigue. "Jimmy, you look so tired," she said with quick concern. "Didn't you sleep well last night?"

"I slept fine." The boy shifted on his feet and glanced around the kitchen with a tense, jerky motion. "I just need to talk to Mrs. McKinney, that's all. It's very important."

"Well, Mrs. McKinney has lots of things to do besides listening to whatever *you* have to say," Lettie Mae told him. "Child, pick up that baby's hammer, for goodness' sake, before she starts yelling."

Jimmy glared at the cook and bent to pick up the red hammer, which Jennifer had tossed out onto the floor and was now regarding with sorrowful concern.

The back door opened at that moment and Cynthia entered, followed closely by her husband. Lisa still wasn't accustomed to the shock of seeing him unexpectedly like this. She glanced up, her cheeks flaming with embarrassment.

"My goodness," Cynthia said in her soft, musical voice. "What an operation. It looks like a pie factory in here, Lettie Mae."

"Lisa's helping me," Lettie Mae announced with satisfaction. "We'll have all these pies made and tucked away in the freezer in two shakes."

Lisa was conscious of Cynthia moving across the room to stand next to her. She was forced to glance up again and smiled nervously as the tall, golden-haired woman dropped a gentle hand onto her shoulder.

Lisa looked at her employer more closely, troubled by the look of distant sorrow on Cynthia's beautiful, finely drawn face. *She should be so happy now, with her husband back home again,* Lisa thought in confusion. But there was something in the depths of Cynthia's dark eyes, a kind of lonely desolation that stabbed Lisa to the core of her tender heart and made her feel like crying.

"Hi, Jimmy," Cynthia was saying. She smiled politely at the boy as J.T. crossed the room to give Lettie Mae a cheerful hug, then poured himself a cup of coffee from the pot on the counter.

"Hi," Jimmy said. "I need to talk to you," he added abruptly, causing J.T. to glance over at the boy in surprise.

But Cynthia nodded and looked at Jimmy with sudden interest. "All right," she said. "Why don't you come by this afternoon? I'm taking Jennifer into the swimming pool, and you can come with us. It's a nice way to spend a hot afternoon."

"Okay," Jimmy said, his face expressionless, though his eyes glittered behind the glasses with some private emotion.

J.T. leaned against the table, watching Lettie Mae's dexterous hands as she rolled out a circle of pie dough.

"You're going to be with Jennifer this afternoon, honey?" he said to his wife.

Cynthia nodded and picked up a piece of apple, munching on it with a small, apologetic glance at Lisa. "Jennifer loves the swimming pool. Don't you, sweet baby?"

J.T. turned to look full at Lisa. "Well, then," he said casually, "maybe that would be a good time for me to have a little talk with Lisa. I'd like to get to know her better."

Lisa drew in her breath sharply, stunned by this unexpected threat. The sharp paring knife slipped in her hands and sliced deeply into the ball of her thumb, causing an immediate gush of bright red blood.

Confusion erupted in the kitchen. Jimmy pressed close, giving loud instructions about how to stanch the flow of blood, while Lettie Mae yelled impatiently at the boy and held a dishcloth against Lisa's hand. Cynthia hurried over to pick up the baby, who had begun to howl in distress.

"Be quiet, all of you!" J.T. commanded, bending to examine the cut with a frown of concern. Gently he pulled aside the bloody dishcloth to look at Lisa's hand, then pressed the cloth back into place. "It needs stitches," he said. "Come on, Lisa. I'll drive you into town."

"Can I come, too?" Jimmy asked, looking somewhat more boyish and likable as he gazed up at J.T. with a pleading look. "Please? I'm very interested in medical procedures."

J.T. shrugged. "Sure," he said. "Why not?"

He kissed Cynthia and took Lisa's arm, hurrying her out the door and into a dusty pickup truck parked by the gate. Lisa felt herself being propelled along, helpless and shaky, even a little sick to her stomach when she recalled the sharp burst of pain and that flow of crimson blood.

At least, she thought with relief, glancing timidly over Jimmy's head at J.T.'s rugged face as he drove into Crystal Creek, the accident seemed to have removed all thought, at least for the moment, of any kind of private discussion between the two of them.

AN HOUR LATER, Lisa came out of the doctor's office and into the hospital waiting room, where Jimmy Slattery was curled up on one of the vinyl benches, his mouth open and his glasses crooked, sound asleep.

"Jimmy," she whispered, bending to touch his shoulder. "Wake up, Jimmy. I'm all finished."

The boy's eyes fluttered and opened. He gazed at her blankly for a moment. Then he pulled himself erect, adjusted his glasses and frowned at her. "I wasn't asleep," he said with dignity. "I was just sort of... concentrating on something."

Lisa smiled. "I know. Where's Mr. McKinney?"

"He had to go to the bank or something. He said when you were done we should go down to the Longhorn and wait for him."

"All right. Are you hungry, Jimmy? It must be past lunchtime by now."

The boy nodded. "Mr. McKinney gave me money for both of us to have hamburgers," he said with an air of importance. "And milk shakes, if we want them."

"Good. Let's go, then. I'm hungry, too, now that this is over with."

Jimmy looked curiously at the bandage on her slim hand. "Did you really have stitches?"

Lisa nodded. "Five of them. You should have seen him stitching it, Jimmy. It was just exactly like sewing."

"Did it hurt?" Jimmy asked, fascinated.

Lisa shook her head. "He gave me some needles all around the cut, like a dentist does to take the pain away."

The two of them walked out through the front doors of the hospital and onto the sun-washed street, moving off in the direction of the Longhorn Coffee Shop.

Jimmy plodded slightly ahead of Lisa, occasionally peering into alleys and through hedges, as if constantly on the lookout for danger. Once he paused and made a couple of entries in his notebook while Lisa waited patiently, watching his stagy movements in amused silence.

He snapped the notebook shut, put it back in his pocket and gazed earnestly up at Lisa, his eyes hidden behind the flashing disks of his glasses. "I saw something last night," he told her.

"Did you?" Lisa asked absently. Her hand was beginning to throb a little, and for some reason, she was starting to feel a little nervous out here in the open. She was anxious to get into the shaded depths of the coffee shop.

Jimmy nodded and moved off down the street again with a pompous stride. "It was something that's never before been witnessed by human eyes," he said.

Lisa hesitated, at a loss for words. He really was an odd little boy, she thought. Her brothers weren't anything like Jimmy.

"I can't tell you what it was," he went on firmly, as if she'd pleaded for more information. "It's a matter of international security."

"Jimmy, I don't know what—"

"Besides," he added, looking grim and secretive, "you probably wouldn't believe me anyhow. Nobody's ever going to believe me."

"Why don't you tell me and we'll see if I believe you?"

Jimmy gave her a haggard glance, clearly longing to unburden himself. Suddenly he stiffened, peering down the street beyond the restaurant. "Oh, *great*," he muttered in disgust. "Here comes that guy again. He's always hanging around."

"What guy?" Lisa asked, looking up, then tensed and paused on the street.

Tony Rodriguez was strolling toward them, wearing faded jeans and a navy blue T-shirt that showed his muscular, tanned arms and his broad shoulders. His dark eyes lighted with happiness when he saw Lisa, and his steps quickened as he approached her and the scowling boy.

"Hi, Lisa," Tony said with a cheerful grin. "What a nice surprise. I didn't think you ever came to town."

"I . . . I cut my thumb," she said shyly, holding her bandaged hand toward him with a childlike gesture.

Lisa's heart was beating crazily and she felt weak and shaky again, but this time it had nothing to do with her injury. These symptoms were somehow related to Tony's laughing eyes, the gentleness of his smile, the way his face sobered as he glanced down at the heavy bandage.

"Did you have stitches?" he asked.

Lisa nodded, unable to speak.

Tony took her hand in both of his and she thrilled to the feel of him, the warmth of his skin against hers, the sureness and strength in his fingers as he drew the bandage aside to frown at the neat row of stitches on her thumb.

"A real good job," he said with critical approval, smiling down at her. "I couldn't have done better myself."

With that same firm tenderness, he set the bandage back in place and took her arm, moving beside her down the street while Jimmy clumped sullenly along behind them.

Lisa trembled at the young man's nearness, overcome by a sudden crazy desire to throw herself into his strong arms, burrow close to him and never, never be frightened again.

With Tony, she thought, a woman wouldn't have to be afraid of anything. Tony was the kind of man who'd take such loving care of a woman, treat her with consideration all the time. Tony was so nice....

"Have you had lunch?" he was asking.

Lisa shook her head. "We were just going down to the Longhorn to eat. We have to wait for Mr. McKinney to finish some business."

"Well, that's real lucky," Tony said, giving her arm a little squeeze, "because I'm going for lunch, too. Now I can have some company."

Lisa smiled up at him uncertainly, thinking how wonderful it would be to eat a meal with Tony, talk and laugh across the table with him like any ordinary girl.

Tony held open the door of the coffee shop, and followed Lisa inside. The restaurant was cool and shady, crowded with people, and Lisa felt suddenly shy and frightened. She drew aside awkwardly, looking around for Jimmy.

"I can't..." she murmured, her cheeks flaming. "I have to... Jimmy's waiting for me."

"No, he isn't," Tony said with a grin, indicating a table near the door, where Jimmy had already seated himself in lofty solitude, like a visiting dignitary among the peasants. He was frowning critically as he examined the menu.

Lisa spotted the boy, then looked up at Tony, whose dark eyes sparkled with amusement. "Who's paying for the kid's lunch?" he whispered, bending so close to Lisa that she could smell the clean scent of his skin.

"Mr. McKinney gave him money to buy lunch for both of us," Lisa whispered back, shivering as Tony took her bare arm again and guided her to a table.

Tony chuckled. "Looks like the kid's planning to make a tidy little profit on this deal," he observed solemnly.

Lisa looked again at Jimmy's spiky round head, then back at Tony. "How?" she asked in confusion.

"Well, because he knows I'm going to buy your lunch," Tony said calmly. "So he can pay for his own and keep the change, and he'll come out ahead. Almost makes up for me stealing away his girl, I reckon."

Lisa stiffened, unaccountably frightened again. "Please," she whispered. "I can't...I can't let you buy my lunch. Mr. McKinney—"

"J. T. McKinney has no say about who I take to lunch," Tony said calmly. "And you're the girl I want to take, Lisa Croft."

His words were so firm, his smile so warm and meaningful that when Lisa overcame her surprise, she became conscious of some other strange emotion, which crept through her body in delicious little fiery trickles.

But then her good sense reasserted itself and she turned away, sinking into the chair he held out and staring down at the menu fixedly.

I'm not the girl you want, she felt like shouting at him. *I'm a dirty Las Vegas hooker, Tony. How do you like that? If you knew the things I've done, you wouldn't want to be anywhere near me. You'd run away just as fast as you could....*

"Hi, there, darlin'," Tony said with a grin as the waitress approached. "Lisa, this is Kasey. Kasey, darlin', give me a Longhorn burger and fries with gravy and a big glass of milk."

"Same as you always have," Kasey Bradley observed, smiling back at him. She was frequently on shift when Tony dropped by, and exchanged pleasantries with him with an easy familiarity. Her blue eyes softened as she turned to Lisa. "And you, honey?"

Lisa hesitated, her panic growing as her emotions raced out of control whenever she looked at Tony's handsome tanned face. "I'll... I'll just have an egg salad sandwich, please."

"Nothing else?"

"I'd like a glass of milk, too," she murmured. "But just a small one."

"Sure thing." Kasey grinned at Lisa and jerked her head in Tony's direction. "This boy here," she said in a confiding tone, "he drinks about a gallon of milk a day. We keep a Jersey cow out back, just for him."

"Come on, Kasey," Tony said, leaning back in his chair. "Give me a break. I'm still growing."

The waitress rolled her eyes. "God help us all," she murmured soulfully, heading back toward the kitchen.

Tony smiled at Lisa, then glanced around at Jimmy, who was apparently complaining to another waitress about the service.

Tony chuckled. "That kid reminds me of one of my brothers," he commented. "Most annoying little sucker I ever met, but there's something about him that tickles me."

"How many brothers and sisters did you say you have altogether?" Lisa asked, trying to picture Tony as a little boy. He would have been such a beautiful baby, with big dark eyes and soft rosy cheeks. . . .

"Seven," Tony said briefly. "One older sister, two younger ones, and four little brothers. It's quite a houseful."

Lisa nodded. "Where are they now? Where did you grow up?"

"On a little chicken farm over by El Paso. I've plucked so many chickens in my life, sometimes I'm afraid I'll get to look like one."

"You don't look like a chicken," Lisa told him with a shy smile, and was rewarded by a grin so warm that she felt almost light-headed again, the way she had when her hand was cut.

"Well, thanks, Lisa. What do I look like?"

Lisa glanced up at him, startled, then down at the table again.

"Come on," he teased. "You started it. What do I look like, Lisa?"

"Like...like a summer day," she whispered, unable to stop the words, although she was horrified at herself for saying them. "You look like a summer day when the sun is shining and there's just a few white clouds drifting in the sky, and it feels so delicious...."

Tony reached across the table and took her unbandaged hand in both of his, holding it gently. "Lisa..." he whispered. "Lisa, you're the sweetest girl I've ever met. I've wanted to tell you that ever since I first saw you. You're so sweet and pretty. I've never met a girl like you."

Lisa looked up at him, appalled by his words, and drew her hand away quickly. "It must have been ..." she began huskily, and struggled to get her voice back under control. "It must have been hard," she went on in a more normal tone, "growing up on a little farm like that and finding the money to go to school for so long. How did you do it?"

He shrugged his broad shoulders. "I applied for every scholarship I could possibly qualify for, and I worked like hell. Summer jobs, after school, all the time. Back when I was ten years old, I knew I wanted to be a vet, and my daddy said I'd better start saving because he couldn't help me. He has his hands full just looking after my mama and the other kids."

Lisa studied the dark young man across from her, awed by his courage and determination. He'd come from a background even more impoverished than hers, but he'd pulled himself out of it by the power of his own will. He hadn't let himself slide into crime and squalor, as she had, or done dreadful things that he was ashamed of....

"How about you?" Tony was asking. "Where's your family, Lisa?"

"In New Mexico," she said tonelessly, looking down at her hands again. "My mama divorced my daddy and got married again when I was seven. I have four little brothers, too. It was . . . like your home," she added, looking up at him frankly. "There wasn't ever much money to go around."

Tony nodded, watching her face. "You and I, we know what it's like to live a hard life," he said cheerfully. "Makes us appreciate things, right?"

She looked away, wondering if anyone could ever grasp how hard her life had been, or how much she valued this sweet new existence she'd been given the chance to enjoy for a little while.

"Yes," she murmured, smiling politely as the waitress brought their food. "It makes us appreciate things."

All at once she stiffened, staring in horror at the door of the coffee shop. A man had just entered and stood silhouetted in the square of light by the front entrance. His hair glistened in the sunshine, dark and finely styled, and his green silk shirt was shimmering like emerald fire.

He stood for a moment, and looked directly at Lisa. At last he smiled, a brief smile that was humorless and menacing. The smile faded and he stared at her a moment longer, with a cold, threatening look that stabbed right to her heart, leaving her desolate and without hope.

Then he turned and strode out of the restaurant, vanishing so completely that Lisa wondered in silent desperation if she'd imagined him.

"What is it?" Tony asked in concern, seeing her expression. "Who *was* that, Lisa?"

He turned in his chair and peered around at the door, where a couple of teenage girls had just pushed their way in behind their boyfriends. The girls made a small commotion at the entry to the coffee shop, laughing and tossing their heads in conscious flirtation.

"Lisa?" Tony asked again, observing her white face and trembling hands.

"Nothing," she whispered, focusing on her sandwich, her face hidden. "It was nothing, Tony. Just . . . somebody I thought I recognized, that's all."

He watched her a moment longer, then picked up his hamburger and began to eat, pausing occasionally to entertain her with stories about his job, about the people he met and the animals he worked with.

Lisa listened and smiled, her heart aching with sorrow as she looked into his shining eyes.

She drifted on a vast, dark sea of sadness and fear, wondering how many happy days were left to her, how long it was going to be before Ramon seized her and dragged her back down into the horror that was his world.

CHAPTER EIGHT

LISA RODE SILENTLY in the truck next to Jimmy when J.T. drove them back to the ranch. She concentrated on the green hills and dry creekbeds flashing by, but the peaceful beauty of the day was lost on her. All she could see was Ramon's face, his cruel stare and cold, mocking smile.

How could she have forgotten what he was like?

Lisa shivered and gripped her hands together in her lap, oblivious to the pain around her injury that mounted as the anesthetic wore off.

She knew it had been childish of her to put Ramon out of her mind and pretend he didn't exist. When she first heard Virginia talk about the well-dressed stranger in town, even though she'd known the man was probably Ramon, Lisa had somehow managed to push the threat to the back of her mind and go on with her life. She'd peeled apples, dusted furniture, sewed and gardened and cared for little Jennifer as if she hadn't a care in the world.

Even more foolish, she'd allowed herself to lie in the darkness of her room at night dreaming about Tony's smile, his lithe, boyish step and broad young shoulders, just like any other love-struck girl. But she couldn't deny Ramon's reality any longer. He was in town, and he knew where she was, and sooner or later he would be coming for her.

Lisa bit her lip and blinked at the tears that blurred her eyes. Maybe she could run away, pack a few things and slip out of the ranch house under a cover of darkness. She had money now, because Cynthia had already given her a paycheck so generous that she'd protested in vain over the amount.

But if he'd tracked her this far, where could she go that Ramon wouldn't follow? Besides, the thought of leaving the enclosing safety of the ranch was terrifying to Lisa. She was fairly certain that Ramon wouldn't take the risk of actually coming onto Double C property. He'd bide his time and plot some other way of getting to her, of luring her away so he could grab her.

Maybe he would even have done it today, if Tony hadn't been with her....

Lisa was so deep in her unhappy thoughts that she was hardly aware of what was happening when J.T. parked by Ken Slattery's house and stepped from the pickup to let Jimmy out. Then he climbed back in, swung the truck around and drove up a dusty trail to a grove of trees above the buildings, getting out to squint at a group of placid Hereford cows in a field nearby.

Lisa watched him through the window, suddenly cold with fear.

J.T. strolled back to the truck, held her door open and indicated a couple of large, flat rocks near the trail.

"Care to sit in the sun and chat with me for a bit, Lisa?" he asked politely. "There's a real nice view from up here."

Her heart pounding, she climbed from the passenger seat and moved haltingly over to the rock, sitting down and holding herself stiffly erect. J.T. lounged on the rock next to her with his booted feet extended, gazing from under the brim of his old gray Stetson at a distant line of hills. Lisa glanced at him quickly and realized in surprise that he was almost as nervous as she was.

Finally she cleared her throat and forced herself to speak. "I'm...I'm really sorry about this, Mr. McKinney," she whispered. "About being here and everything. I didn't...I honestly had no idea...." She faltered and fell silent.

"That the man you met in Vegas and the man you were coming to work for were one and the same?" J.T. finished the sentence for her, eyes still fixed on the horizon.

Lisa nodded miserably. "Virginia said at the bus depot that there was a job available out here, and it sounded so perfect. I had no idea it was in your house. I never even dreamed that you still lived in Crystal Creek, until I saw the picture of you in the sitting room."

"So how did you happen to come to Crystal Creek in the first place?" J.T. asked.

Lisa was still tense, trembling with apprehension, but J.T.'s voice was so calm and without accusation that she felt somewhat reassured.

"It just sounded so nice," she told him wistfully. "That...that night," she went on, awkward again with humiliation, "when you talked about where you grew up, I thought it sounded like the nicest place in the world. So when I got to the bus depot and the guy asked me where I wanted to go, I just...said the name of the town. It was the first thing that popped into my head."

J.T. looked at her with interest. "You went straight to the bus depot after you left me? In that cab?"

She nodded, lowering her head to avoid his eyes. "I was so scared," she whispered. "I knew my only chance was to get away as fast as I could. There was a bus leaving just after midnight, heading for Texas. I got here a couple of days later."

"And met Virginia at the bus depot," J.T. concluded.

"She was seeing somebody off on the bus. Her niece, Angela, was going to Houston for a few days."

"My God," J.T. said in wonder, shaking his head. "What a strange old world it is, Lisa."

Lisa, eyes still lowered, began to finger the edges of the heavy white bandage.

This time it was J.T.'s turn to clear his throat and shift awkwardly on the rough surface of the stone. "I guess you've already figured out," he said at last, "that both of us are in big trouble if anybody ever finds out about that night in Las Vegas."

"Both of us?"

"Well, yeah." J.T. gave her a weary grin. "I love my wife, Lisa," he said. "I love her more than anything in the world. I've never done anything like that before, and I never will again. I just went...a little crazy for a minute or two, I guess. But she might not understand that, if she knew what I did."

Lisa's face was still hot with fierce embarrassment. "You didn't do anything," she whispered, still unable to look at him. "Nothing at all."

"I went with you to your room, knowing what...what business you were in."

"But that was because I begged you to come with me. You didn't really want to."

"We know that, Lisa, but it still might not look that way to my wife. You know what I mean?"

She nodded. "Of course I do. I'm not going to say anything," she added, nerving herself to look directly at him for the first time.

He met her eyes in thoughtful silence.

Lisa drew a deep breath. "I'd never say anything. For one thing, everybody would think...they'd know what I did, and how awful I was," she said, her voice breaking, then steadying. "Besides," she added, "I love Miss Cynthia, too. She's the most terrific person. I'd die before I'd hurt her."

J.T. watched her intently as she spoke. At last he nodded in satisfaction. "I don't mind telling you, I was real worried when I first saw you in my house," he said gently, "but I think those women down there are right after all. They're usually right, those women." He grinned briefly, then sobered. "I think you're a nice girl who's had some bad luck and just needs a chance in life. You're welcome to stay on at my ranch and look after my baby as long as you want."

Lisa nodded, her heart breaking all over again.

Yesterday, those words would have made her happier than anything she'd ever heard in her life. Today, because of the man who had appeared so briefly in the coffee shop, J.T.'s acceptance didn't mean anything. It was all dust and ashes.

"Thank you," she whispered, her voice almost inaudible. J.T. noted she was staring into her lap.

"Is anything else bothering you, Lisa?"

She drew a shuddering breath. She was almost overcome by the longing to tell the whole story to this quiet, powerful man, cast herself on his protection and beg for help.

But, of course, that was impossible. Lisa had already brought enough squalor and ugliness into J. T. McKinney's life. The thought of getting him involved in this, too, was unbearable to her. Besides, she knew what Ramon was like. He'd kill without a qualm, destroy anybody who stood between him and what he wanted. And if anybody on the ranch was hurt because of her, Lisa would never forgive herself.

The only thing she could do was keep the knowledge to herself, carry on and hope that if she never left the ranch again or put herself in an exposed position, Ramon might not be able to get to her. Maybe after a while, he'd get tired of waiting and return to Las Vegas, back to his other girls and all his shady business interests.

It was a frail hope, but it was all she had. She turned to J.T., trying to smile. "No," she said steadily, as she stood up. "I'm not afraid. Not anymore."

He gave her a keen glance, looking deep into her eyes. After a long moment he got up and followed her back to the truck, holding the door for her politely and then strolling around to the other side to climb behind the wheel.

At least J.T. looked more relieved now. His face was calm and relaxed, and he walked with a springing tread that reminded Lisa, with a sudden wrench of her heart, of the way Tony had looked as he'd come strolling toward her in the warm Texas sunshine.

CYNTHIA LIFTED Jennifer clear of the water and held her in the air, smiling up at the little girl. Jennifer laughed and kicked, looking fat and adorable in her tiny flowered bathing suit.

"Want some juice, baby?" her mother asked. "Jen-Jen want some juice and a cookie?"

"Dada!" Jennifer shouted, then beamed down on Cynthia. "Mum-mum-mum," she said.

"Jenny!" Cynthia whispered, overwhelmed by sudden tears of emotion. "You said mama. Sweetheart, you said mama!"

Jennifer dimpled happily. "Mum-mum," she repeated, immensely pleased with herself.

Cynthia kissed the baby's neck and face until she kicked and wriggled with delight, then carried her up the shallow steps and onto the pool deck. She popped the child into the mesh playpen that she and Virginia had set up earlier in the shade of the trees, and rummaged in the diaper bag for a bottle of juice and a cookie.

"Here you are, darling," Cynthia murmured, fitting the baby's sunbonnet on her head and moving her toys closer on the floor of the playpen. "Here's your juice, and your cookie, and Jennifer's nice fuzzy blanket...."

At last the baby was curled up contentedly in the soft folds of the blanket, sucking on her bottle of juice. Cynthia settled herself on a lounge nearby, stretching her long body in the sunlight and burying her head in her arms.

A band of clouds drifted across the sun, casting a shadow over the rolling expanse of land. Cynthia turned her head on the lounge cushion and squinted upward, longing for the cooling rains to bring an end to this brutal summer heat.

Maybe tonight, she thought.

It was getting later in August, and the clouds were beginning to mass along the horizon every day, as tall and white as distant mountains. Maybe tonight the rain would come, washing over the parched earth in a healing flood, and everybody would feel better.

She propped herself up on her elbows to look at Jennifer, who had drifted off to sleep, still clutching the plastic juice bottle against her cheek. Cynthia got up to pull the blanket higher on the baby's bare shoulders, then stretched out again, brooding over her own situation.

She carried the image of Jennifer's sweet face with her, wondering in despair what was going to happen to the poor baby. There was no doubt that Jennifer was soon going to be hurt by her parents' behavior.

Because Cynthia knew now, with miserable certainty, that she was going to leave her husband. She'd made that irreversible decision last night when she'd told him about her idea of selling stock in the winery, and seen the closed, wary look in his eyes.

Cynthia wasn't particularly angry over J.T.'s opposition to her idea. She knew before she made the suggestion that her husband understood very little about creative financing, that he would need to be educated and convinced. No, her marriage had ended when she'd looked into his eyes and seen his fear, and his absolute refusal to let her be involved in the family business.

J. T. McKinney was never going to allow his wife to be a person in her own right, fully and actively involved in a personal and financial partnership. The man simply didn't have it within himself to sustain such a relationship, and Cynthia wasn't able to live any other way. That was the stark reality of their situation, so simple that it seemed incredible to think that two intelligent adults who loved each other couldn't work it out.

But Cynthia had spent a long time analyzing their marriage, and she knew that at the bare bones of the conflict, they were left with nothing. All of her unhappiness had crystallized in that one moment when she'd made a sensible business suggestion and her husband had stared at her with a trapped look of utter distress.

Trapped, she thought. *That's the word. We're both trapped in a marriage that's impossible for us just because of the way we think. There's really, truly no hope for us.*

But even as she framed the thought, Cynthia was flooded again with weariness. How could she possibly leave him? Even apart from the fact that she still loved and desired him, probably always would, how could she go about disentangling their two lives?

There were so many complications. She certainly wouldn't want to stay in Texas if they weren't married anymore, and he'd never leave his ranch. So how would Jennifer manage to maintain a healthy relationship with both her parents? Would J.T. have to fly up to Boston every weekend to see the child that he adored? Or would Cynthia be forced to leave the little girl here for extended periods of time, establish some kind of cumbersome joint-custody situation that would leave Jennifer feeling rootless and confused, and Cynthia worried all the time?

The clouds broke apart and the hot sun beamed onto her shoulders again. Cynthia frowned, trying not to cry as she thought about the ranch house that she'd come to love, and would soon be leaving. What about all the furniture? Would she take the new dining room set they'd bought, or leave it behind? It looked so perfect there in the dining room. But she'd chosen it with such loving thoughtfulness, and she certainly cared about it more than J.T. did.

And there was the matter of the flowered chintz sofa and love seat in the morning room. They'd been custom-made, designed personally by Cynthia and shipped down from a little shop in Georgetown. They were the nicest she'd ever seen....

Cynthia frowned as she rolled onto her back, fitting her dark glasses in place and applying a fresh coating of sunscreen.

She knew that all this preoccupation with furniture was just a device to keep her from thinking about J.T. Because if she let herself remember her husband's dark eyes, his lean smiling face and tall body, the gentleness of his hands and his sweet lovemaking, Cynthia's heart was going to break. She could almost feel it breaking now, ripping apart and shattering into a thousand pieces within her breast.

"Mrs. McKinney?" a tentative voice said nearby.

Cynthia leaned up on her elbow and saw Jimmy Slattery standing on the pool deck, squinting at her. She sat hastily erect on the lounge, reached for her white terry-cloth robe and belted it around her waist, running a hand through her damp hair.

"Hello, Jimmy," she said, trying to smile as she swung her legs over the edge of the lounge. "Sit down," she added, indicating one of the deck chairs nearby. "How are you today? Did you bring your swimsuit?"

"I climbed up the hill last night," he said abruptly, seating himself on the extreme edge of the cedar deck chair and staring at her with concentrated intensity.

Cynthia nodded. "I thought you might," she said, giving him a reproving smile. "Jimmy, you promised you wouldn't do that. It's dangerous for you to be up there alone at night. What if something happened to you, and we wouldn't even know you were—"

"I saw them," he whispered hoarsely, ignoring her lecture. He leaned forward, his body taut with emotion.

Cynthia stared at him blankly and took off her dark glasses.

"The aliens," he muttered, glancing around nervously at the silent terrace. "I saw the aliens."

"Oh, Jimmy..." Cynthia searched for words, smoothing the belt of her robe awkwardly between her fingers.

"I *saw* them," the boy repeated, his eyes glittering wildly behind the glasses. To Cynthia's astonishment, tears began to roll down his cheeks. "I knew you wouldn't believe me," he murmured in despair, turning away from her. "Nobody's ever going to believe me."

"Maybe you should tell me everything that happened," Cynthia said gently. "Start at the very beginning, and don't leave anything out, all right?"

He looked up at her, brushing impatiently at his tears. "Are you going to believe me? Because I don't want to tell if you'll just laugh at me."

"We'll see after you're finished," Cynthia told him solemnly. "Look straight into my eyes, Jimmy, and if you're not telling me the truth I think I'll know."

Their eyes met and held for a long moment. At last the boy nodded, looking so pale and intense that Cynthia began to wonder what really had happened to him up on that moonlit hilltop.

"I started up there before midnight," he began tonelessly, "but it took a long time to get to the top. Prob'ly a couple of hours."

"It must have been such a hard climb," Cynthia murmured, trying to be sympathetic, but Jimmy cast her a glance of cold impatience and went on with his story.

"Just when I was getting close to the top, I saw the light start to flash."

"I saw it, too," Cynthia whispered, staring at him. "Around one o'clock, I think it was. I . . . I couldn't sleep, so I got up and looked out the window. The light was only there for a little while, though, not like last time. I almost wondered if I'd imagined it."

"It was there," Jimmy told her grimly. "It flashed all different colors and then stopped. I was right up close when it started."

"Oh, Jimmy..." Cynthia studied him, wide-eyed, and felt her hands begin to tremble.

"That hill, it's kind of flat on top," Jimmy told her. "There's all kinds of rock formations and big caverns in the limestone, really spooky."

He fell silent, staring down at the pool deck with a brooding expression.

"Jimmy?" Cynthia prompted. "What happened when you got to the top?"

The boy took off his glasses, making his face seem suddenly childlike and vulnerable. He squinted up at Cynthia with a look of pleading. "I saw them," he whispered.

"What? What did you see, dear?"

"It was kind of light up there," Jimmy muttered, his voice muffled. "There was a light in one of the caves or something. It wasn't very bright. And these ... these things were moving around."

Cynthia's stomach tightened. She licked her lips nervously. "What kind of things, Jimmy?"

"Sort of like people, but not the same. They were silvery, and weird shapes. One of them came so close to me I thought it was going to grab me. I hid behind a rock...."

The boy began to cry, his shoulders heaving silently. Cynthia reached for his hands and drew him over beside her on the lounge and put her arms around him, rocking him as tenderly as if he were Jennifer's age. "Don't cry," she murmured to the distraught child. "Don't cry, dear. It's all right. Whatever you saw, it can't hurt you now."

"It was...it was so *weird*," he whispered in agony. "It had eyes, kind of, but all glassy and funny, and a sort of head that was really big and knobby, and kind of arms with things stuck into them...."

He began to cry again. Cynthia held him and looked absently over his spiky head at the cattle grazing in a nearby field, wondering what to make of this incredible story.

There was no doubt the boy believed what he was telling her. Cynthia knew that Jimmy had enough imagination to manufacture the strange creatures on the hilltop, but she didn't think he possessed the dramatic ability to pretend this sort of emotion about something he'd fabricated.

And his distress was certainly genuine. As he spoke about the weird monster that had approached him, his body began to quiver with terror. Still holding him close, Cynthia could actually feel his heart racing and thumping against her.

"What should we do, Jimmy?" she asked him quietly. "Should we tell somebody?"

"No!" He squirmed away and stared at her with wild-eyed panic. "No!" he repeated. "Not yet. Not till we know what they are."

"But... how can we find out?"

"You can go with me," the boy said, his face pale and taut with purpose. "You can see them and tell people. They'll believe you, but they'd just say I was a stupid kid and laugh at me."

Cynthia looked down at him, suddenly gripped by a desperate excitement. It was such a relief not to think about J.T. and all the miserable decisions that had to be made in the next few weeks. Much more comfortable, she thought with a small, bitter smile, to think about monstrous silvery aliens invading the earth....

"Can we?" Jimmy asked her tensely. "Can we go up there together?"

"When?"

"Tonight," he said with rising excitement. "We need to go tonight. We got no idea how long they'll stay up there. They looked like they were... doing experiments or something. They had all this silver stuff like... like ribbons, or something, and they were spreading it around...."

Cynthia nodded, biting her lip and frowning. "All right," she said at last, throwing caution to the winds. "We'll go tonight. I'll meet you by the windmill at midnight, and we'll start climbing then. Should I... should I bring a lunch or something?" she added.

Jimmy looked at her disdainfully, beginning to recover his equilibrium now that a decision had been made. "It's not a *picnic*," he told her.

She stifled a grin at his change of tone, and nodded solemnly. "You're right, Jimmy. This is serious business. I'll wear my hiking boots and try not to slow you down too much."

He got up, brushed surreptitiously at the tears still drying on his cheeks and squared his shoulders. "Midnight," he told her in a tone of brusque command, turning away and heading off across the terrace. "Don't be late."

"I won't be late," Cynthia promised. She watched him thoughtfully as he moved out of sight, then settled back on the lounge. She was still breathless and afraid as she focused on the towering limestone cliff above the ranch. But Cynthia knew that the mystery on the hilltop, no matter how terrifying, didn't frighten her nearly as much as the other problems that were tearing at her heart.

IT WAS TONY'S TURN to stay late and close up the veterinary clinic. He finished tidying up, sterilized and put away the last of the equipment, then washed his hands and took off his white lab coat, hanging it neatly on a hook in the corner.

He stepped outside, locked the little building that he worked in with Manny Hernandez and started off up the street in the summer twilight, thinking about Lisa.

Every time he saw the girl, Tony fell a little harder.

There was something about her that stabbed right to his heart, and left him as weak and quivery as jelly. He wanted to hold her, kiss her, lie with her in the darkness and talk all night long. He wanted to tell her every single thing that had ever happened to him, and hear all about her life, down to the smallest detail. He wanted to watch her smile, kiss her eyelids, reach out to lift the little tendrils of dark hair that curled around her cheeks.

Tony groaned and shifted his big shoulders in an agony of longing.

He didn't know why she affected him so much. He'd met lots of girls who were prettier, more talkative, more consciously charming. But there was something about Lisa's air of fragile purity, her stillness, the soft light in her eyes and the gentle curve of her mouth, that made him crazy. He was like a man bewitched, and he had no idea how to deal with his emotion.

"Hey, Tony," a cheerful voice called, interrupting his brooding thoughts.

Tony looked up to see Sheriff Wayne Jackson crossing the street toward him. Wayne was off duty and out of uniform, his long body looking relaxed in jeans and a soft plaid shirt. He nodded amiably as he approached the younger man.

"Nice evening," he drawled, falling into step beside Tony.

"Sure is. Where's that pretty lady of yours?" Tony added, the topic of women being generally uppermost in his mind these days. "How come you aren't home for supper?"

"She left me," Wayne said, looking so mournful that Tony paused and regarded him in alarm.

Wayne grinned. "Just for tonight. She's doing a show in Austin."

"I thought she wasn't performing in public anymore."

"She isn't," Wayne said with another fond smile. "But she's a pushover for a sob story. She can't resist a charity show for crippled kids or homeless puppies, that sort of thing. This one's for the new women's shelter in Austin. Jessie and Nora Slattery are all involved with the committee."

"So you're a free man tonight."

"Yeah," Wayne said gloomily. "And it's sure not as much fun as it sounds like. I'm just heading down to the Longhorn for some supper."

"Me too. Might as well eat together, since there's no ladies who want to eat with us."

"Sounds good. How's that colt of Lynn's? I heard it got cut up pretty bad."

The two men moved off down the street, talking companionably in the slanting rays of sunlight.

Suddenly Wayne paused and glanced through a shop window, his big body tense and still, poised as alert as a cat. After a moment, he shook himself a little and moved on, his face grim.

"Something wrong?" Tony asked, looking curiously at his friend.

"I don't know. It doesn't smell good to me, that's all."

"What doesn't smell good?"

Wayne shook his head again. "Did you see that guy in the menswear store? He was by the till, paying for something."

"What did he look like?"

"Oh, he's a big-city dude," Wayne said with distaste. "Drives a black sports car all over town, looks like a movie star, with real pretty hair and a green silk shirt."

Tony stiffened, remembering his lunch with Lisa earlier in the day, and her strange moment of distress when the silk-clad stranger had stepped briefly into the coffee shop. "Yeah," he said curtly. "I reckon maybe I've seen him around."

"Reckon you have. He's hard to miss, that one."

"What's he doing in Crystal Creek?"

"Now that," Wayne said grimly, "is something I'd really like to know."

"Why don't you ask him?"

"I did." The sheriff gazed reflectively at a couple of teenage boys careening down Main Street on their bikes.

"And?" Tony asked, still feeling vaguely tense and uneasy, though he had no idea why.

"And he told me it's a free country, and a man can have a holiday if he likes. Said he's interested in local flowers."

"Flowers?"

"Yeah," Wayne said with a bitter smile. "I guess it's not so surprising that a snake would be interested in flowers, come to think of it."

"Wayne..." Tony began slowly. "Do you know this guy from somewhere?"

"I sure do. At least, I think I do. I never forget a face, and I'm pretty damn sure I ran into this lowlife a few times back when I was on the city force in Las Vegas. If I've got the right guy, I think he's part of a real dirty scene out there."

"What kind of scene?"

"A bad scene. Drugs and girls, mostly."

Tony's hair prickled and rose on the back of his neck. "Girls?"

"Yeah, girls. Hookers. Where do you think the creep gets the money for those pretty silk shirts? He's sure no working stiff, and I doubt that he's even got a grade school education."

"So," Tony repeated doggedly, "what's he doing here? There's no action like that out here."

"Damned if I know what he's doing. But I aim to find out," Wayne said, his face still grim as he pushed open the door of the Longhorn and strode inside.

CHAPTER NINE

CYNTHIA STOOD next to J.T., watching Hank's leathery face on the pillow. The old man looked so fragile these days, she thought sadly. He was hardly a person anymore, just a delicate little bundle of bones and skin, so light and insubstantial that a stiff breeze would carry him away.

But there was still nothing delicate about his spirit. "Go away, both of you," the old man growled. "I'm fine. Quit starin' at me, fer God's sake!"

Ever since Hank had grown so weak, the family members had taken to stopping by in the evening, just to make sure that he was safely tucked in bed for the night and there was nothing he needed.

Cynthia had tried more than once to get the old man moved into the ranch house, where he would be better supervised and she wouldn't have to worry about him all the time. But the last time she suggested the move, he'd resisted with such force that he made himself sick, and she'd backed off.

"You sure you're okay, Grandpa?" J.T. asked patiently. "Nothing you want us to get for you?"

Hank rolled his head on the pillow and looked around with a peevish expression. "Where's my cat?"

"He's over in the rocker," Cynthia said. "I think he's asleep."

"Bring him," Hank demanded. "I like having him here in bed with me at night, lyin' on my belly. He's a nice warm cat."

"But, Grandpa Hank, don't you think maybe he'd be more comfortable in—"

"Bring him!" Hank growled, and Cynthia hurried to obey.

Cautiously, she lifted the heavy mass of orange fur into her arms, thinking how fortunate they were that Hagar was such a sweet-natured cat. He never seemed to get impatient with the old man's demands, and suffered Hank's foibles and erratic personality with unruffled calm.

She carried the cat back to the wasted figure in the bed, placing him gently on Hank's sunken abdomen. The old man's skinny hands closed over the cat's body and he sighed in pleasure, then looked up at Cynthia, his ancient dark eyes suddenly knowing and alert.

"Don't go up there," he whispered hoarsely.

Cynthia stared at him and felt a little prickle of fear twisting along her spine. She glanced quickly at J.T., who was across the room, drawing the drapes over Hank's bedroom window.

"Grandpa Hank, I'm not sure what you mean," she murmured, leaning close to him.

"You know what I mean." His eyes dropped shut, the lids creased and hooded. His lips were barely moving, and Cynthia had to lean close to hear him. "Stay in bed with your man, where you belong," he muttered. "You got enough sorrow an' trouble ahead of you without climbin' that goddamn hill. You'll just come to grief if you do. Turrible grief."

J.T. returned to the bedside, took Cynthia's arm and drew her gently away before she could question Hank further. With a troubled frown, she forced herself to put the old man's warning out of her mind, concentrating only on getting through the rest of the evening.

Cynthia and J.T. walked in strained silence through the summer twilight to the ranch house. She remembered how easy it had once been for them to talk together. There'd been a time when words had flowed effortlessly between them like sweet wine. Now they were just a pair of courteous strangers, exchanging stilted comments about the weather and the food.

Cynthia was becoming weary and oppressed by the weight of things they weren't saying, by all the unspoken fear and anger that crowded around them when they were together. She shivered, hugging her arms.

J.T. looked down at her in concern. "Feeling cool, Cynthia?" he asked politely.

She shook her head. "No, I'm fine, thanks. But I'm really tired," she added. "I think I'll make it an early night."

"All right." He held open the front door for her and followed her into the hall. "I have some business to tend to in my office. I'll come up in a little while."

Cynthia nodded, relieved, and made her escape up the stairs. By the time he came to bed she'd be safely tucked away in the darkness, pretending to be asleep. J.T. would climb in beside her and drift off almost immediately.

He was always able to sleep, Cynthia thought bitterly. No matter what was going on his life, J.T. didn't miss his sleep.

And he slept so deeply, he'd never notice when she slipped out of bed and left him to get dressed in the clothes she'd hidden away in one of the downstairs bathrooms.

Her plans were going ahead without a hitch. But most of her relief with the present situation was related to the fact that if they didn't go to bed at the same time, there'd be no awkwardness about making love.

Cynthia wasn't at all sure that she could control herself if her husband made a physical advance to her. And she really had no idea what her reaction would be. She might betray herself by giving in to her body's hunger and letting him do whatever he wanted. Or her anger might swell to the point where'd she'd start screaming and never be able to stop.

WHEN SHE'D MADE her careful plans for this late-night expedition, the one thing Cynthia hadn't reckoned on was bad weather. But when she finally slipped out the front door and started across the darkened ranch yard, clouds were rolling over the night sky, dark and brooding. There was a heavy, sulfurous scent in the air, and lightning crackled in the west, sending ominous rumbles of thunder drifting over the hills. The first heavy raindrops came swirling against her face, carried on a wind that was growing colder all the time.

Cynthia ducked her chin lower in her jacket collar, and shivered as she approached the windmill with quick, silent steps. Jimmy was already there, huddled in the darkness by the fence.

"Jimmy," Cynthia said breathlessly over the howling of the wind, "we can't go up there tonight. It's going to pour. We'll get soaked."

"I *know* that," he muttered furiously, his voice hoarse with disappointment. "I don't think we could even climb up that trail if it's wet, anyhow. It'd be too slippery."

Cynthia thought suddenly of old Hank's strange warning and felt so much relief that she was surprised by her own emotion. Surely she didn't take his words seriously? But then, he'd been right so many times....

She looked down at Jimmy's dim outline and wondered what she really believed about the mystery on the hilltop. She'd told herself that this was all just a game, a silly summertime adventure in which she was consciously joining into the child's fantasy to keep her mind off her own problems.

But did she truly consider it a fantasy? Or did she actually believe, at some level of her consciousness, that those flashing lights indicated an alien presence high up there on the limestone cliff, and that old Hank had somehow seen that mysterious presence as a threat to her?

Cynthia shivered again and touched the boy's shoulder. "I'm really sorry, Jimmy," she whispered. "We'll go the very first night it isn't raining, all right?"

"Yeah, sure," he muttered sullenly.

"Now you'd better go home and get into bed before somebody notices that you're missing. Ken and Nora would be really worried if they thought you were out in this storm." She watched him plod off toward the Slattery house until his stolid form was swallowed up in the darkness. Then she turned and hurried back through the rain to the ranch house, letting herself in silently through the kitchen door and tucking her hiking boots away in the closet.

Cynthia paused for a moment, listening to the old house breathe and shift as the wind rose and the rain began to hammer on the roof. She was still too keyed up to sleep, so she hung her jacket away and padded into the morning room in her stocking feet. She switched on the television with the sound turned low and curled up on the love seat, watching without comprehension the ghostly, flickering images on the screen.

Tiffany wandered into the room and leapt onto the couch beside Cynthia, purring noisily.

She gathered the cat to her as gratefully as old Hank had with Hagar, resting her chin on the silvered fur. "Nice Tiffany," she murmured, her voice breaking. "Nice, nice cat."

Cynthia was bereft, disappointed that the brief diversion of the nocturnal adventure had been taken from her, and terrified of the uncertainties that lay ahead. But she was determined not to start crying. Tears had no place in all the hard decisions that she would soon be making. From now on she would have to be levelheaded and practical, firm and cold, emotionless. She needed to cling to her anger, hold it around her like a protective cloak and never let anybody see that her heart was breaking.

She needed to... Cynthia tensed, hearing a drowsy complaint from upstairs. With a weary, automatic gesture, she set Tiffany aside and started to get up from the couch, then sank back again with a sigh of relief when she heard Lisa's quick footsteps on the stairway.

"Bless the girl," Cynthia whispered to her cat, wondering if it would be possible to take Lisa with her to Boston. She'd certainly be needing some help, and she couldn't find anyone better than Lisa, not if she searched forever.

Cynthia drew Tiffany's warm body against her for comfort, marveling at the enormity of these thoughts in her mind. Could she really be planning to leave her husband and home and take her baby out into that lonely world?

LISA LIFTED the fretful baby from her crib and rocked her gently, stroking the downy little head with her free hand.

"Poor baby," she whispered. "Poor little Jennifer. Are you afraid of the storm? It's nothing to be afraid of. Nothing can hurt you. See, it's just a nice cool rain, and everything's going to look so clean and fresh tomorrow."

Jennifer hiccuped and stuffed part of her fist in her mouth, blinking up at Lisa with wide frightened eyes.

"Mum-mum?" she asked. "Da?"

"Mama and Daddy are sleeping in their beds, just like you should be. There's nothing for you to be afraid of, sweetheart."

Just then a bolt of lightning ripped across the sky in a long, jagged spear of fire, followed almost immediately by a deafening clap of thunder. Jennifer stiffened in Lisa's arms and began to whimper with terror.

"Oh, baby," Lisa murmured, still rocking the child and kissing her cheek. "It's not scary. It's just lightning. See?"

She carried the frightened child to the window and held her up, showing her the rain driving against the glass and a sudden bright flare of lightning beyond the hills.

Jennifer gazed out in awe, straining in Lisa's arms to see better. Another bolt of lightning split the heavens and the baby laughed in delight. "Li," she murmured huskily.

"Yes, it's certainly a big light. And it's pretty, isn't it? Nothing to be afraid of. Jennifer's safe in her room and nothing can ever hurt her. Now, sweetie, let's..."

All at once Lisa stopped speaking and watched, horrified, as a low-slung black car entered the rainwashed yard. The vehicle drifted toward the front of the house, its engine inaudible in the roar of the storm.

The car's headlights were turned off and it seemed to float on the warm currents of rain like some ghostly pirate ship, eerie and menacing. While Lisa peered out, holding her breath and biting her lip to keep from screaming, the car parked right at the front entrance and sat glimmering in the rain, silver-blue in the occasional flashes of light. Lisa stood, holding Jennifer tightly in her arms, so deep in anguish and terror that she couldn't even move, while the car rested there in the night and taunted her silently with its presence.

See this? it seemed to be whispering through the storm. *I can come right to where you live. I'm here in the middle of your safest place. There's no way you can hide from me.*

Lisa gulped back a sob of fear and turned away abruptly to lower the drowsy baby back into her crib. For a long time, even after Jennifer had fallen deeply asleep, Lisa stood by the bed, rubbing the child's delicate little back, her eyes dark and haunted in the muted glow of the clown-shaped night-light.

LIKE MOST of the women in his household, J.T. was also sleeping fitfully on this stormy night. He tossed and turned, hot and restless despite the cool flow from the air conditioner. Somewhere deep in his consciousness he registered the sound of Jennifer's sleepy complaint, and Lisa's quick steps out in the hallway, then her soft voice and the baby's husky replies. They seemed to be punctuated by another sound, an engine churning suddenly and then dying away in the night.... J.T. frowned and opened his eyes, wondering if he'd really heard a vehicle or if it was just the noise of the storm.

Maybe one of the ranch hands, he thought, slipping home after a late night on the town.

But he was sure the sounds had been leaving the ranch buildings, not approaching.

He rolled his head on the pillow and reached out for Cynthia, yearning so desperately for the comfort of her body that he forgot for a wistful moment the tension between them. His hand fell on an empty pillow and he sat up in alarm.

"Cynthia?" he whispered, with a quick glance in the direction of her bathroom.

But the little room was dark and silent, and so was the rest of the master bedroom. J.T. sank back against the pillows and lay staring at the ceiling. From long habit he put a hand over his heart, as if he could protect that vulnerable part of his body.

But there was no way to protect himself from the kind of hurt that threatened him now. He could watch his diet, pay attention to exercise and keep his blood pressure down, do everything the doctor ordered. But he couldn't keep his poor old heart from breaking apart if Cynthia left him, and he was afraid she was planning to do just that.

J.T. stirred restlessly in the bed, his long body aching with need and loneliness as he lay thinking about his wife.

He knew, of course, why she was so upset. He'd known the moment it happened, when she suggested that crackbrained plan about selling shares in the winery, and he'd been fearful that she was pushing her way back into his business again. J.T.'s jaw tightened stubbornly as he remembered the conversation.

There truly were limits to what a man should have to endure, no matter how much he loved his wife. Why couldn't women ever seem to learn that there were things they needed to leave alone, parts of a man's life that were his concern and his alone?

But that was the essence of their problem. Cynthia didn't believe any part of his life wasn't her concern, and she'd never change her mind. She wanted to share the whole burden of his business, walk shoulder to shoulder with him, be a full and equal partner, and J.T. felt a harsh wave of panic when he even contemplated the prospect.

He didn't know how to have that kind of relationship with a woman. It wasn't in him, never had been. It wasn't part of his heredity or upbringing or personal philosophy, so how could she blame him for his feelings? Dammit, she'd known when she married him just what she was getting into. She had no right to start complaining now.

But his burst of anger faded when he looked again at her empty pillow and wondered where she was. Maybe, he thought wistfully, she'd just gone down to tend to Jennifer. Maybe it was Cynthia's footsteps he'd heard out in the hallway, not Lisa's.

But he knew that wasn't true. With a deep, sure instinct, J.T. sensed that his wife was already gone from him, off into some private world that he had no part in.

Like, for instance, a secret relationship with another man? He groaned and rolled his head in agony on the pillow, trying not to think about the engine he'd just heard leaving the ranch yard. He couldn't bear to think about her in the arms of another man. The image seared him with fiery torment whenever it crept toward the outer edges of his mind. He pushed it away with a panicky dread that made him feel sick and cold.

Still, though J.T. could acknowledge the problems in their marriage, he was stubborn enough to keep on refusing Cynthia what she wanted. He'd knuckled under lots of times in the past, but he couldn't give in to her now, not on something so important.

While he lay tormented in the dark, Cynthia tiptoed into the room, fully dressed and carrying her nightgown. J.T. tensed in the bed and narrowed his eyes to slits, pretending to be asleep as he watched her.

She glanced in his direction, her face ghostly in the sudden flare of lightning at the window. Then, apparently satisfied that he was asleep, she let herself quietly into the bathroom and emerged a little while later in her white silk nightgown.

J.T. kept his eyes resolutely closed as she slipped into bed next to him and rolled over to face the window, turning her back on him. But his mind was boiling with questions.

Where had she been? Who was she seeing on this stormy night?

His throat ached with the need to shout at her, to scream out his rage and fear, batter her with the pain he felt. But he was so afraid. If he turned to her now and accused her, told her what he suspected, things would be said that neither of them could ever take back. He'd lose her for sure. And J.T. knew absolutely that he couldn't go on living if he lost her.

He turned his back, as well, and lay there, staring blindly at the red numbers on the digital clock while the rain hammered noisily on the roof. He couldn't believe he was behaving this way, letting his wife cheat on him and not saying a thing about it. He'd always felt that the wronged parties in marital adultery, like poor Mary Gibson when Bubba was playing around, were kind of pitiful creatures, victims who weren't strong enough to defend their own interests and keep their mates at home.

If it were his marriage, he'd always maintained, he'd do something about the situation before things got to that state, even if it involved a screaming three-way battle.

But J. T. McKinney was beginning to learn a painful truth: Relationships between men and women weren't all that simple. Apparently there were some problems you couldn't solve just by applying force and shouting louder than anybody else. The reality was, there were situations you couldn't fix without giving up big pieces of yourself, and the misery of it all was just too much for a man to endure.

LISA PICKED her way across the crushed rock in the ranch yard, surprised that there wasn't more mud after all that rain. But the ground was so parched that the moisture had all soaked away, rippled off through dry creekbeds and sunk down into the earth, leaving merely a trace of dampness behind.

She paused with a cold shiver of distaste next to the place where the black car had parked last night, and glanced fearfully around before bending to peer at the ground. But there was no sign of the car, no tracks or tire marks of any kind.

Maybe she was so frightened of Ramon that she'd just imagined the whole thing, had a bad dream about him driving up to the house in that storm and sitting there in his car, staring up at the windows....

Lisa shivered again and hurried on through the fresh, rain-washed morning, heading for the barn.

"Tiffany?" she called anxiously, looking into the silent depths of the big building, breathing in the pleasant scent of hay and horses. "Tiffany? Are you out here? Miss Cynthia's getting..."

Suddenly she gasped and put a hand over her mouth with a little cry of fear.

A man had appeared behind her, tall and dark in the ray of sunlight beaming across the floor. He moved slowly toward her while she stood rooted in place near one of the box stalls.

As the man drew nearer, he blocked the glare of light behind him so she could see his features.

"Lisa? What are you doing out here?" he asked, and she almost collapsed with relief, sagging against the front of the stall.

"Tony," she whispered. "I didn't...I didn't know you were here this morning."

"The van's parked down by Ken's place. I just came to check the colt again," he added, smiling down at her. "His cuts are healing real nice."

"Cuts?" she asked blankly, looking down at her hand.

Tony grinned. "On the colt," he said, taking her hand gently and moving closer to her. "Those stitches of yours will have to stay for a little while longer, I reckon."

She met his eyes, hardly breathing as he lifted her hand with its clumsy bandage and held it against his cheek, then turned it over to kiss her fingers.

"Lisa," he whispered huskily.

She trembled, staring at him in panic, but unable to turn away.

Tony put his arms around her and pulled her close to him, bending to kiss her forehead and cheeks, her eyelids and throat and lips, with lingering, gentle kisses that took her breath away.

She could feel his body shaking as much as her own. His muscles were quivering like those of a fine young horse, which longed to run but was being held and curbed. Lisa understood the depths of passion that he was holding in check out of consideration for her, and her heart ached.

"You're so sweet," he whispered against her mouth. "So sweet . . ."

Lisa's mind was flooded by a vague series of impressions, all tied up in the warmth of the damp summer morning, humming drowsily with insect sounds, the rich scents in the barn, the sweetness of Tony's lips and the strength in his body, the delicious, soaring feeling of being in his arms.

This is the nicest thing that's ever happened to me, she told herself. *This is the sweetest feeling I've ever had.*

But just as that thought occurred to her, she came abruptly back to reality and pulled away from him, turning aside in confusion.

"I was... I'm looking for Tiffany," she faltered, her cheeks hot with embarrassment.

He fell into step beside her as she moved toward the door. "Who's Tiffany?"

"She's the house cat. Miss Cynthia's cat. She must have slipped outside early this morning when J.T. went out, and nobody's seen her since. She didn't come home for breakfast."

"I see. And what does she look like, this Tiffany?"

"She's... small and dainty, kind of a grayish tortoiseshell, you know?"

Tony nodded solemnly. "I think I've seen her," he said with a chuckle.

"Really? Where is she?"

"Down by the haystack, eating a mouse."

"Eating a *mouse?*" Lisa echoed in horror.

He grinned and put a casual arm around her shoulders as they paused in the doorway of the barn. "It's a natural thing for cats to do," he said cheerfully.

"I know, but I don't think Tiffany is supposed to eat mice. I'd better not tell Miss Cynthia. I'll just say she's playing with the barn cats."

"Sounds good."

"Would you... would you like a cup of coffee or something?" Lisa offered shyly. She was unable to look at him, still overwhelmed by the blinding sweetness of that kiss.

"What I'd like," Tony said with quiet deliberation, "is for you to go out with me tonight, Lisa. I'd like to take you to the movies or something. Is that possible, do you think?"

She forced herself to look at him then, stabbed cruelly by the image of what he was offering. He was suggesting that she could have a normal, happy relationship with a decent and attractive young man. How simple it seemed, and how completely impossible it was for her!

"No," she whispered miserably. "No, I'm afraid I can't do that, Tony. Not ever. Please don't ask me again."

She fled before he could say anything else, running wildly across the yard to the ranch house, as if she were being pursued.

Tony leaned in the doorway of the barn, his smile fading as he watched Lisa disappear around the corner of the house. He shifted restlessly, still aching with desire after their kiss.

Finally, he turned aside and wandered into the barn again, sinking onto a hay bale and dropping his face into his hands.

Lisa's kiss had seemed so innocent, as sweet and shy as a child's caress. Everything about her was flowerlike and pure.

And yet...

Tony shook his head, his face twisted with pain and uncertainty.

He didn't know anything for sure. All he had were suspicions, a few things the sheriff had said, coupled with that stranger's presence in town and Lisa's obvious terror of him. Most significant, though, were Lisa's own words, her insistence that life was over and that a normal relationship wasn't possible for her.

Tony had heard a lot of gruesome stories about the kind of things that happened to runaway girls in Las Vegas. He just couldn't square those shadowy images with the reality of someone like Lisa.

Could any of his suspicions possibly be true? Could she be one of those girls Wayne Jackson had spoken of, somehow involved with a creep like that silk-shirt guy? Could her body have been fondled and caressed by lecherous strangers, sold for money on those gritty streets?

"*No,*" Tony whispered in agony. "No, I don't believe it. It's not true."

A little cat came into the barn, stepping daintily among the scattered wisps of hay. She sat near Tony, regarding him with solemn, yellow eyes while licking fastidiously at her front paws.

Tony realized that this was probably Tiffany, the missing house cat. He looked into its wide, inscrutable eyes, lost in thought about Lisa.

After all, nothing had really changed, had it? If the Las Vegas creep hadn't come along, and if Tony had never learned anything from Wayne Jackson about the guy, he'd have gone on thinking she was the sweetest girl in the world.

"Because she is," Tony told the cat, who listened gravely and began to groom her back paws as well. "If she got mixed up in anything bad, it couldn't have been her fault. She's not that kind of girl."

But despite his loyal words, a wave of jealousy and disgust rose within him, almost sickening in its intensity.

"Dear God," he muttered, cradling his head in his hands again while the little cat watched him curiously. "God, help me be a man about this. Please help it not to hurt so much."

When he finally looked up, Tony's young face was haggard and his cheeks glistened with tears. But his eyes were calm and steady, his jaw firm. In those few moments of agony, Tony Rodriguez had left his boyhood behind forever.

A FEW HOURS LATER the doorbell rang, just when Lisa was giving Jennifer her morning bath in the downstairs washroom next to the kitchen.

She paused, her hand braced on the baby's slippery back, waiting for somebody to answer the door. But then she remembered that Lettie Mae was in town doing the grocery shopping, Cynthia was helping Virginia get settled in her new house and J.T. was out around the ranch somewhere. The doorbell sounded again, a long, insistent ring in the morning silence. Lisa swept Jennifer out of the tub and wrapped her in a big white towel, bundling the little girl up so just her damp head and her soft pink toes were visible.

She hurried down the hallway to answer the door, then drew her breath sharply and swayed a little on her feet, instantly nauseated.

Ramon stood quietly in the morning sunlight, looking through the screen door at her with a dark expressionless gaze. "Hello, Lisa," he said.

"Go away," she whispered, reaching out automatically to lock the heavy aluminum door that protected her from the man outside. "You can't...they won't let you take me away," she told him with a small show of defiance, forcing herself to be brave. "I live here now, and they'll look after me. If you touch me, you'll be in big trouble."

"I have no intention of touching you," Ramon said coldly. "I'm inviting you to come back to work, and I think you're going to accept my offer like a sensible girl. My car's just outside, and I can't wait for very long."

Lisa stared at him, so surprised by his words that her terror ebbed away for a second or two. "Why would I go back there with you? Nothing on earth could make me do that."

Ramon's eyes flicked from her to the damp, sweet-smelling baby in her arms. "You like the little kid, Lisa?" he asked softly.

Her dread came flowing back, hotter and stronger than ever. She clutched Jennifer's wriggling body tightly in her arms and tried not to give way to tears.

"Because," Ramon went on in a quiet, hypnotic voice, "if you don't come with me, that kid's not going to have a long life, sweetheart. Her mama's going to find her hanging up there one morning." He jerked his head toward the stately columns of the veranda.

"Oh, God . . ."

"Hanging like a piece of meat," Ramon concluded softly, smiling at the baby.

"Dada?" Jennifer asked with her most enchanting grin, and reached toward him.

Lisa drew the child firmly back into her arms and stared at Ramon, her mind faltering with horror.

She knew beyond a shadow of doubt that he meant what he said. And there was no way for the McKinneys to protect themselves from someone like Ramon. He'd find a way to creep into the house some night, and he'd take this sweet baby and kill her with no more compunction than a man shooting a rat or squashing a bug. A picture flashed into Lisa's mind of Jennifer's dear little body, mangled and torn, lifeless. . . .

She moaned aloud and buried her face in the fragrant softness of the towel. After a moment, she squared her shoulders and looked up at him.

"I can't go with you right now," she said. "There's nobody here to look after her."

"Do you really think I give a damn?"

"No, Ramon," she said coldly. "I don't think you give a damn about anything or anyone. But I'm not leaving this baby alone. I'll go with you tonight. Just tell me when and where to meet you.''

He flashed her a warning glance, his face twisting unpleasantly. "You'd better not try anything, Lisa. If you take off, even if they find something to arrest me for, they can't hold me more than twenty-four hours and then I'll be back, and that kid will be dead. And maybe a few other people around here, too. Killing's easy, Lisa. I like killing people. It gives me a rush."

She looked up at his handsome face, the cold depths of his eyes, and recognized the truth of what he was saying.

"Just tell me where to meet you," she repeated tonelessly.

"Tonight at midnight, out by the front gate. Be there waiting when I drive up, and don't tell anybody that you're leaving. If we drive all night, we'll be halfway to Vegas before they know you're gone."

"All right," she said in that same flat voice. "I'll be there."

"You're being a real smart girl, Lisa."

"I hate you," she whispered, holding the baby and staring at him through a blur of tears that she fought back with fierce pride. "Dear God, how I hate you."

"That's okay. Other people hate me, too. But I invested a lot of money in you, sweetheart, and I want you back at work, and that's what's going to happen."

Lisa had a sudden grim memory of herself doing the "work" he spoke of, the drunken smiles and grasping hands and bitter humilation. She closed her eyes and drew a deep, shuddering breath of revulsion.

As if he could read her thoughts, Ramon gave her one of those frozen, lazy smiles that never touched his eyes, then turned and strode off down the front walk, his red silk shirt glimmering like fire in the warm sunlight.

CHAPTER TEN

WHILE LISA WAS ALONE with Ramon, absorbing the horror of his brutal threats against the people she loved, she'd felt that there was nobody who could help her, nobody in all the world who even knew that this nightmare was happening.

But she was wrong. Someone was nearby, listening to every word.

Jimmy Slattery had spent most of the morning in one of his favorite surveillance spots, under the veranda of the big house. Weeks ago, he had discovered an easy access to this hidden place through a couple of broken slats at the side of the veranda behind the rosebushes. At first he'd been afraid of entering the darkened space, worried that it would be cold and slimy, possibly even infested with snakes. He'd forced himself to explore beneath the veranda only because he recognized it as an ideal place to eavesdrop on private conversations, and had been pleasantly surprised when he first crawled inside.

The cavern beneath the veranda wasn't wet at all. It was dry and cool, and on really sunny mornings there was even enough light under the floorboards to read and make notes without a flashlight. That was what Jimmy was occupied in at the moment. He was planning the midnight expedition up the limestone cliffs, trying to think of everything in advance so Mrs. McKinney would be totally impressed with his competence.

Jimmy had just begun to list the supplies he needed to take in his backpack when he heard a car stop out front, followed by hard, confident footsteps directly over his head.

Jimmy frowned, hating to be interrupted while he was concentrating. He heard Lisa's soft voice, and a man's deeper tones. Jimmy's mouth fell open in shock as he gradually absorbed what they were saying.

After the man left the veranda, Jimmy sat huddled in the shady cavern. He stared at his notebook, gnawed on the pencil and then began to make feverish notes. At last, when he was sure the man's car had left the ranch yard, Jimmy crawled out through the prickly rosebushes and ran to look for Mr. McKinney.

J.T. STOOD LEANING on the corral fence, watching while Lynn ran a big bay stallion through his paces out in the paddock.

He had to admit that these Thoroughbreds were showy animals, high-stepping and pretty in their movements. J.T. had always been prejudiced against the breed because they were so temperamental. He really disliked a head-tossing, skittish kind of horse.

"A horse isn't worth the saddle you strap on him," he often told his daughter, "if you can't count on him to settle down and work for you when you need him."

But Lynn had assured him that the skittishness of Thoroughbreds could usually be attributed to bad handling, especially by people who wanted them to run at any cost. Her horses were treated with such loving care and tenderness that they were as gentle as big dogs, ambling happily around the pasture when she rode them and paying close attention to every small command from her legs and hands.

J.T. smiled, enjoying the summer morning and the warmth of the sun, for a brief moment forgetting about the growing tensions in his marriage and the bitter unhappiness this silent conflict was causing for him and his wife.

He heard rapid footsteps behind him, and frowned when he saw Jimmy Slattery approaching the corral. Jimmy clutched his notebook, looking pale and solemn behind his thick glasses.

"I have to talk to you, Mr. McKinney," the boy said abruptly when he reached the corral fence. "Something bad is happening."

J.T. was tempted to tell the boy that something really bad was going to happen if Jimmy didn't start minding his own business and leaving people alone, but he curbed the impulse. "Yeah, Jimmy?" he asked with a tolerant smile, turning his attention to the boy. "What's happening?"

Jimmy squinted up at him, the sunlight reflecting off his glasses in disconcerting fashion. "A man came to see Lisa," he reported. "Just a few minutes ago. He talked to her at the front door of the ranch house, and said some really bad things to her."

Again, J.T. was strongly tempted to ask the kid just how he'd happened to be in a position to overhear Lisa's conversation. Ever since that girl from Crystal Creek had hung around the ranch spying on Tyler and Ruth, J.T. had had a dread of anyone's privacy being invaded.

Suddenly the child's words registered in his mind. He looked down at Jimmy sharply. "A man?" he asked. "Saying bad things to Lisa?"

Jimmy nodded and flipped open his notebook. "The conversation began at 10:17 a.m.," he read aloud. "They were..."

"All right," J.T. said impatiently. "Never mind the details. What man was this? Somebody from the ranch, or from town?"

Jimmy shook his head with an important air, clearly gratified that J.T. was finally taking him seriously. "I don't know," he said, consulting the notebook again. "He drove a late-model black Corvette and wore a red shirt."

"I see," J.T. said quietly. "And what did he say to Lisa?"

"He said she had to go with him to Las Vegas. He said he wanted her to go back to work."

"Did he, now? What did Lisa say about that?"

"She said she wouldn't go. She said the people at the ranch would look after her, and the man couldn't make her go."

"Good for her. What did he say then?"

"He said if Lisa didn't go, he'd kill Jennifer. He said he'd hang her from the veranda like a piece of meat."

J.T.'s stomach churned with loathing. He stared at Jimmy's freckled face, appalled by the boy's words and the gruesome image they evoked.

Jimmy glanced up at him cautiously, then continued reading from his notebook. "After he said that, Lisa sounded like she was crying. She told him she'd go with him. She said she couldn't leave right now because there was no one to look after Jennifer."

J.T. swallowed hard and gripped the top rail of the corral fence, battling a tide of fury so powerful that he felt sick and shaky.

"The man told her to meet him at the front gate at midnight, and not tell anybody what she was doing. He said they'd be halfway to Las Vegas by the time people knew she was gone."

J.T. bent and stared into the boy's face.

"Jimmy, listen to me," he began, slowly and distinctly. "You listen to me, and you do exactly what I say. Do you understand?"

Jimmy gave a brief, frightened nod. He licked his lips nervously and stared up at J.T.

"Don't you tell a soul what you just told me," J.T. whispered softly. "You hear me, Jimmy? Not a living soul. Not ever. Will you promise me that, son? I need you to be a real man about this."

The boy studied the tall rancher like a small bird mesmerized by a rattlesnake. He nodded again, his face so pale and tense that his freckles stood out in stark relief.

"Good," J.T. said softly. "I knew I could count on you, Jimmy."

Jimmy's chest swelled and his face warmed at these words of praise. "Will you do something about it, Mr. McKinney?" he asked. "Will you stop him from taking Lisa?"

"Not a word," J.T. repeated in a warning tone, then patted the boy's spiky cowlick. "But I think I can tell you, Jimmy," he added in that same gentle voice, "that we don't take real kindly in these parts to men who go around bullying women and hurting little kids. You understand what I mean?"

Jimmy thought this over and gave J.T. a brief, solemn nod, then turned away and marched back toward the ranch buildings.

J.T. watched the boy's progress, his mind still reeling when he thought of that vicious threat to his baby girl. "Jimmy," he called.

The boy turned and gave him an inquiring glance.

"Thanks, son," J.T. said, nodding gravely to him across the dusty ranch yard. "Thanks a whole lot."

By now, Jimmy's composure seemed to have fully returned. He made a lofty gesture, like a man who is accustomed to doing his job and expects no thanks for it. Then he turned and vanished into the mesquite behind the windmill.

J.T. ATE A SANDWICH in his office for lunch, from a tray brought to him by Lettie Mae. He tried to concentrate on the sheets listing weights and prices of the last load of cattle he'd shipped, but the figures blurred and shifted before his eyes, flowing into a picture of Jennifer, crying and screaming with pain, helpless in the hands of that evil son of a bitch....

Finally, he shoved back his chair, reached for his hat and left the office, his face hard and set. He paused for a moment in the hallway, then walked into the kitchen, where Lettie Mae was filling the dishwasher and Lisa was feeding Jennifer her lunch.

J.T. smiled automatically at the baby. Jennifer sat in her high chair with a pink bib tied under her chin, and strained peaches smeared over most of her face.

"Dada," she greeted him cheerfully, waving a little spoon that she liked to hold while eating, although J.T. was fairly certain that she had no concept as yet of how to use it.

"Hi there, sugar," J.T. said, moving across the room to stroke his daughter's fluffy head. He felt a surge of love, primal and overwhelming. "Sweet baby," he murmured, then dodged instinctively as a small blob of peaches sailed through the air and landed on the floor near his boot.

Jennifer braced her fat hands on the tray of the high chair and leaned forward to examine the mess on the floor. She looked at the spoon in her fist with amazement and delight, then puffed in excitement and drummed her bare heels against the base of her chair.

This is a tool, she seemed to be thinking. *With this object, I can send food flying through space. This is wonderful!*

"A light dawns. I reckon that's how we first crawled down out of the trees and started developing technology," J.T. told Lisa, who nodded without smiling, and got up to wipe the orange stains from the floor.

The poor kid, J.T. thought with wrenching sympathy, observing her pale face and the shadows darkening her eyes. *She's been carrying this burden around with her for such a long time. Now it's caught up with her again, and she can't even tell anybody. What a hell she's lived through....*

"Damn," he said aloud, giving Lettie Mae an apologetic smile. "I left those lunch dishes in my office. I'll just go get them, Lettie Mae, so you can put them in with this load."

"You'll do no such thing," Lettie Mae told him firmly, as he'd known she would. She gave him an indignant glare and marched briskly from the room, heading for his office.

Alone with Lisa and the baby, who was struggling to load more peaches onto her spoon, J.T. stood by the table in awkward silence. Lisa had her hair pulled into a casual ponytail today, and her nape looked

vulnerable and childlike. Another flood of protective, fatherly concern washed over J.T., almost iden-
tical to the emotions evoked earlier by little Jennifer.
But this time his anxieties weren't for his own child.
They were for this shy young woman who'd so
quickly become a treasured part of his household.

"Lisa," he said gently, "you know how much we
all care about you."

She cast him a brief, startled glance, and he was
wounded by the depths of pain and sorrow in her
eyes.

"Thank you, Mr. McKinney," she murmured almost inaudibly, and turned back to Jennifer.

"What I mean to say," J.T. continued, "is that if
you're ever bothered by anything, you know you can
come to us, don't you? Cynthia and I, we feel that
you're just about like one of our own. We really care
about you."

A couple of tears glimmered on her eyelashes and
slipped down her cheeks. She brushed at them fur-
tively and stirred the baby food with intense concentration while she fought to regain her composure.

But when the girl looked at him again, her face was
quiet and distant, pale with resolve.

She wasn't going to say anything, J.T. realized. She
was afraid to get the family involved, because she
took that creep's threats seriously. She was planning
to sacrifice herself without a word to anybody, just to
get Ramon safely away from the ranch and this family.

J.T. contemplated her, awed by her courage and selflessness. But he knew there was no point in talking to her. They couldn't eliminate this threat merely by talking about it. Some kind of action definitely needed to be taken, because J. T. McKinney had no intention of leaving his family at the mercy of scum like Ramon.

He hesitated a moment longer, then bent to kiss Jennifer's forehead, the only part of her face that wasn't smeared with peaches, and walked out into the noonday sunlight.

He drove his truck into town, passing the little cottage he'd bought for Virginia, and wistfully noted the midnight blue Cadillac parked outside. Cynthia was still there, helping Virginia with her move. J.T.'s thoughts curled protectively around his wife as he brooded over the danger to his family if he didn't handle this situation properly. It almost drove him crazy, the thought that someone had dared to threaten his loved ones.

Cynthia, he thought, visualizing her lovely dark eyes, the patrician beauty of her face. *Cynthia, I won't let anybody hurt you. I'd die before I ever let them hurt you....*

But, he realized in bleak sorrow, that wasn't true. He was hurting her himself, more than she'd ever been hurt in her life, and he didn't seem to know how to stop doing it.

This sleazy Ramon was at least an enemy that could be seen and dealt with, not like the invisible specters that were haunting J.T.'s marriage, stealing away his wife and his happiness.

Still deep in his troubled thoughts, J.T. parked by the Longhorn and strode inside. As he'd expected, a few of the late lunch crowd were still there, chatting jovially at tables and booths in the cool depths of the coffee shop. J.T. saw Bubba and Mary Gibson in a booth near the entry, holding hands over the remains of their meal.

"Hi there, you lovebirds," J.T. said, grinning down at them as he passed. "Try to behave yourselves in public, okay?"

His neighbors smiled delightedly, then returned to their happy absorption in each other.

J.T. caught sight of Wayne Jackson's familiar uniform at a table near the back, but his heart sank when he recognized young Tony Rodriguez across from the sheriff. He hesitated, then moved forward and seated himself with the two men.

"Hi, J.T." Wayne drawled. "How are you feelin' today?"

"Not bad," J.T. said automatically. "Fact is," he muttered, leaning toward them and dropping his voice, "I've got some trouble out at my place. I need to talk to you, Wayne."

"Trouble?" the sheriff asked, suddenly alert. "What kind of trouble, J.T.? Not more cattle rustling?"

J.T. shook his head, acknowledging young Tony's alert expression with sick reluctance. He knew how the new veterinarian felt about Lisa. There was hardly anybody in town who didn't know, because this young man wasn't the kind to be secretive about his feelings. Tony was as straightforward and honest as the sun, and he sure didn't deserve the kind of hurt that was about to come to him.

But what else could be done? While J.T. hesitated, Tony cast a quick glance at both his table companions, then began to get to his feet. "Well, I'd better mosey along," he said casually. "Manny's going out of town this afternoon, and I'm handling the clinic alone."

"Wait, Tony," J.T. told the young man, his voice abrupt. "I want you to hear what I've got to say. This concerns you, too."

Tony sank back into his chair, startled and a little worried. J.T. paused, wondering in agony if there was a gentle way to say what needed to be said. For the life of him, he couldn't think of any.

"It's about Lisa," he began.

Tony's handsome face tightened and his eyes took on a wary look.

"I reckon I know what this is about," he said after a tense silence. "That silk-shirt dude, he's here to get Lisa, right? He's been following her."

J.T. and Wayne Jackson both turned to the young man in surprise. "Yeah," J.T. said at last. "That's why he's here. How did you know, Tony?"

"I just put two and two together. Did she come here from Las Vegas?"

J.T. nodded miserably. "Matter of fact, I...sort of ran into her there when we all went on that trip to California. Just met her on the...on the street," he added hastily. "It was the damnedest coincidence. She was there doing...what she was doing...when I met her," he went on, beginning to falter when he looked into Tony's blazing eyes. "It was a terrible situation. She'd been trapped and beaten into doing it, poor kid, and when she finally managed to run away, she came here to Crystal Creek and got a job at my place without even knowing that we'd ever run into each other. It was a real strange thing."

Wayne placed a gentle hand on J.T.'s shoulder. "All that stuff doesn't matter, J.T.," he said quietly. "I figure you probably had a hand in helping the girl get away from Vegas, whether you want to take credit for it or not, but the main thing is what's happening now. This dude...he's come to get her, you think?"

J.T. nodded. "I know he has. You recall Ken's nephew, that little kid who's staying at my place?" He cast a questioning glance at the other men, who both nodded.

"Well, Jimmy was under the veranda when the guy came. He heard him threaten Lisa. Actually," J.T. added, his face twisting, "the bastard threatened Jennifer. He said if Lisa didn't go back with him tonight, he'd kill my baby girl."

Wayne reached for his hat. "That's enough for me," he said coldly. "I'm taking him in."

"Hang on, Wayne," J.T. said. "We need to think about all this for a bit. We need to step real careful. My family's involved here, and I want a say in what's going on."

"But," Tony whispered in agony, "what about Lisa? She can't just...go away with him!"

J.T. looked at the young man. "Does it make any difference to you, Tony? Knowing about all this, does it change how you feel?"

Tony was silent a moment, his head lowered so the others couldn't see his eyes. When he looked up, his face was pale and haggard. "Sure, it makes a difference," he muttered. "How would you feel, either of you, if you had to hear something like this about a woman you really cared for?"

Both the older men were silent, watching his struggle.

"But it doesn't change the way I feel," Tony said finally. "I think I've come to know Lisa pretty well. If she got involved in something like...like what you say," he whispered, hardly able to get the words out, "then I think J.T. was right. She was forced into it, and nobody can judge her for what happened. I'm sure not judging her."

J.T. took a quiet measure of Tony's handsome young face. "You're a hell of a man, son," he said at last.

"I...I really care about Lisa," Tony murmured, his cheeks flushing under his tan. "I care a whole lot. I figured maybe she had something like this in her life, even before I saw the guy who's after her. She didn't ever want to go out and do anything, and she told me once that she felt like her life was already over. I knew something bad had happened to her, but I don't think it was her fault. I still feel the same about her."

"Tony, even if we get her away from this guy," Wayne cautioned him, "it's going to be real hard for her to believe that you care about her. I saw a lot of this crap when I worked in the city. Young girls get hurt so bad by guys like that, it's hard for them to trust anybody afterward."

Tony's jaw set stubbornly. "She can trust me," he said. "And I mean for her to know it."

The sheriff grinned briefly. "J.T.'s right, kid," he said with gruff approval. "You're quite a man. Now, let's make some plans. I'm taking both of you on as temporary deputies, all right?"

CYNTHIA DROVE into the ranch yard and glanced anxiously at her watch as she parked the Cadillac in the garage. It was past five o'clock, and she'd left before midmorning. She couldn't remember when she'd been away from Jennifer for such a long time.

Thank God for Lisa, she thought fervently, hurrying toward the house. Without Lisa's competence, a day like this would have been impossible for Cynthia. And it had been such fun, helping Virginia to hang curtains and move furniture around, exploring all the delightful nooks and crannies in the little house....

When she thought about it, Cynthia couldn't tamp down a wistful envy for Virginia. The housekeeper was spending her first night all alone in her charming, vine-covered cottage, free to do whatever she pleased without the constant worry of negatively affecting somebody else, or painfully adjusting to another's personality.

Of course, Cynthia wouldn't be all alone when she left. She'd have Jennifer with her, and hopefully Lisa as well, so she wouldn't be able to be completely selfish. But it would still be restful to be free of J.T.'s domineering presence, and his stubborn insistence that she become the kind of woman she could never make herself into.

Her pleasure at the day's activities began to ebb away and weariness settled over her again as she approached the ranch house, with all its problems and sorrows. Much as Cynthia loved the house, it was beginning to seem more and more like a prison. And now she faced another endless night of lying sleepless in the wide bed, staring at the window while J.T. slept beside her, his handsome, withdrawn profile mocking her with all the sweet love that could have been, that would never happen now....

Not tonight, Cynthia thought suddenly, her heart lifting with childlike anticipation as she mounted the steps. Tonight she and Jimmy were climbing up the hillside to visit those mysterious silvery beings on the top of the limestone cliffs.

She grinned, feeling irrationally cheered by this thought. Cynthia, by now, had dismissed all her earlier fears about Hank's dire warning and Jimmy's obvious terror and agitation. Of course there was nothing unusual on the hilltop. It was ridiculous ever to have suspected that something might be up there. But she still wanted to have the adventure, the sheer diversion of climbing up there at midnight full of breathless anticipation, and the deliciously scary thought that *something* waited for them up there.

Besides, anything was better than lying beside J.T. throughout another endless night.

As Cynthia approached the front door, Jimmy appeared around the side of the veranda, making her jump. The boy was also clearly startled by her arrival. He bent in awkward fashion to brush dirt from the knees of his blue jeans, then clutched his notebook and stared up at her.

"Hi, Jimmy," Cynthia said cheerfully, puzzled by his defensive look. "How are you? All ready for a little walk later on?" she added in a lower tone, moving closer to him and giving him a conspiratorial wink.

Jimmy shifted nervously on his feet. "It might start raining again," he said. "Maybe we shouldn't go tonight."

"Rain?" Cynthia looked at him blankly, then surveyed the clear blue sky, dusted softly with mare's tails of light cirrus cloud. "Oh, I don't think so, Jimmy. I think it looks really clear. And there's even going to be a full moon," she added with satisfaction. "I checked the calendar this morning."

Jimmy clutched the notebook tighter. "Something else is happening tonight," he said, with a quick furtive glance over his shoulder.

"Something else? What's happening?"

"It's very, very secret. I can't talk about it. But I really think I should be on the scene to monitor the situation."

Cynthia laughed. "Oh, come on, Jimmy. What's going to be happening at midnight? You promised me," she added, almost feeling a little embarrassed by her own persistence. "You said we'd climb the cliff tonight. I want to go, Jimmy. I want to see what's up there making that light. And if you don't go with me, I'm going to climb up that hill all by myself."

Jimmy paused, clearly torn. "All right," he said at last, his voice heavy with reluctance. "I'll go up the hill with you."

Cynthia grinned. "Good for you. See you later," she added, and watched with a smile as Jimmy trudged off toward the Slattery place for supper.

Then she turned and hurried into the ranch house, heading for the kitchen. A little guilty apprehension clutched at her when she thought about her poor abandoned Jennifer, who had probably spent the whole day crying pathetically for her mother.

But, of course, she needn't have worried. Jennifer was happily enthroned in her high chair, banging her spoon on the tray and crowing at her father. The baby wore her most adorable outfit, a pair of pink corduroy overalls patterned in dinosaurs, and a darker pink T-shirt with a row of tiny dinosaur-shaped buttons at the shoulder.

J.T was seated on a kitchen chair in front of his daughter, spooning food into her mouth while she beamed at him and tried to grab his hair.

"Ow!" J.T. yelled, to please her, when her little fist finally managed to grasp a handful of crisp dark hair. "Ow, stop that! You're killin' me!"

Jennifer chortled and sat back in the chair. She ducked her head and gave her father a coy smile, covering her eyes with her hand and peering bright-eyed though her spread fingers.

"No," J.T. said sternly. "We're not playing peek until you finish your mashed potatoes. Lisa, how do you get her to eat?"

"I think maybe she's had enough to eat now," Lisa said quietly from her seat at the table, where she was busy with her seemingly endless task of folding cotton diapers.

Cynthia paused in the doorway, troubled by something in Lisa's voice. During the brief time the girl had been in the house, Lisa had already become so familiar that Cynthia was sensitive to her voice and moods, and she could tell that Lisa was deeply unhappy about something. Her pale cheeks, the droop of her head and the listless movements of her hands all spoke of sorrow and worry.

I'll talk to her later, Cynthia thought. *Maybe I can get her to tell me what's . . .*

"Mum-mum-mum!" Jennifer shouted, catching sight of her mother and waving the spoon in radiant delight. "Mama!"

Lettie Mae turned from the counter, where she was cutting pastry dough to make sausage rolls, and J.T. and Lisa both looked up from their tasks.

"Hi, everyone," Cynthia said cheerfully, moving across the room to lift her baby from the high chair. "How are things at home? I feel like I've been gone a week."

Jennifer hugged her mother ecstatically, burrowing against her and butting her soft head into Cynthia's shoulder. Cynthia held the baby and patted her back automatically.

"How's Virginia?" Lettie Mae asked, returning to her pastry. "Changed her mind yet?"

Cynthia smiled. "I don't think so. I think Virginia's really happy with the way things are turning out. It's a beautiful little house," she added, looking over the baby's head at J.T., who gave her a distracted nod. "That was really a smart purchase, J.T. I wish . . ."

Cynthia was alarmed to catch herself on the verge of saying that she wished she could live in the little house herself. She bit her lip and nuzzled against the baby's neck to hide her expression, but her resolve hardened.

This simply couldn't go on. She needed to have it out with her husband, let him know how she felt and what she planned to do. Cynthia couldn't stand any more of the uncertainty of her life, all this creeping around under a dark cloud of resentment and worry.

Maybe tonight, she thought, and then remembered the expedition up the hillside, which had begun to take on some kind of mythical significance in her mind. The midnight climb was seeming more and more like an odyssey that had to be completed before she could move on to the next phase in her life.

Tomorrow, then.

She'd make certain that tomorrow morning she and J.T. could have a long, serious talk, and she'd tell him that she was leaving and taking Jennifer. And then she'd really go, first thing in the afternoon. It wouldn't be so complicated. Once she'd made the actual break, everything else could follow. Maybe she'd get a room in Austin for a few days and come back for the things she needed, or arrange to have them shipped....

"I won't be here for supper, Lettie Mae," J.T. was saying. When all three women looked at him in surprise, he shifted awkwardly in the chair, reaching up to take Jennifer from Cynthia's arms.

"Where are you going?" Cynthia asked, forgetting entirely that she was planning to leave this man, that within hours his comings and going would no longer be any of her business.

Again, he looked strangely uncomfortable as he bounced the baby on his knee. "Well, a bunch of the guys are getting together to play cards and have steaks at the country club," he said, his eyes darting from Cynthia to Lettie Mae. "Sorry. I reckon I should have said something earlier."

Lettie Mae sniffed and looked injured. "I'm making sausage rolls with cream sauce. It's your favorite," she pointed out, waving a floury hand at the pastry on the counter.

"It sure is," J.T. said humbly. "Sorry about that, Lettie Mae. Maybe you can warm some up for me tomorrow."

"Warm them up!" the cook muttered. "These sausage rolls never taste good warmed up like they do fresh from the oven."

"Sorry," J.T. repeated.

Cynthia leaned against the counter, watching as Lisa quietly finished her pile of diapers. "What guys?" she asked.

"Beg pardon, honey?"

"What guys are playing cards?"

J.T. shrugged. "Ken and Tyler, Wayne Jackson, Warren and Vernon Trent . . . just a few of the neighbors, that's all."

Another wary, evasive look crossed his features, causing Cynthia to wonder what exactly was going on. But she was too absorbed in her own problems to care very much, and her primary response was relief. If J.T was playing cards all evening, he'd be getting home very late, too tired to take any notice of her. She could probably slip away, climb the hill with Jimmy and be back down and in bed without her husband ever realizing that she'd been gone.

In fact, since J.T. wasn't going to be home, she'd be able to get hold of Jimmy and suggest that they leave earlier, maybe around ten-thirty or eleven, giving them lots of time to get back down at a decent hour....

Cynthia was so encouraged by this new plan that she hardly noticed when J.T. settled the baby back in her high chair, gave his wife a polite kiss on the cheek and strode from the room.

Lettie Mae followed, heading out to the garden to pick some fresh greens for their evening salad, still muttering darkly about her sausage rolls.

Cynthia turned to Lisa, who had lifted Jennifer from the chair yet again and was checking the condition of her diaper. "That baby gets cuddled and passed from hand to hand all day long," Cynthia observed, trying to smile. "She's going to be spoiled rotten before she starts walking."

"I don't think people get spoiled from being loved," Lisa murmured, keeping her face hidden. "I think it's just the opposite."

"Is everything all right, Lisa?" Cynthia asked gently.

The girl nodded without looking up. "Everything's fine," she said, so quickly that Cynthia suspected she'd deliberately misunderstood the question.

"She fussed a bit when you left, but then I gave her a bath and put her down for her nap and she was fine when she woke up. She ate a really big lunch."

"That's good," Cynthia said automatically. She lingered by the table, wondering if she should persist with her questioning. Something was clearly bothering Lisa, but if the girl wasn't ready to talk about it, Cynthia could hardly force her.

Besides, Cynthia told herself bleakly, who was she to be giving anybody advice? She couldn't even manage her own life, let alone tell somebody else what to do.

Finally she bent to kiss Jennifer, gave Lisa a sad little smile and turned to leave, trudging slowly up the stairs to her room.

CHAPTER ELEVEN

NIGHT FELL across the ranch, and the full moon slipped over the horizon, climbing the starry sky until it hovered directly above the limestone cliffs. It glowed a golden orange, huge and iridescent in the blackness of the summer night. A few of the lacy clouds still lingered in the sky, drifting like dark blue cobwebs across the face of the full moon, giving it a shrouded, mysterious look.

Lisa stood in the shadows by the front gate, silently contemplating the golden moon. Her mind was carefully blank because if she had allowed herself to consider what lay ahead, the pain of her musings would surely have killed her.

She knew what she was going back to, and what her life would be like from now on. The only way to endure such an existence was to shut off all reflection, completely and permanently, and move through her days like an automaton. If she was lucky, some kind of violence would overtake her, ending her life before too much time could pass.

Violence was all too common on the gritty back streets of Las Vegas. And that was all she had to hope for, now that Ramon had found her again.

Lisa shivered and hugged her arms close to her body, unable to stop herself from worrying about Jennifer in her crib upstairs in the silent ranch house. Lisa was always alert to nighttime sounds, and she was fairly certain that she'd heard Cynthia creep down the stairs and out the back door a little while earlier.

Likely Miss Cynthia couldn't sleep, she thought, all alone in the big bed with her husband away in town, and she'd gone out for a walk under the warm summer moon. But she hadn't come back yet, and that left only Lettie Mae in the house. Lisa wasn't sure that the cook would even hear Jennifer if she woke up and cried. Lisa could hardly bear the idea of the baby crying, hot and frightened in her crib, and nobody coming to tend to her.

But, of course, she couldn't worry about that now. Jennifer would be in far more danger if Lisa didn't leave and take Ramon away as well. The family would just have to manage on their own from now on, caring for the baby and all the other duties in the big house. And Virginia wasn't there any longer....

Lisa pushed the anxieties from her mind and shifted from one foot to the other, her face shuttered, waiting for him to come.

At last she spotted the headlights on the road, heard the low, powerful throb of the car engine as Ramon swept up the deserted stretch of highway. He passed Lisa, pulled the car in an abrupt circle on the shoulder of the road and came up beside her, leaning over to flip the car door open.

"Get in," he said curtly.

Despite her resolve, it was all Lisa could do not to begin sobbing when she got into the car and heard the cold finality of the door slamming, sealing her once more into Ramon's world.

She was painfully sensitive to everything about him, all the remembered impressions that were burned into her brain. The glimmer of the dashboard lights on his cruel profile, the sound of the car's engine, the smell of leather and expensive cologne and a kind of sweet corruption that lingered around Ramon wherever he went....

Lisa shuddered and gripped her hands together in her lap, hoping desperately that she wasn't going to be sick. Ramon would be so angry if she threw up on his expensive leather seats.

"I should slap you silly," he was saying harshly as he lit a cigarette and waved the match to extinguish the small flame. "Causing me so much trouble, wasting all this time.... "

Lisa stared ahead of her in silence, still battling the waves of nausea.

"I bet you wonder why I even bothered, right?" he went on, turning to look at her with an unpleasant smile. "There's lots of girls in Vegas, right? Why spend so much time tracking one little bitch who runs away?"

Lisa bit her lip and focused out the side window at the rolling moonlit fields behind vine-covered fences.

"Well, I'll tell you why," Ramon went on, ignoring her silence and puffing smoke through his nostrils. "I don't want any of those other bimbos getting the idea they can take off on a little trip any time they feel like it. After they talk with you, sugar, they might change their minds about traveling anywhere."

Lisa supposed she should be concerned about this threat, but she wasn't. What could he do to hurt her more than this? Having taken everything from her that had any meaning or value, what more could he possibly take?

"I don't care what you do to me," she said aloud, surprising herself. "There's nothing you can do to me anymore."

He cast her a quick glance, his face tightening. "Yeah? We'll see about that, angel face. We'll just see about that."

Lisa glared at him, meeting his eyes with courage. "I don't care," she repeated. "I hope you kill me. I'd rather be dead than live like this."

"I don't plan to kill you, sweetheart," Ramon countered, his lip curling again as he smiled. "I got other plans for you."

Lisa turned away and her mind filled with a sudden image of Tony. She envisioned his laughing eyes, recalled his decency and gentleness and strength.

I love him, Lisa thought in childlike astonishment, her eyes burning with tears. *I really love him. I wish*

I'd had the chance to tell him so. I wonder what he's going to think when he hears I've run away without even saying goodbye....

All at once her failure to say goodbye took on a huge, dark significance. Tony might spend the rest of his life wondering why. Or J.T. would tell him who she was and what she'd done. When Tony knew all that, he wouldn't care about her anymore. He'd be glad she was gone.

Suddenly, Ramon swore loudly and hit the brakes on the powerful sports car. Startled, Lisa peered through the windshield, wondering what had provoked him. They were well past Crystal Creek now, across the river and out on the lonely road heading west. But the road, Lisa began to realize, wasn't so deserted after all. To her shocked amazement, a ghostly roadblock had appeared from nowhere to straddle the dark, tree-lined expanse of highway.

A row of pickup trucks, parked bumper to bumper, stretched across the road and down into both narrow ditches, making it impossible for Ramon to get past them. He shifted the gears viciously into reverse and swung the car around, then swore again as another couple of trucks moved swiftly into position from behind the trees, blocking the rear access as well.

Lisa gaped out the window in bewilderment, at a loss as to what was happening.

Half a dozen male figures emerged from the vehicles and started cautiously toward the stranded car. The men moved in eerie silence; they wore dark clothes and bandannas covering their lower faces. Lisa's nightmarish sense of unreality deepened when, in spite of the disguises, she was almost certain that she recognized J.T.'s lithe stride, and the lean, ambling shape of his foreman, Ken Slattery.

Suddenly, her heart leapt into her mouth as another man walked out from the shadows, his face also concealed. But this was a body that Lisa would have recognized anywhere.

Tony, she thought with deepening dread. *Oh, Tony...* She must have made some kind of sound, a whimper or muffled sob, because Ramon looked over at her wildly. Then he opened the door, grabbed her arm and dragged her with him across the gearshift console, reaching into the compartment at his elbow for the gun that he always kept in the car.

Lisa felt the gearshift scrape brutally on her legs, and almost screamed with pain at the harshness of his grasp. But her concern wasn't for herself. She was thinking about the gun in Ramon's hand, the look of fury, almost madness, on his face, and Tony standing quietly out there in the moonlight....

She sensed a coolness on her hot cheeks, a soft rush of midnight wind and the silver touch of the moonlight. One of her shoes had come off, and the sharp pebbles on the shoulder of the road dug cruelly into her bare foot. Ramon continued to clutch her arm, pulling Lisa close to him and jamming the gun barrel against her side.

She heard Tony's voice, surprisingly near to them. "Put the gun down, creep. Just put it down, slow and gentle, or I'll blow you away."

Lisa was almost paralyzed with terror. If she looked up, made any kind of move at all, she might startle Ramon and cause him to shoot Tony. But she couldn't help herself. She hungered to see that beloved face one more time, look into Tony's eyes once again before she died.

She raised her head and drew in a sharp breath. Tony stood just a dozen feet away from them, holding a rifle trained steadily on Ramon, who laughed harshly and shoved his gun harder against Lisa's body.

"You make a move and I'll kill her," he said. "I'd like to kill her. She's a lazy, dirty little bitch. Lies and cheats all the time."

Lisa was tense with emotion as she turned to Tony, willing him silently to go away, to listen to Ramon and back off before he got hurt. But even behind the concealment of the bandanna, she recognized the cold resolve in him. With a sinking heart, she realized that Tony wasn't ever going to yield ground to a man like Ramon.

"If you hurt her," Tony said softly, "there's a half dozen rifles besides mine pointing at you right now. You'll die like a dog, right here in the road, and they'll never find your body. I don't think you want that, do you, creep? After all, you're too pretty to die."

Lisa could sense Ramon's hesitation, the slight loosening of his grip on her arm. He cast a panicky glance around, stiffening with alarm when he realized that this masked vigilante was speaking the truth. Lisa, too, could see the moonlight glinting on the circle of leveled rifle barrels, the menace in all those silent, watchful eyes beneath the shadowy hat brims.

"We've got a deal to offer you," Tony went on in a reasonable tone. "Me and my friends, we don't normally like to deal with snakes. You should be real tickled that we're making an exception in your case."

Again she could sense Ramon's hesitation. He quickly surveyed the quiet circle of masked men, then looked back at Tony. "Who are you?" he asked with a show of bravado. "Why are you bothering me, you bastards? I haven't done anything wrong. This woman is my..."

"Shut up," Tony whispered savagely. "Just shut up and listen, because you're making a life-or-death decision here. Now, if you hurt that girl or any of us, you'll die in a heartbeat. That's one choice, but I don't reckon you'd consider any woman worth dying for, would you, Ramon? If you let her go, you'll live. That's the deal. You take lots of time to think it over. We've got all night."

Lisa held her breath, petrified to move or make a sound. She stood silent in Ramon's grasp, biting her lip until the pain was almost unbearable, staring in fixed silence at Tony's level eyes.

At last, to her amazement, she felt Ramon's grip slacken. He gave her a brutal push, sending her sprawling to her knees on the graveled shoulder of the road, and glared defiantly at the watchful circle of men. "If she's worth that much to you all, you can have her," he said with scorn. "She's practically used up anyhow. The men who pay, they like their women fresh."

Lisa huddled on her knees in the cold moonlight, painfully conscious of Tony standing nearby, of the way his hands tightened on the gun barrel and his body stiffened. He was clearly fighting for control. Lisa half expected him to lose the battle and shoot Ramon where he stood.

Another man stepped forward, the one she'd recognized earlier as J.T. "Give me the gun," he said curtly to Ramon, holding his rifle cocked and ready. "Hand it over butt first, nice and easy."

Ramon tossed the revolver contemptuously into the tall weeds that filled the ditch. "How about if you crawl down there and look for it, cowboy?" he asked with a sneer.

"Oh, I don't think I want to do that," J.T. said mildly from behind the bandanna. "Come on, Ramon. We're taking you out for a nice moonlight ride. You're gonna love it."

"What?" Ramon licked his lips and glanced around nervously as the men closed in on him. "Come on, cowboys," he protested, his voice rising to an incongruous note of pleading. "You said you wouldn't hurt me. You said all you wanted was the girl, and you got her, so let me go, okay?''

"We aim to let you go," J.T. said amiably. "We just have our own ideas about how we're fixin' to do it, that's all. Come on, fellers," he added, gesturing to the silent group of masked men. They formed a circle around Ramon, escorting him down the highway and onto a graveled side road.

Two of them separated from the others and hurried to move the parked vehicles off the road and into the ditch. At last the sound of engines died away and all the men vanished into a field beyond the highway, leaving Lisa alone with Tony on the moon-washed road.

She crouched on her knees in the dusty gravel, her shoulders heaving.

"Go with them," she choked out, unable to look at him. "I'll be all right. Please go away."

"Come on, Lisa," he said quietly, reaching to help her to her feet. He pulled down his bandanna and hovered over her, then brushed at her dusty knees. He eyed her bruised bare foot and a long rip in her shirt with concern.

She hugged her arms and shivered in the cold, wanting him gone so she could be alone with her shame and torment. To have Ramon say those words in front of everybody, say them to Tony's face, so there could never be any doubt about who she was or what she'd done....

Lisa shuddered violently and gave a little strangled moan of anguish.

"What's the matter?" Tony put his arm around her and held her close, trying to warm her with his body.

"It's just..." Lisa stiffened in his arms. She didn't want to let herself yield to his strength and warmth. He wasn't meant for her, and both of them knew it. She didn't deserve a man like Tony.

"What?" he urged, his face hard and taut with worry. "What's the matter, Lisa? You're safe now. He won't ever bother you again."

She shook her head, unable to speak. She wanted to push him away, force him to leave her alone so she could try to pick up the scattered pieces of herself and decide where to go and what to do next. But she couldn't find the words, and she was still trembling like a chilled kitten, barely able to control the chattering of her teeth.

Suddenly, a light flared above the pasture next to the road, rising and spilling across the trees as an engine throbbed powerfully overhead. Lisa looked up, startled and frightened by the flashing lights that filled the sky. She bit her lip nervously and glanced at Tony. "What's happening now?" she asked in a small voice. "What are they going to do with him?"

Tony's expression was grim and haggard in the flickering light. "They're taking him for a ride," he told her curtly.

"In a plane? Where are they taking him?"

"It's a chopper, not a plane. Warren Trent's got a commercial helicopter license. A few of the guys are with him, and they're taking our friend Ramon down to Brewster County. I reckon they should be getting there around sunrise."

"Brewster County?" Lisa echoed blankly, staring at him. "But that's..."

"Mountain and desert," Tony said with a satisfied smile. "The most godforsaken place you'll ever see. Not a living thing down there but snakes and buzzards and polecats for a hundred miles in every direction. Old Ramon should feel right at home."

Lisa's mind was moving sluggishly. She was struggling to comprehend what he was saying.

Tony put his arms around her and drew her close to him again. Lisa still wanted to resist, but her strength was fading as the shocking terror of the night's events began to ebb away, leaving her empty and weak.

"See, Lisa," Tony murmured against her hair, "we thought about this whole thing a long time, planned it out real carefully. We had to figure out what to do with this guy when we caught him. I wanted to kill him, but Wayne said he couldn't let us do that. J.T. figured that if a man's spent his life treating women like cattle, we should give him a taste of his own medicine, slap a branding iron on him and leave him tied up in the cactus somewhere."

Lisa stared at the young man, her eyes wide with astonishment. "J.T. said that?"

Tony nodded. "Among other things. None of us felt real crazy about this guy, sweetheart. But Vern Trent had the best idea. Vern's kind of a thinker," Tony added with a quick grin. "He's a neat guy, that ol' Vern."

Lisa was silent, enumerating how many of these men might know of her private shame.

"Vern said that since this creep has stolen so many girls and dropped them in a wasteland, left them to die among the varmints, we should do the same thing to him. We decided to get Warren to fly him down to Brewster County and drop him off in the ruggedest, most isolated canyon he could find. We're nicer than Ramon ever was, though. We're giving him a full canteen of water and letting him keep his shoes."

Lisa's head began to spin when she heard Tony saying these incredible things so matter-of-factly. "What . . . what will happen to him?"

Tony shrugged. "Who cares? Chances are, a few years from now some hikers will stumble onto a few bleached bones in a canyon somewhere, scattered by the coyotes, and wonder what they are. Or it could be he'll manage to stay alive, fight his way out of there after a few weeks and get somebody to help him. That's his business. The main thing is, he won't ever bother you again, Lisa. Not ever. He's gone."

The import of Tony's words slowly began to blossom in her mind. She became dizzy and light-headed with amazement. "Never again?" Lisa whispered, staring at Tony. "He's gone?"

"He damn sure is. You can bet he won't be back in these parts again. The sheriff will send his car out to Vegas with a note saying it was abandoned here, but we don't reckon he'll be picking it up anytime soon. He's gone."

Gone. Ramon was gone.

The words reverberated in Lisa's mind, almost too wonderful to grasp. She stood watching as Tony got into the sports car and drove it down into the ditch. He retrieved the handgun from the weeds and put it back into the compartment, rearranged everything neatly inside the car, then put the keys under the floor mat and locked the doors.

Lisa noted that he'd pulled on a pair of plastic surgical gloves before he handled anything. His actions confirmed what he'd told her about how carefully and thoroughly this group of local vigilantes had thought out their whole midnight operation.

"Tony..." she murmured awkwardly when he strode back up the ditch. "How did everybody know that he was...coming for me tonight? I didn't tell anybody, because he said he'd...he'd hurt Jennifer if I..."

Her voice trailed off as she recalled that dreadful threat.

"I know. Jimmy Slattery was hiding under the veranda when Ramon came to talk to you. The kid heard the whole thing and told J.T., and then J.T went looking for some help."

"So these other men—they all know about me?"

Tony looked down at her anxiously while she stared at the pavement, unable to meet his eyes. "I reckon they have a fair idea what happened," he said quietly. "J.T. told us what he did to you."

"They know that I was..." Her voice trembled and broke. She stopped speaking and bit her lip, trying to hold back tears of shame.

"They know that you're a nice, sweet girl who's real good with kids, and that everybody loves you," Tony said gently. "They know that you ran into this creep and he hurt you, but you got away. That's all, Lisa."

"But," she faltered, her cheeks hot and wet with the tears she couldn't hold back any longer, "now everybody's going to know. They won't let me look after the baby anymore, when they..."

Tony reached out to draw her close again, but this time she was able to resist. She shook his hands away and stood alone in her sorrow while the cold moonlight washed over them, and the throb of the helicopter engine died away into stillness.

"Lisa, none of these guys will ever talk about what happened here tonight. They promised they wouldn't, not even to their wives. And believe me, these are all men who take a promise seriously. We wouldn't have asked them to help otherwise."

Her face registered her surprise when she finally raised her eyes to his.

"As far as this community is concerned," Tony went on calmly, "you're a sweet kid who graduated high school and came here from New Mexico to get a job. That's the truth, Lisa, and it's the whole truth. That creep is gone, and so is that part of your life. Nobody will ever mention it again.''

Lisa looked briefly away, her mind whirling with the wonder of the night's events.

Could it possibly be true? Was her nightmare really over?

"Will I be able to stay at the ranch?" she asked Tony, her voice trembling. "Will I be able to look after Jennifer, just like before?"

"Damn right you will. And you won't have to be afraid to go to town anymore, or out on a . . .''

Tony stopped abruptly, leaving the words hanging on the night air. He turned aside and took her elbow in his hand. "Come on, Lisa," he murmured. "I'll take you home now. You're getting chilled."

She nodded and fell into step beside him, absorbing what he'd said.

Part of her rejoiced at the marvelous word *home,* at the thought of sweet little Jennifer, and Lettie Mae's smiling dark face, of Cynthia and J.T. and all the others who'd grown so dear to her, and whom she'd fully expected never to see again.

But part of her whimpered with pain at Tony's unfinished sentence. He'd been about to say that she could go out on a date without fear, but he'd caught himself in time.

Because, of course, Tony would never want to take her anywhere now. Not now that he knew about her, and knew that all his friends were aware of her history as well. In his kindness, he'd try to be gentle about it and let her down easily, but he'd make it clear that nothing like that could ever exist between them. Lisa climbed into his truck and huddled by the window, concentrating on the shadowy silhouettes of the trees.

"Are you all right?" Tony asked, glancing over at her as he pulled his truck out onto the highway, and headed for the ranch.

"I'm fine," Lisa said tonelessly, still not looking at him. "I just can't believe it's all over."

"You should have told me," Tony muttered, staring ahead down the road. "You shouldn't have tried to get through something like this all on your own. I'd have helped you, Lisa, if I'd known."

"I was so ashamed," she whispered. "I didn't want anybody to know. And I was afraid that if I told anybody, he'd hurt them, too. I couldn't bear to think about him hurting anybody I . . . I cared about."

She fell silent and peered ahead into the darkness, watching for the familiar safety of the ranch gates. As they came glimmering into view, Lisa acknowledged clearly for the first time that she didn't need their protection anymore. Ramon's evil threat was gone forever. She could live her life the same as any normal person, could come and go entirely without fear.

She sighed at the familiarity of the high stone gates as Tony's truck passed through, then at the sweeping drive into the ranch and the stately, pillared facade of the big house. There was a world of warmth and happiness in there, of laughter and acceptance and sweet family life.

Lisa held herself grimly under control and swallowed hard, trying not to give way to emotion now that the danger was past. She wanted to escape from Tony's disturbing presence, to be alone in her little room so she could think.

But Tony parked away from the house, down near the stables in the shadow of the barn. He rested an arm along the seat and turned to look at her, but didn't touch her.

"Tony..." Lisa ventured nervously, alarmed by the sudden silence and by his nearness inside the cab of the truck. "I really should be getting inside," she added, her cheeks flaming with embarrassment. "Jennifer might...she might wake up and need me."

"She can get along without you for a few minutes," Tony said calmly. "Besides, her mama can look after her if she cries."

Lisa was about to tell him that she wasn't sure Cynthia was home, but she caught herself in time. The comings and goings of her employers were not her business to chatter about. Besides, Tony didn't look as if he would be interested. He was studying her with a fixed, intent look, his eyes gleaming softly in the fading light.

She huddled beside him, afraid to look at him again, her whole body on fire with a love that was too terrible to endure. She remembered how she'd felt when Ramon was taking her away, how sorry she'd been because she hadn't ever had the chance to let Tony know she loved him. And now she never would.

With bruising clarity, Lisa pictured herself sprawled on her knees in the gravel before that silent group of men, and heard again Ramon's mocking voice declaring that she was almost used up, and men liked their women fresh.... She shuddered deeply, then drew herself together with an effort when Tony said something to her.

"What?" she asked, turning wide-open eyes to him. "What did you say, Tony?"

"I said that I love you," he repeated quietly. "I love you more than anything, Lisa. I just want you to know that."

"You...you love me?" She continued to gape at him in blank amazement, feeling clumsy and stupid. Of all the things he might have said, this was the last she'd ever expected to hear.

Tony gave her a shy, boyish grin. "Now," he suggested, "you're supposed to say that you love me, too. That's what happens in the movies."

"But, Tony...how can you love me?" she asked him in despair. "You know all about me. You know what I did. You can't possibly *love* me, after all that!"

"Obviously you don't know much about love, sweetheart," he told her with another quick grin. "I guess I'll have to teach you, won't I?"

Lisa shook her head, wondering how he could joke about something so momentous. But when he leaned across the seat and drew her into his arms, she realized that he wasn't joking at all. He was trembling with the strength of his emotion.

"Lisa, you don't stop loving people because of what happens to them," he whispered against her hair. "That's what they mean when they say 'for better or for worse.' If bad things happened to you that weren't your fault, why should they change the way I feel about you? You're still the same person, and you're the only girl I've ever wanted."

She nestled in his arms, lost in wonder at this unexpected turn of events. But while her mind churned, the rest of her was already operating on instinct. Her body cuddled shyly against him, glorying in his warmth and sweetness, delighting in his strength and scent and the wonderful, manly feeling of him.

"So what do you think?" he whispered, his voice husky in her ear. "Do you think you could love me back, or am I going to have to go around with a broken heart for the rest of my life?"

Lisa smiled against his shirtfront. She blinked back tears of happiness and nerved herself to glance up at him. "It would be terrible for you to go around with a broken heart," she countered solemnly.

"Why?"

"Because you have such a nice smile, Tony. Such a beautiful smile."

He looked down at her in surprise, then realized that she was teasing. "Yeah?" he asked with a delighted grin. "You like my smile?"

"Yes, I do."

"Do you like anything else about me?" Tony asked, pulling her close and bending to kiss her mouth. "Anything at all?"

Lisa smiled, her heart overflowing with joy. "Oh, maybe a couple of things," she told him primly.

"Tell me," he demanded, kissing her again until she found it hard to concentrate on the conversation, or her soaring happiness, or anything in the world but loving him.

"Hmm?" she said softly .

"Tell me what else you like about me."

Laughing, misty-eyed with joy, Lisa lifted her head and began to whisper in his ear as a lonely owl called softly from the trees near the river.

CHAPTER TWELVE

J.T. STOOD in the field with his foreman, Ken Slattery, and his son Tyler, watching the helicopter lift and circle in the night sky. The Trent brothers were both up there, along with the sheriff, taking Ramon off for his meeting with destiny.

J.T. nodded to himself in quiet satisfaction, confident that they were doing the right thing.

He'd been deadly serious earlier in the day when he'd suggested slapping a branding iron on the man and leaving him tied up in the blazing sunshine among the cactus and the army ants. Ramon certainly didn't deserve gentler treatment, not after the cruelty he'd inflicted on so many others.

But J.T. had to admit that he liked the symbolism of what they were doing now, setting the man down in a wasteland to battle the elements and struggle for survival. There was a kind of balance and symmetry to the whole thing that pleased his orderly mind.

In fact, he thought, watching the helicopter lights wink away until they were lost among the stars, the entire night's adventure had been thoroughly exhilarating. After J.T.'s recent nagging worries and small miseries, this had been a welcome diversion, a chance to feel like a young, strong man again.

He only wished Bubba could have been with them. It had been a long time since he and Bubba had enjoyed an escapade together, and his old friend would have loved being part of this one. But, with considerable regret, the group had voted not to include Bubba Gibson among the vigilantes.

For Lisa's sake, and for the sheriff's as well, it was essential that no word of this midnight kidnapping ever leak out into the busy gossip mills of Crystal Creek. And despite how much they all loved Bubba, they were sadly aware that he couldn't always be counted on for total discretion, so they'd chosen not to involve him.

"Heading home soon, Daddy?" Tyler asked at his elbow, interrupting J.T.'s thoughts.

J.T. turned to his son and smiled. "I reckon it's time. I sure wish I could have gone with them, don't you?"

Tyler nodded grimly. "I'd like to see that snake dropped into a canyon in his shiny, tasseled loafers. It's a real shame to miss it."

They turned away and walked together in the direction of their vehicles, with Ken Slattery falling into step beside them. The three men were silent, lost in their own thoughts. The bandannas now hung loosely around their necks, and their rifles rested easy in their hands.

They stepped out through a gap in the trees and onto the shoulder of the road, where the row of trucks waited silently in the clear night. J.T. noted with relief that Tony had already parked Ramon's sports car in the ditch and taken Lisa away. "Poor kid," he said half-aloud, feeling a wrench of sympathy when he remembered her kneeling in front of them in the gravel. "Oh, God, the poor kid."

"Will you ever tell Cynthia about any of this?" Tyler asked, after Ken had strolled away to get into his truck.

J.T. looked at his son. "I doubt it," he said. "I don't want Cynthia to know what we did to him. That's too much responsibility to dump on someone who's not involved."

"But will you tell her anything about Lisa?"

J.T. shook his head. "I don't think so. Lisa can tell her own story if she chooses to. It doesn't make any difference to us now. It's all over."

Tyler smiled privately and clapped his hand on his father's shoulder. "I love you, Daddy," he said quietly.

Then, as if to protect both of them from the awkwardness of their emotion, Tyler turned abruptly and strode off toward another of the pickup trucks. He climbed inside and waved casually at J.T.

"See you in the morning," he called, backing the vehicle around and heading toward the ranch.

J.T. waved at him and watched his taillights fade in the distance, deeply moved by his son's rare display of feeling.

The vanishing taillights reminded him of the helicopter, carrying both friends and enemy into the rugged wilderness. Alone in the ditch, J.T. approached his truck, but instead of climbing in, he leaned against the door, pondering men like Ramon and the pain they caused to women by their greed and cruelty. His mind drifted onto the subject of women in general, and the suffering they endured at the hands of men. It wasn't just the Ramons of this world, J.T. realized with bleak compassion, who caused anguish and suffering for women.

Standing there in the summer night with his rifle in his hands, J. T. McKinney was struck by one of those rare, stunning moments of total clarity, of absolute empathy. He finally understood, from the depths of his soul, what it really meant to be a woman.

All his life, he'd taken his power and freedom for granted. He'd moved through his days with an easy confidence that he was able to go where he pleased, do what he wanted and answer only to himself and the people he chose to involve in his decisions.

But what if he'd been born a woman? What must it be like, having to put your life in the hands of someone else, trusting someone with your happiness and security, being expected by society to subject yourself and your future to the will of another person?

J.T. frowned, hardly able to contemplate that kind of limitation on his freedom.

Maybe, he thought ruefully, there was something to all this equality stuff that women kept demanding, and that men were so bitter about. For the first time, J.T. seriously entertained the possibility that women might have a legitimate complaint after all, considering how they'd been treated all through the years.

There were, of course, millions of wretched, exploited girls like Lisa, who suffered untold cruelties at the hands of men, simply because men were more powerful and far more ruthless. And it was so unfair. After all, women didn't do things like that to men. You never heard of a man being held captive and forced to endure humiliation from a group of women.

Not that women didn't have their own ways of being cruel, J.T. told himself, trying to be fair. But they didn't use power as a weapon. Maybe, he realized with another painful moment of clarity, because they didn't have a lot of power. The prevailing social climate had, after all, been more or less designed to keep women from having power.

J.T.'s sympathies had been triggered by the plight of an innocent young woman like Lisa, and the horrors she'd suffered at the hands of men. But even a woman like Cynthia, who was more sophisticated, better educated and probably smarter than her husband, lacked the essential power to control her life as she chose. She lived in his house and had to adjust herself to his choices. She bore and nurtured his child, and was expected to rearrange her priorities to accommodate that responsibility.

Apart from being more fulfilling and certainly more comfortable, J.T.'s life hadn't changed in any significant way when he got married. His wife's very identity, on the other hand, had ceased to exist. She had been Cynthia Page, a Boston investment banker, and had been forced to change, literally overnight, into Cynthia McKinney, a Texas housewife.

J.T. heard her despairing cry echoing in his mind, her claim that she didn't *exist* anymore, and was embarrassed to recall his own impatient reaction. He thought of his friend, Don Holden, who had been a sympathizer with the feminist movement long before such a choice was fashionable. And he recollected Don's quiet voice as he told J.T. that maybe he just wasn't listening.

His friend had been right, J.T. told himself in agony. His wife had tried so hard to tell him how she was feeling, what her life was like, and he hadn't paid any attention. He'd followed the classic male pattern of hoping that she'd "snap out of it," meaning she'd let go of her own needs and identity and get on with the important business of blending her existence into his.

He felt a hot flood of shame when he analyzed his behavior in his marriage, and what he'd done to the strong, intelligent woman he'd chosen as his partner.

The very qualities that had attracted him the most were the ones J.T. had immediately set out to destroy, in his relentless struggle to make Cynthia conform to his own stereotyped image of what a wife should be. In his own way, he'd been as cruel and exploitive as Ramon up there in the helicopter.

"I'm sorry, sweetheart," he whispered to the warm night air, picturing Cynthia's beautiful face, her thoughtful, serious smile. "I'm so sorry...."

And he was.

Now that his understanding had been fully illuminated, J.T. could no longer escape from the reality of his situation. There would be no slipping back into the old ways, not anymore. He felt deeply ashamed, full of remorse for his behavior, and he wanted to go to her right now, this instant, and beg her forgiveness. He wanted to sit down with her and figure out how they could make it right, how they could build a life together that would be as rich and challenging and satisfying for her as it was for him.

But part of him was terribly afraid that it was too late.

Now that he could comprehend how he'd behaved, J.T. also had a clear, grim image of how his wife must feel about him. Seen in this new light, it amazed him how patiently women bore the limitations that men placed on them, how long they suffered and endured in the hope that their men would see the light and things would somehow improve.

But a lifetime of experience had taught him that when a woman finally snapped, she didn't tend to get over it easily.

J.T. admitted to himself that he'd been aware of the exact moment his wife reached that point. It had been the night he got back from California and she'd tried to talk to him about financing the winery. He recalled their conversation, her shy, eager suggestion and his panicky concern that she might be pushing her way back into the business affairs of the ranch again.

His mind had returned a number of times to that conversation in recent days, knowing that it held some kind of dark significance for Cynthia. But he'd always excused his own reaction, justified himself by claiming that there were things a man just shouldn't be expected to put up with....

Again, he was flooded by remorse and humiliation. He groaned aloud and turned to rest his face briefly against the cool side window of the truck. "God, what an ass I am," he whispered. "What a sad, sorry bastard."

For a long time he stood in the fading moonlight, his rifle hanging limp in his hands, and gazed in bleak silence at the graceful wisps of silvered cloud swirling across the blackness of the sky. Finally, he put the rifle on the rack in the cab, climbed inside and headed for the ranch.

J.T. was in the grip of a cold fear, unable to think any longer about what had happened to him or rehearse the words he was going to say to his wife. All he could see was her face in the starry darkness, and the way she used to smile in the days when she loved and trusted him.

If he lost this woman, his life was over. Nothing would ever mean anything to him again, not after her sweet love had filled the lonely corners of his life and spread sunshine everywhere.

"Don't leave me, girl," he muttered to the night wind that whipped through the open window and flowed across his face. "Don't leave me yet. Please give me one more chance."

And yet he feared she'd already gone, that it was too late to save their marriage. When he ran up the stairs to their room and saw the empty bed, neatly made up and silent in the cold predawn light, his only reaction was sorrow.

He stood in the doorway, staring at the bed for a long time, then moved slowly across the room and sank into a chair by the window, burying his face in his hands.

WHILE RAMON WAS STANDING in terror on the edge of the deserted highway, watching the circle of masked men who held their rifles trained on him, Cynthia was battling another kind of fear.

By that time, she and Jimmy were already well embarked on their journey up the hillside, and it wasn't at all the jaunty, childlike adventure she'd been picturing. For one thing, the trail was brutally steep, and it took all her strength just to keep climbing upward, following Jimmy's sturdy form as he toiled ahead of her.

She really needed to get more exercise. So much of her time had been taken up with the baby, and she hadn't yet recovered the strength and suppleness she'd lost during pregnancy. Cynthia recalled her friend Sally, who always maintained that pregnancy was a dreadful insult to a woman's body, and that if men had to bear children, the human race would have died out in two generations.

The memory of Sally's vivid face cheered Cynthia for a moment, but then her foot slipped and twisted on a loose rock and her mood darkened again.

She couldn't seem to banish from her mind the image of old Hank and his dire warnings about this journey, and the "terrible grief" that would come to her if she dared to climb the hill.

Maybe Hank had gotten it wrong. Perhaps the grief he'd seen in her future was nothing more than the pain she was already enduring as she made her plans to leave her home and husband, and go back out into the world on her own. That was certainly grief enough, Cynthia thought miserably, peering upward at the dim shape of her young companion. After what she'd been through these past weeks, whatever waited on that hilltop would be nothing more than a diversion.

Monsters, laser guns, sinister aliens . . . bring them on, she thought with sudden recklessness. What was all that compared with the unhappiness she was about to wade through when morning came?

In fact, their misery was likely to start as soon as she got home. J.T. was going to be back before she was, and neither of them would be able to ignore that empty bed. He'd be furious, and demand to know where she'd been, and she was going to tell him firmly that her activities were no longer any of his business, that she was leaving the next day and taking Jennifer with her.

And then the fight would start.

Cynthia lifted her head briefly to scan the remote, craggy hilltop. Maybe there really *were* aliens up there, she thought hopefully. Maybe they'd kidnap her and Jimmy and fly them off through a black hole into some other world, some distant place that was unimaginably beautiful, and none of these other dreadful things would ever happen. Maybe...

Panting and stumbling, haunted by thoughts of the unhappiness to come and torn by conflicting emotions, Cynthia continued to struggle up the rock-strewn trail in the chilly moonlight.

Jimmy turned and shone his small flashlight back down the trail, looking at her anxiously as he waited for her to catch up. "Are you okay?" he whispered, sounding manly and competent. "This is pretty steep right here. It's prob'ly the hardest part."

"I certainly hope so," Cynthia panted. "I'm just about worn-out, Jimmy."

"Do you want to wait here and have a rest while I go up to the top?"

Wistfully, Cynthia considered this suggestion, then looked down at Jimmy's pale, freckled face, gleaming faintly in the moonlight. "I thought you wanted me to come along as a witness."

He hesitated and looked nervous. "Maybe there's nothing up there anymore," he suggested awkwardly. "Maybe they've already left."

Cynthia regarded the boy thoughtfully, wondering if he'd deliberately invented the whole story about the silvery, misshapen beings on the hill, and was now hoping to cover his tracks.

While she hung back, a light began to shine from the hilltop. It spilled down over the tumbled rocks and scrub mesquite in an eerie flood of silver, laced with glimmers of red and green and purple that shone ghostly and iridescent in the blackness of the night.

Jimmy began to shiver violently, but turned to look up at the hilltop. Cynthia moved closer and put her arms around him.

"It's okay, Jimmy," she whispered to the trembling child, putting her own fear aside in her urgent need to protect him. "Let's just go back down. We don't need to climb up there."

He pulled away and his eyes narrowed. Cynthia could see a strange mixture of emotions at play on his face...annoyance with her pampering, panicky terror of the unknown beings he'd seen on the hilltop and a stubborn determination to carry on with the mission.

"You don't need to come if you're scared," he said firmly, turning back to the trail. "But I'm going up there."

"Oh, Jimmy..." Cynthia lingered on the path, torn by fear and indecision. She looked at the lights up among the limestone, now flaring and glimmering away into the starlight, and saw Hank's leathery old face.

"Turrible grief," he warned her softly in the night. *"Stay with your husband. Don't go up there...."*

Jimmy was moving away from her, rapidly vanishing into the darkness as he toiled upward. At last, with a little moan of terror and despair, Cynthia drew herself together and began to climb after him.

She was so tense that every sound, every movement was exaggerated. She could hear her own breathing, loud and sibilant in the starry blackness, almost drowned out by the noisy pounding of her heart and the scrapes and rustles of their feet on the loose rock. The night wind felt clammy against her hot face, leaving her chilled and a little sick. Even her sense of smell was more acute, so that she was sharply conscious of the nighttime fragrance of crushed sagebrush, of damp leaves and soil and a strange, indefinable scent, faintly metallic, unlike anything she'd ever smelled before.

Cynthia forced her emotions under rigid control, struggling to suspend her thoughts and keep herself from giving way to panic, largely because she felt such a terrible responsibility for this young child who was with her. She'd used him, Cynthia realized with shame. She'd exploited his credulous little boy's sense of adventure, merely to provide herself with a diversion from her own adult unhappiness. Her behavior toward Jimmy Slattery had been irresponsible, completely unforgivable. And now, because of her selfishness, both of them were climbing toward something too dreadful to imagine.

Cynthia wanted to grab Jimmy by the shoulders, force him to come with her away from that menacing light, flee back down the hill to safety. But they were so close to the top now that she couldn't risk an argument, or make any kind of noise for fear that their presence would be detected.

She watched Jimmy hoist himself over the lip of the limestone outcropping and roll quickly away out of sight. Biting her lip, trying not to whimper with fear, Cynthia did the same, and felt her body coming to rest next to his.

When she opened her eyes she realized that they were huddled behind a huge boulder near the edge of the summit. Beyond them was a flat, rocky expanse. In the distance she could see the outer walls of the limestone caverns Jimmy had spoken of, filled with a ghostly, flickering light.

Jimmy got up on all fours and crept to the edge of the boulder. Cynthia did the same, peering out over the top of the child's head, and almost fainted with fright.

The caverns were alive with shadowy figures, strangely shaped beings that glistened and flared silver as they moved slowly in front of the light. "Oh, God," Cynthia whispered, stuffing her hand into her mouth to keep from screaming. "Jimmy, come back here! Don't look at them!"

Jimmy scrabbled away from the edge of the boulder and flung himself into her arms, sobbing in terror.

"They're just the same!" he whimpered against her jacket front. "Just like what I saw. They're going to kill us!"

Cynthia soothed him automatically, holding him and stroking his soft brush of hair. She tried to think, to come up with a plan that would rescue both of them from the danger she'd foolishly placed them in, but her mind wouldn't work. Like Jimmy, she had a fatalistic sense that this was the end of everything. Old Hank had been right again. She should never have come up here, and now there would be no escape for her or Jimmy.

Lost in sorrow, she held the child and rocked him in the moonlight, whispering soft words of comfort as she waited for the inevitable to happen. She had a deep, terrible certainty that those alien beings already knew of their presence, that it was only a matter of time until she and Jimmy were captured.

She was hardly surprised when a harsh light beamed onto them, pinning them like frightened insects against the looming boulder. Jimmy screamed aloud and huddled frantically against her. Cynthia continued to hold him, staring defiantly up into the light that dazzled and burned her eyes.

"Turn that thing off!" she shouted, her fear giving her a reckless courage. "Can't you see that this child is terrified?"

To her amazement, the light flickered and dimmed. She crouched over Jimmy's sobbing body, holding him tightly, waiting for whatever came next. Pain, decompression, floating...possibly just darkness and the end of everything. Cynthia wondered, in a strangely detached fashion, what would happen, and how it would feel.

But there was only silence, then a sinister scuffling noise. When Cynthia finally dared to look up, she could see that the creature holding the light had been joined by a number of others. Her eyes were still blurred from the brilliance of the light, but the aliens seemed to be much as Jimmy had described them. They were silvery and huge, with grossly misshapen heads and dangling appendages. Their massive domed heads turned slowly and they appeared to communicate with one another although Cynthia couldn't detect any audible sounds.

At last the front one stepped closer, shone the light at an oblique angle along the ground and bent in a stiff, awkward fashion to bring its huge round head nearer to the cowering woman and child.

"Could Ah ask yo' name and yo' bidness up heah, ma'am?" the creature asked, in a Southern drawl so warm and broad that Cynthia forgot herself and gaped upward in astonishment.

Gradually she realized that the silvery torso and domed head were not a body but a form of suit, and that the being inside had a distinctly human appearance. The dome, in fact, was a metallic globe fronted with glass, and the face behind the glass was young and cheerful, blue-eyed and covered with freckles as clearly defined as Jimmy's.

"What...who are you?" she whispered, licking her lips and studying that face behind the glistening visor.

"Sergeant Walter Cheevers, United States Air Force, ma'am."

"Air Force?" Cynthia echoed blankly.

She felt Jimmy pull himself out of her arms and sit upright, brushing a hand across his tearstained face. Cynthia gripped his arm and began to collect herself. "What are you doing here?" she asked.

"I believe I just asked you the same thing, ma'am."

He was speaking to her through an opening in his face shield, Cynthia realized. The others, grouped in the shadows beyond them, must be conferring by means of some kind of intercom system built into their helmets, because Cynthia could sense their conversation, although the night remained eerily silent.

"I'm...I'm Cynthia McKinney," she faltered, feeling as young and helpless as Jimmy. She struggled to her feet, slapped at her dusty jeans and faced the young sergeant with a brave attempt at dignity. "My husband owns this property. Jimmy and I...we came up here because we were...worried about the lights. We wondered what they were."

"Mr. McKinney was notified of this operation before it began," the sergeant told her calmly.

Cynthia's head began to whirl. "He was?"

"Yes, ma'am. An unidentified object tracked through our radar screens and disappeared up here on August third. We sent a team down to the base at Killeen to examine the site and determine what the object was, and notified Mr. McKinney before we landed on the property. He was in California at the time."

"He...he never said anything about it to me. Not a word."

"We asked him not to, ma'am. We didn't want anybody getting all worked up and calling in the media. There's always lots of hysteria around UFO's," the young man added, kindly refraining from looking directly at Cynthia's dusty clothes and the tears-tained face of the child at her side.

"I see," Cynthia said, feeling a growing annoyance with J.T., who'd known about this all along. She looked down at the rocky ground, wishing herself a thousand miles away from this silent group of men in their metallic space garb.

"What was it?" Jimmy asked suddenly. "Why are you guys dressed like that?"

The young man lifted his face shield to smile down at the boy, a gesture that was incongruously human and gentle in this eerie moonlit stillness. "Well, son, we finally figured out that it was just a stray bit of a Russian communications satellite that broke up in orbit and fell down here. But we couldn't take any chances of contamination until we knew for sure."

"Why did it take so long?"

"We didn't find it until tonight. It was wedged down in some rocks over there on the far side of the hill. And we had a few nights of heavy rain, too. That held us up some."

Jimmy eyed the young sergeant, looking defiant and skeptical. Now that the danger was past, Jimmy's normal buoyancy had fully returned. In fact, he appeared to be disappointed that there was such a simple explanation for the mystery on the hilltop.

"How did you get up here?" he asked suspiciously. "You must have come in a helicopter or something. How did you land so quiet?"

The man bent toward Jimmy, stiff and awkward in his bulky protective clothing. "Son," he whispered solemnly, "don't you tell anybody, but the U.S. Air Force has helicopters so quiet they could land on your bed and you wouldn't wake up."

Jimmy gazed back at him earnestly. Cynthia sensed with growing alarm that the boy was about to ask if he could look at the helicopter.

"Come on, Jimmy," she muttered, grasping the child by the hand. "Let's leave Sergeant Cheevers and his men to get on with their job, shall we?"

"Sorry to have troubled you, ma'am," the freckled young man said courteously, dropping his face shield back into place. "We'll be leaving soon."

Cynthia nodded and turned away, dragging Jimmy along with her while the silent group of military personnel watched them leave.

Jimmy lagged behind her, stiff with reluctance. "Do we have to go right away?" he pleaded. "Can't we just stay and watch while they—"

"No!" she snapped. "Jimmy, we're lucky they weren't more upset with us. We're not supposed to be here at all. Come on, let's hurry."

Miserably conscious of the quiet circle of glass-fronted faces, Cynthia scrambled over the edge of the cliff and started off at a run down the steep trail. Jimmy pounded along behind her, still muttering. At first, her only emotion was relief that their lives weren't in danger after all and Earth wasn't threatened by some unknown terror.

But gradually she felt a resurgence of anger at J.T., who had known about this since the beginning and, as usual, hadn't bothered to share the information with her.

As she panted down the trail, heading for the darkened sprawl of the ranch buildings, her anger gave way to misery. Now she was experiencing, in full force, the "terrible grief" that Hank had spoken of.

Cynthia was stunned by the depths of her sorrow. She felt as if her heart had been physically wrenched from her and tortured. The whole night's adventure took on a kind of dark symbolism, representing the degree to which she was excluded from J.T.'s confidence and all his decision-making processes, and how wasteful and unfair it all was.

Their lives could have been so different if he had only chosen to include his wife. But he wasn't able to, and so their marriage was impossible. It was over, beyond hope of repair.

Not until Cynthia thought these words in her mind did she realize that up to now she'd still been clinging to the hope of some kind of miracle, something to avert disaster at the last minute.

But it wasn't going to happen. If this dreadful night had taught her anything at all, it was the fact that miracles didn't happen no matter how much you longed for them. Not in the real world.

Tears burned at her throat, choking her so that she was unable to continue. "Jimmy," she faltered, struggling to keep her voice even, "you go on home, all right? We're almost back, anyhow. I'll just rest a bit and then go down to the ranch house by myself."

He glanced up at her, but the moon had set by now and his face was an indistinct blur in the darkness. "Are you okay?" he asked.

"I'm fine," Cynthia said, longing for the child to be gone so she could give way to the tears that were threatening to overwhelm her. "I'm just a little winded. I'll see you in the morning."

He nodded and moved off reluctantly, swallowed up almost at once in the intense darkness that came just before the summer dawn. Cynthia waited until the sound of his feet died away on the trail.

Then she sank into the soft dirt and leaves on the hillside, buried her head on her folded arms and began to cry.

CHAPTER THIRTEEN

CYNTHIA HAD no idea how long she huddled there, mourning the end of her marriage. The sky was beginning to lighten in the east when she finally sat up, rubbed her swollen eyes and gazed bleakly at the clouds of mist that swirled around the base of the cliff.

As she was preparing to heave herself to her feet, she heard rapid footsteps approaching up the trail and saw a tall form come looming out of the dusky haze. Cynthia peered at the man, then stiffened in alarm.

It was J.T.

She sank back into the soft carpet of grass and hugged her knees moodily, waiting for him to draw near. They might as well get this over with now, she thought. No point in putting it off any longer.

But when he reached her and knelt in front of her, there was no anger in his face, just concern and sorrow.

"Are you all right, darling?" he whispered, putting his arms around her. "Jimmy came and told me where you were and what you've been doing. He thought you might be hurt or something. I was so afraid—"

"I'm fine," Cynthia said curtly, pushing him away and averting her face so he couldn't see her reddened eyes. "I just feel like an idiot, that's all."

"Why? Cynthia..."

"Why? Because there were military personnel on the ranch and you never bothered to tell me a word about it, that's why!" she told him furiously. "Because you let me climb up there like a...like a..."

"I'm sorry," J.T. said quietly. "It was stupid of me not to tell you. I was wrong."

"You certainly were. You..." Cynthia paused in midsentence, struck by his words and his tone. In all their time together, she had never known J. T. McKinney to admit that he'd been wrong, or to sound so humble and sincere in an apology.

"I was raised to believe that there were things the womenfolk shouldn't be told," J.T. went on, regarding her intently as he knelt in front of her. "It's insulting to a woman like you, Cynthia. I'm sorry."

She raised her eyes to his, forgetting the ravages her tears had made, confused by his odd behavior. He gave her a sad little smile and cocked an eyebrow at her.

"I thought you were off with a boyfriend," he told her. "You can't imagine how relieved I was to find out you were tracking UFO's with a ten-year-old kid. I love you so much, sweetheart."

"Don't make fun of me!" she snapped, stung by his teasing look. "It's not a bit funny."

"No, it isn't," he agreed, his grin fading. "I'm sorry this had to happen. There's something else I should tell you," he added, moving over to sit beside her, but looking off at the swirl of pastel colors above the eastern horizon. "I wasn't going to tell you all this, but from now on I don't want to keep anything from you."

While Cynthia listened in shocked amazement, he told her all about Lisa and Ramon. Cynthia sensed that despite his new frankness, her husband was still holding something back, probably some details about his first encounter with the girl in Las Vegas. But she didn't care. Her concern was all for Lisa, for the anguish the girl had suffered and the danger she'd been in.

"And this . . . he's gone for sure?" she asked when J.T. finished talking. "He won't be back?"

"No. He likely won't survive. And if he does, he sure won't be coming back here."

Cynthia hugged her knees in silence, appalled by the story.

Gradually her horror faded, to be replaced by a growing wonder. J.T. had trusted her with these facts, details that could endanger all the men involved in the vigilante operation. Particularly the sheriff, Wayne Jackson, whose job and future were at stake. Her husband had placed all of them in her hands and was counting fully on her intelligence and discretion. She'd never known him to behave this way before.

"J.T.," she whispered with a painful wrench of sadness, "you've finally decided to treat me like a grown-up, and it's too late. If you'd started out this way, maybe we'd still have a marriage."

"Don't we have a marriage anymore, Cynthia?"

"No, we don't. I'm leaving tomorrow...today, I guess," Cynthia corrected herself, glancing at the lightening sky. "And I'm taking Jennifer. I can't live this way, J.T. I can't stand it any longer."

She held her breath, waiting for him to explode and shout at her. But he nodded thoughtfully and looked down at the ranch buildings, gradually emerging from the gray mists of dawn. "I don't blame you," he said quietly. "Nobody should have to live that way."

Cynthia stared at him with a growing sense of astonishment, a kind of dizzy unreality. Was this her husband, or some stranger wearing his face and body?

He smiled at her briefly, then looked off into the distance again. "After they took that guy away in the helicopter, and Tony came back here with Lisa, I started thinking what life is really like for women," J.T. told his wife. "I thought about men like that who abuse and exploit women, and how the way I've treated you hasn't been all that different. I didn't tie you up and torture you, but I sure did hurt your soul, didn't I?"

Cynthia stared at him, speechless.

"And it was wrong. A woman like you should be treasured for her abilities and allowed to contribute, not shoved in a box and told to behave. I'm so sorry, darling. I can understand you not loving me anymore, and not wanting to live with me, but I wonder if I could interest you in a business proposition.''

The conversation was growing more and more bizarre. Cynthia floundered like a swimmer out of her depth, without the slightest idea what to expect from him next. "A . . . a business proposition?''

J.T. nodded. "You don't have to live with me if you don't want to. We could make some kind of arrangement for you to live in town, or in Austin if you prefer. But I'd like to offer you a partnership in the winery. I think we should form a company and take you and Ruth in as full partners. I haven't talked it over with Ruth and Tyler yet, but I'm sure they'll agree.''

"What would be our roles in this partnership, the four of us?''

"Well, I'd provide the land and some of the business capital. Tyler would contribute the energy and the management skills. Ruth is the expert on wine making, and you'd handle the financial end. I think we'd be a dynamite team, don't you?''

Cynthia was gradually beginning to understand that he was completely serious. Something momentous had happened to her husband in the hours since she'd seen him last. He'd clearly experienced one of those shattering, life-changing flashes of illumination that make everything different from that moment on.

He looked sad but at peace with himself, as if he'd made his choices and was willing to live with them. There was no anger or tension in him, no insistence that things be done his way. He was giving her the power to call the shots, offering her a full partnership entirely on her terms, even if those terms excluded him from her life.

Cynthia's heart stirred and lifted. She held her breath, hardly daring to look at him, and then shook her head slowly.

"J.T. . . . what's happened to you?" she whispered at last. "I've never seen you like this."

"I've realized a few things, that's all," he repeated calmly. "And you know something else I realized tonight?"

Cynthia shook her head again, feeling dazed and numb.

"I realized that I need a holiday. I haven't been away from this place for a real holiday in years. Would you like to come with me?"

"J.T., I don't know if . . ."

"No pressure," he told her, looking as shy and awkward as a young boy on his first date. "I mean, you wouldn't have to share a room with me or anything. We could just get away sometime soon and have some fun together. We've always been good friends, Cynthia, even if I haven't been much of a husband."

"Where would we go?"

He shifted nervously on the grass and looked a little abashed. "You know something I've always wanted to do?"

"I can't imagine," Cynthia said dryly, a small smile beginning to tug at the corners of her mouth. "J.T., I truly can't imagine."

"I've always wanted to go on one of those cruise ships up the Canadian shore to Alaska. I think that would be a wonderful holiday."

She stared at him, searching for words.

"There'd be glaciers, and snowcapped mountains," J.T. said, his eyes on the misty sun that was climbing above the horizon off to the east.

"It would certainly be nice and cool this time of year," Cynthia agreed wistfully, imagining miles of ocean and glistening, snowy peaks.

"And you know what they say?" J.T. turned to her with a boyish smile. "The whales come right up close to the ship at night, and you can hear them singing. I'd love to hear that."

Cynthia studied her husband's sculpted face, his tanned cheeks and strong jaw, and felt a surge of love more powerful than anything she'd ever known in her life.

"J.T. . . ." she whispered, her voice shaky.

"Yeah?" He looked down at her, his eyes still dreamy and faraway, filled with images of glaciers and singing whales.

"̇he cruise sounds lovely, but I don't know
: midnight sun."

He cocked an eyebrow at her in puzzled silence.

Cynthia looked away so he couldn't see her face. "If I were to go on a romantic holiday like that with my husband," she murmured, "I think I'd want the nights to be dark and long. *Really* long."

He smiled down at her, and when she finally met his eyes she could see the happiness dawning in them like the morning sun.

"We could ask for an inside cabin without a porthole," he whispered. "It'd be dark all the time."

"In that case," Cynthia told him huskily, moving into his arms, "then maybe I'll agree to go with you."

He held her and kissed her with a gentleness so sweet that it took her breath away. Cynthia nestled in his arms while the warmth of the sun's rays began to flood over them, and looked at the Texas dawn with a sense of wonder and joy.

For the first time in their brief, turbulent marriage, she had the feeling that she'd finally, truly come home.